ECHOES OF THE GODDESS

ECHOES OF THE GODDESS

TALES OF TERROR AND WONDER FROM THE END OF TIME

DARRELL SCHWEITZER

THE BORGO PRESS
MMXIII

ECHOES OF THE GODDESS

Copyright © 1982, 1983, 1984, 1985, 1987, 1988, 1991, 2013 by Darrell Schweitzer

FIRST EDITION

Published by Wildside Press LLC

www.wildsidebooks.com

DEDICATION

To Steve Behrends, whose enthusiasm, support, and nagging contributed substantially to bringing about this book's existence.

Contents

DEDICATION	5
ACKNOWLEDGMENTS	9
PROLOGUE	11
THE STONES WOULD WEEP	13
THE STORY OF A DADAR	32
THE DIMINISHING MAN	57
A LANTERN MAKER OF AI HANLO	92
HOLY FIRE	105
THE STOLEN HEART	159
IMMORTAL BELLS	195
BETWEEN NIGHT AND MORNING	211
THE SHAPER OF ANIMALS	222
THREE BROTHERS	239
COMING OF AGE IN THE CITY OF THE GODDESS	257
ABOUT THE AUTHOR	273

ACKNOWLEDGMENTS

"The Stones Would Weep" originally appeared in *Fantasy Tales*, Winter 1983. It has been revised for this book. Copyright © 1983 by *Fantasy Tales*. Copyright © 2013 by Darrell Schweitzer.

"The Story of a Dadar" originally appeared in *Amazing Stories*, June 1982. Copyright © 1982 by Ultimate Publishing Co., Inc. Copyright © 2013 by Darrell Schweitzer.

"The Diminishing Man" originally appeared in *Fantasy Book*, September and December 1984. Copyright © 1984, 2013 by Darrell Schweitzer.

"A Lantern Maker of Ai Hanlo" originally appeared in *Amazing Stories*, July 1984. Copyright © 1984 by TSR, Inc. Copyright © 2013 by Darrell Schweitzer.

"Holy Fire" originally appeared in *Weirdbook* #17. Copyright © 1983, 2013 by Darrell Schweitzer.

"The Stolen Heart" originally appeared in *Weirdbook* #26. It has been revised for this book. Copyright © 1991, 2013 by Darrell Schweitzer.

"Immortal Bells" originally appeared in *Weirdbook* #18. Copyright © 1983, 2013 by Darrell Schweitzer.

"Between Night and Morning" originally appeared in *Weirdbook* #20. Copyright © 1985, 2013 by Darrell Schweitzer.

"The Shaper of Animals" originally appeared in *Amazing Stories*, July 1987. Copyright © 1987 by TSR, Inc. Copyright © 2013 by Darrell Schweitzer.

"Three Brothers" originally appeared in *Weirdbook* #23/24.

Copyright © 1988, 2013 by Darrell Schweitzer.

"Coming of Age in the City of the Goddess" originally appeared in *Fantasy Tales*, June 1985. Copyright © 1985, 2013 by Darrell Schweitzer.

PROLOGUE

The Goddess is dead. The Earth is very old. The fabric of time itself has worn thin. Who knows what might be glimpsed through it?

—Opharastes, *After Revelation*

At long last, she died. The Goddess of Earth, the Mother of Centuries, the dual mistress of dreams and nightmares, of the burning light and the impenetrable shadow, *died.*

It was revealed. The prophets knew, but did not proclaim it. There was nothing left to prophesy, save that in some remote, unimaginable future, the godhead would be reborn yet again in a form too strange to be described, like a storm once more gathering strength out of dissipated winds.

But for now, in the interregnum, would be an age of random portents and incoherent miracles.

The priests knew, but kept silent. They heard the divine voice fading away like an echo in a vast cavern.

About this time a certain soldier was mustered out of the army in Ai Hanlo, the capital of the Holy Empire. Wasting his money in taverns, drunk, exhausted from one last debauch, feeling desperation in his soul, he wandered across the plains, into the hills, without seeming direction or purpose, without any goal except to seek rest, to find peace. In his nightmares, all those he had slain in battle pursued him, screaming, their red wounds gaping. He cried out in fear and awoke in darkness, amid the spray of winter rain, but even while he was awake, the dead men proclaimed the news to him, saying, "Our deaths are as nothing. Behold. Look up."

And he looked up. The clouds parted, and he saw the Goddess falling across the sky, her hair trailing like a comet. To such an unworthy man as he, this vision came, while around him the ghosts of his enemies dissolved like soft clay in the rain.

The soldier abandoned his name, or perhaps forgot it, and lived namelessly until he felt himself worthy, and then assumed another name, Telechronos. Because he happened to dwell in the land of Hesh, he was called the Heshite, though even he no longer knew his exact origin. It was given to him to explain to mankind how, in the fullness of time, even the Goddess must perish, how the fragments of her divinity are scattered across the world like drifting ashes, some of them taking the forms we call the Bright Powers and the Dark, miraculous and dreadful yet not alive, like shadows that can speak.

He explained, too, why young men dream dreams and old men see visions, but the dreams and visions are without any intelligence or meaning, directionless, even if they are still holy.

For in the time of the death of the Goddess the worlds roll aimlessly in the dark spaces, without any hand to guide them. The Powers roam the earth and sky, working merely arbitrary wonders, leaving men to make what sense of them they may.

Let the many voices of these times speak.

Let the stories be written.

In the time of the death of the Goddess—

THE STONES WOULD WEEP

In the time of the death of the Goddess, there lived a boy named Ai Harad, who wanted to be a singer. He was the son of Thain, who had been a soldier, was himself the son of Scidhain, also a soldier, who had served in the Golden Legion of Ambrotae IV, the Guardian of the Bones of the Goddess. When the Goddess was yet living, the Harads had tilled the soil since time's beginning.

But change was in the air. All things were in upheaval in the time of the death of the Goddess. Signs and wonders multiplied. It was whispered that soon men would be free from caste, no longer subservient to lords, that the world would be remade. Therefore Ain Harad aspired to be a singer.

Now when Thain saw his son grow to be slight and slender and not very tall, he knew that the boy would never bear arms. Therefore he put him to work in a field, minding a herd of goats. The days were long and lonely in that field. The goats only acknowledged Ain's presence when he poked them with a stick, or stood up and shouted. Although beasts were said to have obtained the ability to speak in the aftermath of the Goddess's passing, they never revealed the secret to him. He and they regarded one another with close-mouthed contempt and not a little boredom.

To fill the hours, Ain would play upon a kind of lyre, which he had made out of a shell and some string, and sing songs of his own devising. This was his true calling, as anyone who had ever heard him could attest, save for the goats, who offered no opinion. When he sang, he forgot all that was around him, and seemed in a different world. It was as if some fleeting, beautiful spirit possessed him. Perhaps one did. Those were unsettled times.

It was said that when he fell into his trance and played, even the stones would weep at the sound. It was said that the trees bowed down and the streams stopped following, pausing to listen. Many things were said in those days.

And it was also said, or at least observed, that when Ain was enraptured in his music and paid no attention to anything else, the goats would wander off in search of tastier pastures.

One evening in his fifteenth year, he came to himself again after playing, and there was not an animal in sight. He rose, put the lyre into the goatskin bag he wore over his shoulder, took up his staff, and set out patiently to round up his charges. One by one he found them, until he drove the mass of them before him up and down the dry, brown hillsides of Randelcainé, but by then he was far from home, and by the position of the Wolf as it swung around the bright star that was its eye, he knew the hour was very late. The sun would rise soon. Therefore he resolved to wait, and return home in the morning.

He brought the goats into a cave and set a fire at its mouth to keep the dread things of the night away. Then he took out his lyre again, and softly touched the strings, and sang a song about sailors drifting in an open boat on a wintry night. All are frozen to the oars, stiff, nearly dead as they sit. The darkness around them is impenetrable, the sea black, but flecked with foam-capped waves. The wind chills them to the very bone, until the sensations of land beneath one's feet or the warm of a fire, seem impossible, half-forgotten dreams. But then a light appears, and brightens. It is a watchtower. The mariners take heart, the vessel leaps forward as if it had wings, and they reach the harbor and all are safe.

The goats huddled quietly as he sang. They had heard other versions of this one before, about men lost in the desert, about mountaineers, or the folk of Randelcainé venturing into the forbidding forests of the far north.

Ain looked out over the flat countryside to where the Endless River curved like a vast, gleaming serpent in the starlight. To the east, it passed through mountains beyond which he had never gone. To the west, it vanished in the horizon. Both the beginning and ending of the River were mysterious. He had once been told that it flowed in a circle, engirdling the world. He wondered about that dimly, but did not really care, save that someday he might make a song about it. He had a verse already:

> *Oh Endless River, return your waters,*
>   *return your waters, to where they sprang.*
> *Oh Endless River, return your waters.*
>   *The Goddess made you, to bring us home.*

Then, after a pause, he was moved to make another, different song. He scarcely had words for it, but he sang, and the words came. He sang of a longing for something more beautiful than anything on Earth, something to transcend human conceptions of beauty, and he wanted to be raised to this new level, to be reassured, to understand.

There was a tiny portion of his mind which was not involved in the song, which could analyze the wonder which had settled upon him; and this portion looked out through his eyes and beheld the landscape.

A light, which was not a reflection of a star, appeared in the middle of the river, and began to drift to the nearer bank, a point of faint blue, with a hint of rosy pink, the color of the twilight that precedes the sunrise. Then it moved onto the shore, a little larger, yet no more distinct; definitely approaching him. As it climbed the hillside it brightened. All this while he sang, his fingers dancing over the strings. That detached, calculating part of his mind remarked, *As if a fisherman had caught the sun on his hook and were reeling it in.*

More intense grew the light, and still Ain sang, unafraid. The moment of transition was imperceptible, but there was a distinct moment in which only a growing bubble of light drifted up the slope and another in which a procession of figures moved slowly and gracefully within an illuminated sphere.

Still he sang.

He had never seen such people before. There were knights in plumed helmets and golden armor, bearing lances with flowers on their tips instead of blades. An old man, robed in white, led the group, bearing in one hand an ivory staff from which auroras flickered. There were tall musicians too, not all of them human, some with lacy wings that they could beat in time, or with four arms, enabling them to play upon the tambang and the zootibar and other unearthly instruments. One had a face like an elephant, with lips extended a full arm's length in front of the face, forming a trumpet. At last came she for whom all this was an entourage, beside whom all paled into drabness, a lady clad in a gown of woven light, the burning white of noontide, the pale blue of a summer sky, the crisp oranges, reds, and yellows of autumn, the glittering silver of winter ice. She rode a shapeless beast which rippled over the ground like a wave and flashed the brilliant, harsh blue of electric fire. When she came to a stop and dismounted, the creature vanished, and all the company fell silent, and knelt before her.

They waited just beyond the mouth of the cave, silent as mist, armor and jewelry and brilliant gowns gleaming with light.

Still Ain Harad played and sang. He should have been speechless with awe, terrified, but the music burst forth like the ocean out of the earth when the spear of the Goddess struck it, on the first day of her reign and her epoch. He had passed a threshold. There was no turning back. He drifted, like a leaf in a torrent, unable to understand what was happening to him or why, unable to care.

Then the Queen—for obviously she was—bade her followers rise, and the musicians joined in the boy's song, and she danced in the middle of the circle of her knights, who banged their lances on the ground in time to her steps.

Now he had before him, concretely, the source of his inspiration, and in her honor, to praise her, he sang with greater voice, struggling to describe her in a song when mere words were not enough, and she leapt and whirled, and she rose to fill the sky, touching the ends of the world, clad in the auroras.

Somehow, Ai gradually recovered some sense of himself. He became fully aware of what he was doing, and he truly saw what his singing had conjured up. And as he watched the lady in amazement and wonder, his concentration broke, and he missed a note.

The dancer paused in midstep. The ghostly musicians were again silent. Still filled more with pride and awe that he had summoned such a one than with any fear, he asked, "Is the great lady pleased with my song?"

At this the whole company turned toward him, as if noticing him for the first time. The Lady looked down on him. Their eyes met. He was sure that her expression was that of an adult reproving a child who has begun well, but gone on to make an utter fool of himself.

She might have smiled. He could not tell. The movement was so slight that before the image could register in his brain, all of that company vanished into the night like sparks cast off from a burning log.

* * * *

In those days the Earth was disordered, and the Goddess newly dead, and things were changing, but this didn't stop Ain's father from screaming furiously at him when he arrived home in the middle of the afternoon, dazed, dreamy, stumbling, and missing at least half of the goats. Zadain, the boy's elder brother and the very image of the soldier Thain in his youth, was equally wroth. The two of them seized switches and chased Ain around the yard in front of their farmhouse.

"Fool!" cried Thain, striking.

"Idiot!" added Zadain, striking.

"Good for nothing!" (Thwack!)

"Brainless cretin! The goats should be taking care of *you*!"

All the boy could try to do was shield himself and evade the blows, not very successfully. When Patek, his mother, wife of Thain, came out from behind the barn where she had been feeding the chickens, the boy looked to her for sympathy but got none. "To think I wasted myself nursing such a dolt! Quick! Give me another switch!"

It was a very bruised and miserable Ain Harad who spent long hours climbing through briars, limping across stony plateaus, scaling hillsides in search of the missing goats. He found them, one by one, but was sure the imps of evil had spent all that morning placing the creatures in the most inaccessible places. There was a pillar of stone in the middle of a plain. It was said to be part of a palace from some ancient time, before the age of the Goddess. It was smooth on all sides. Sure enough, there was a goat on top, gnawing on a weed that grew there.

He was not allowed to sleep in the house that night. When he got home, his family wouldn't feed him. They had barred the door. So he sat out under the stars, and tried to play a song. It was a simple one, something he had known for years. But for the first time he could remember, he could not play. It was terrifying. All the music was wrung out of him.

Only after many hours of sleepless sorrow did anything come. It was as if breath had returned. He thought of the lady, of the song he had played for her. He could not remember it wholly, but he recalled brief parts of it, and the memory of the dancer was his inspiration.

* * * *

On the day before he was to leave for the wars, Zadain came upon his younger brother as he sat in the middle of a pasture with his face held between his fists. The boy was so caught up in his brooding that he did not notice the goats scattering at his brother's approach. Nor did he mark Zadain's dress: tall, leather boots, a blue tunic, a kilt set with metal strips, and a round helmet.

Said the elder to the younger, "Brother, you've always been a bit distracted, and I've always said that maybe your head isn't right. But I know that something special troubles you. I'm not sure I'll be back, where I'm going, so I'd like to set everything right between us before I leave. So tell me what your trouble is."

When Ain saw that his brother was sincere, he unburdened himself of the whole story, but his trust was shattered when Zadain burst into laughter.

"*You're haunted by some dancing hussy you met in the hills? Do you mean that, after all the years in the world, after the Goddess has lived and died, you've finally discovered sex?*"

"No! No! It isn't like that at all!" The goats scattered as Ain shouted.

"Oh, I see. You mean to say that some lofty, ethereal creature appeared out of heaven, which can never be seen by any of us insensitive, vulgar mortals. Except you, of course—"

"Yes. I mean, no. I mean—not exactly—"

"*Goat crap!* Now look here, idiot little brother—" Zadain grabbed Ain by the front of his shirt and shook him. "I'll show you what sort of girl she is. I'll go up in those hills this very night, and if she's still there I'll bring her back over my shoulder, like any other piece of loot—"

"No! You can't!"

"I think I can." Zadain shoved him to the ground. The lyre fell out of Ain's bag and rattled over some stones. "Listen, little boy, when and if you ever grow up, you'll find out what that thing between your legs is good for. You don't play music on it!"

Helplessly, Ain watched his brother stalk off in the direction of the hills. And he watched the sun set behind those hills. The stars came out. He stayed in the field, allowing the goats to wander where they would. When he was sure that the new glow in the hills was not moonlight, he ran in that direction, stumbling over the rough terrain and falling painfully, but always pressing on. His father's anger didn't frighten him now. Nothing else mattered.

At last he reached a spot where, through a trick of echoes, he heard a dim strain of music. He was certain. And there was another sound. It was the lady. He was certain of that too. Was she angry, frightened, startled? No, she was laughing.

The light went out.

* * * *

Ain returned to the farm, again without most of the goats, just as the sun rose, but before his parents could reach for the switches, Zadain arrived. The elder brother was not visibly harmed, but he seemed diminished, *emptied* of all but a rudimentary awareness. He walked like a corpse rooted out of its grave. His face was blank. He only spoke when spoken to, and then without any feeling.

The younger brother looked on with knowing dread, but at the same time he was sure this was Zadain's punishment for his blasphemy. *He* would not end up like this....

Then Thain exchanged glances with Patek his wife, and they grabbed Ain by either arm, dragged him out of Zadain's hearing, and demanded of him what he knew. The tale was recounted, and afterward the father spoke in a low, grim voice.

"And what do you think your lady will make of you *now*? After this?" He pointed to his elder son.

"Father, I don't imagine. I can't imagine. But I've heard old stories, about people who loved ladies like that, and I am sure that if she is pleased with my music, she'll come to me again."

Thain struck him in the face.

"You blind *fool*! Can't you see that your brother is bewitched? I think you are too. I think your brain has melted away. Know this: I've heard of creatures like this lady before, and I haven't been listening to idle stories or poetry. I *know* what she, or *it*, really is. She is one of the Bright Powers. The Bright Powers move about with the changing of the seasons, like clouds, like wind or the sun. They have no minds. Their outward forms are illusions. They are fragments of the Goddess, shards, splinters, motes of glittering dust. When a great image falls, it breaks into a million tiny pieces. These are the Bright Powers. They are remnants of the fair aspect of the Goddess. She had a dark side too, from which come the Dark Powers. People say that the Dark ones are more dangerous, but as you can see, this Bright one didn't do your brother any good."

"Father, I am sure you're wrong. She is a lovely lady."

Thain struck him again.

"Listen! I am not wrong! Foolish boy, know this from more years of experience than you're ever likely to see! This is my judgment: I forbid you to make music, or to sing when you are in the fields, or otherwise to summon this Bright Power. If you do—" he looked back to where Zadain stood, still as a statue, then into his wife's face, then back to Ain. His voice broke. He seemed about to weep. "If you do… If you do, then I have no more sons. You shall be turned out from this house, driven from all Randelcainé, as is the law. Understand?"

"Yes, Father. I do."

Then Thain took the lyre and hung it on a peg inside the house. "There it stays," he said, "until you're over this madness."

A little while later the thing that had been Zadain rose, took up shield and spear, and departed for the wars.

* * * *

The boy tended the flock for another two days, and he remained silent all the while, in obedience to his father. But then he knew that the time had come for him to go to the Bright Lady. This could not be blasphemy, he told himself. It could be no violation of the law. He would not summon her, as any village conjurer summons a spirit out of a tainted well. No, he would go where he had seen her last, and wait. Perhaps he would perish in the waiting, but he would wait all the same, so strong was the compulsion within him.

So he drove the goats home on the evening of the second day, and sat with his parents on the doorstep after supper, in the cool breeze. At first the talk was slow and faltering, as all were reluctant to mention Zadain, but then words came quickly and easily. Ain and his parents spoke of everyday things. Thain and Patek were pleased to see their son behaving sensibly once more. Ain was tense, but he dared not reveal it. He was about to go away, as Zadain had gone, but much farther, and perhaps he too would never return. He wished his brother could be with him.

It was nearly midnight when they retired. He lay above his parents in a loft which seemed vast and empty, now that Zadain was gone. But for all the unhappiness it might bring, he knew what he had to do. He put his ear to the boards beneath him and listened to his mother's gentle breathing and his father's snoring for a long time. Then he sat up, tied on his shoes, wrapped a cloak around himself, and climbed carefully down out of the loft. He paused in the darkness over his sleeping parents. He wanted to lean over and kiss his mother goodbye, but dared not, so he merely slipped away, into the kitchen, where he gathered some bread and cheese and dried meat into a bag, and slung a water skin over his shoulder. With tense, breathless stealth, he lifted his lyre down from the peg. Then he was gone. The night received him.

In darkness he walked toward the hills. The moon was just up and the sky very clear, so he could see the slopes before him, but the light did not reach into the lowlands yet. Each tree and boulder stood in black outline like some silent sentry in the land of the dead. But he knew the way intimately, having wandered over this ground since he was old enough to walk. Before long he came to the bank of the Endless River. This he followed until he came to where the land sloped upward. He followed the path he had taken on that first night.

He looked up at the cave mouth and saw a light. Fear shot through him. Bandits? Then he saw how foolish his fear had been. The light was a steady glow, not the flickering of firelight, and in it, lesser lights drifted up and down. As he neared it, he could make out upright figures moving. Some of them he recognized.

The Bright Lady was waiting for him. He stood before her, all terrors forgotten.

"I am pleased that you have come again," she said. "When the other came...it was not you."

This was the first time that he had heard her voice. She spoke the words in human fashion, but there was something else, like an after-echo, just beyond the range of hearing, a quality of sound not of Earth at all.

He did not ask if she wanted him to play again. He merely did, and at once the four-armed musicians joined him on the tambang, the zootibar, the kabukkuk, and others for which the languages of men have no names. Once more the Lady danced, whirling the auroras around her, and a great force came over Ain, something as elemental as any which moves the Earth or causes the seasons to change. He could not comprehend the vastness of it, but he felt it in his music, and played on.

The Lady began to move away. The white-robed man with the staff approached Ain, becoming like a cloud, drifting over and around him. Then the boy felt himself rise up. He was caught in the spell of the music, and even that part of his mind which was still conscious knew better than to hesitate for even the tiniest instant; but still he perceived that he was being borne aloft on a litter by some of the winged musicians, who held long, curling horns in their free hands. The knights with the flower-tipped lances were his honor guard. The Lady circled him like a bright planet in its course. For a time he seemed to be high in the air. The Moon was very close, but then the horizons whirled. The stars spun like beads in a top. The ocean rose up to meet him, but there was no coldness, no splash. He had been translated into some other form of being, not wholly material. Still he played his song, as the company passed down through the earth.

At last he came to a place few men have seen even in visions, where all solid things, all soil and stone melted away and only light remained, not blinding, but bright beyond seeing, bright on a whole new scale of perception. Brilliant against brilliance, there were shapes and forms, and gradually Ain discerned an overall pattern as he approached the center of the realm of light: a huge, burning rose unfolded before him, swallowed him up, filled the core of the world. This was the home of the Bright Powers.

* * * *

It seemed that he sang forever, without stopping, and that he *had* stopped, as if he were separated into two Ain Harads. There was no sense of time. He could dimly make out the Powers as they gathered around him, as he drifted suspended in light. Sometimes a shape would flash intensely blue or red or green, then fade away, like an afterimage in his eyes.

* * * *

Once he drifted through a long, wide place lined with many pillars. Fountains spewed gold. He sang. The Bright Lady sat on a throne before him, flanked by her knights. The musicians hovered above, high among the pillars like bright moths.

An image came to him: a tiny fish in a glass bowl, being passed from hand to hand among the splendidly garbed lords and ladies of the court. They talked and laughed and made intrigues, and the fish in the bowl, only faintly aware of them, understood nothing. He was that fish.

* * * *

Beautiful? he said to himself. There were no words, no sounds, no sights, no memories, but something beyond all senses, which could not be encompassed by eye or ear or mind.

* * * *

He sat by the Lady's side in a small boat, motionless on a mirrored lake, his lyre in his hand, the strings strangely solid to his touch, more substantial than anything else. He ran his fingers over them gently, then paused. Of their own accord, they made music.

The Lady wore something around her neck. She leaned forward, holding it up for him to see. It was a sphere of blue glass. Inside, a tiny boat lay on a mirrored lake. A boy sat beside a lady, playing softly on the lyre. He could hear the music, coming out of the glass sphere. The lady sitting inside it, beside the other boy, held up something, and within that yet another lady and boy sat, and the lady held up a gleaming sphere, and the scene was repeated endlessly, as if in a procession of mirrors; and somehow his eyes were made able to see all that tiny detail, into infinity, and his ears could hear the vast harmony of the music made by endless fingers.

* * * *

Once he awoke and was astonished to feel the chill night air and a lumpy mattress beneath him, and to hear straw rustle as he sat up in the loft in his parents' house. Eagerly he opened the trapdoor. More than anything else he wanted to behold his parents sleeping down there, to know that they were real and solid and not some kind of dream—

He set foot on the top rung of the ladder—

—and the light—

—the burning rose, slowly unfolding—

—he awoke into the light, and the Lady spoke inside his mind:

"Ain Harad of Randelcainé, son of Thain, surely you have known since you arrived here that all your ideas about this place are…to use an example from your world…like the efforts of a worm to describe the running deer. You *are* someone special. Your music alone, of all the productions of your race, has attracted the notice of the Bright Kind. Do not ask how this has come to be. It is from within you. You may never be able to comprehend the source, but the miracle and the mystery are within you. You thought to move me and win my love. That cannot be, but nevertheless I am pleased, in a simple way. Now your song is part of the great dance which is our world. For this I am grateful.

"No, no, do not ask anything more. No questions. No wishes, no granting of boons. It is not like that. Do not presume to raise yourself any higher than you are, for it cannot be done. We are of the substance of the Goddess, whose nature and death even we cannot understand. Your words have no meaning. They cannot encompass such thoughts as would be meaningful to us.

"I wish you no ill, Ain Harad. In a small way, you have pleased me. But now, think of something else from your own world. Think of a lady who holds a beautiful songbird in a cage. After a time, she has heard its song and grows tired of it, but she does not hate it. Therefore she sets it free. Think now, focus your mind, on the world from which you came, to which you must return. The door to the cage is open."

* * * *

—and flying on wings of light, the two of them soared or descended or moved in some direction which Ain Harad's mind could not grasp, through the center of the great, burning rose. He felt the Lady's hand on his. There was an illusion of solidity and warmth, though in some abstract way he knew it was an illusion even as he experienced it.

He thought of stony hillsides and grass-filled plains, of rivers and forests, of men and their noisy cities, of marching armies, ships under sail, of gulls drifting on columns of air; of the winter when a dog snatched his slippers and he had to run after it, out into the darkness in his bare feet. As he recalled that particular sharp, clear sensation of cold, the familiar world became more substantial to him, more tangible. He smelled the smoke of a hearth fire. He reached out with his mind, grasping the place of his birth, his home, his parents' house, with all his, drawing himself toward it, like a moth toward a distant light.

For just an instant he had a vision of something else, of a realm equal and opposite to that of the Bright Powers, where a dark rose gleamed at the world's heart, facing into the night, but the Powers dwelling there were no more as his father had described them than the running deer or the stars of the midnight sky can be described by the worm that crawls in the mud.

The Lady led him inward, his beacon on the dark way, until at last he seemed to be rising from the depths of a murky sea. There were pinpricks of light above.

Imperceptibly, his motion stopped. There was solid ground beneath him, and his body seemed solid once more. He held his lyre in his hands, and stood, rather unsteadily, in the middle of a flat, grassy meadow under a clear midnight sky.

Light flickered behind him and he turned, and beheld for the briefest instant the image of the Bright Lady, like a candle flame snuffed out. He was sure—he forced himself to believe—that she was smiling. Then he was alone and blind in the darkness. It was a long time before his eyes adjusted and he could again see the pale stars overhead.

* * * *

Ain Harad walked out of that field, into a town where a strange tongue was spoken. The people there saw by his manner, by the look in his eye, that he had been touched by something beyond nature. They provided him with food and drink, did him reverence, and hurried him on his way. He passed thus through many lands, unmolested but never encouraged to linger, seeking his home.

For a long time he delighted in the simplest things, the feel of the dusty road beneath his feet, the good green woods, the chatter of birds as they heralded the day's dawning. Sometimes he would sit for hours by a stream listening to the rushing waters, or watching tiny fish in a pool. He had words of cheer for all he met, but most folk avoided him, taking him for a holy pilgrim deep in thought, or else a Power clothed fleetingly in material form, or else merely a lunatic.

More than anything else, in those days, he wanted to see his parents again. This drove him on. He thought of his brother Zadain, off in the wars. He even thought of herding goats with more a sense of regret than not.

As long as he focused his mind on such things, he continued on his way. But one evening, after a long climb up a steep mountain road, he paused at the summit to watch the sunset, and the fading light reminded him of the Bright Lady and her kingdom.

It was as if he had awakened from a stupor. The memories came flooding back, overwhelming him. With them came a flash of pride. He would be the greatest of all singers when he told of the Lady in song. He would be, indeed, her equal. She had said otherwise, but she was wrong about that, he was certain.

The memories filled his mind. He went deeper into his trance than ever before. That last, detached part of his consciousness was also filled, like a final housetop submerged in a flood. He thought of his parents and his homeland no more.

He came down the mountain singing. The music was far stronger than any human music. It sustained him. He knew no need of food, drink, or rest. Wild beasts bowed down before him, and, yes, the stones wept.

The people of towns and cities left their homes to follow him, scarcely aware of what they were doing. The strange procession trampled fields of crops and interrupted battles, yet no voice was raised in protest. He crossed stilled seas, walking on the water, and the great masses followed in ships, on rafts, anything they could contrive. Islands were depopulated as they passed.

When at last he came into his own country, the folk of Randelcainé saw before them the largest army ever assembled. The dust from these countless feet filled the sky. This throng joined with another, streaming out of the holy city of Ai Hanlo, as all were drawn to the boy's music and to his singing.

Beneath Ai Hanlo Mountain, the bones of the Goddess stirred.

Then the Guardian of the Bones, lord of the city, called

together what few of his counselors who had not already joined the listeners, and said:

"In the days of our forefathers, the body of the Holy Goddess plummeted from heaven, trailing light across the sky like a comet, crashing deep into Ai Hanlo Mountain. Out of the chasm made by that fall, the newly formed Bright Powers, fragments of the Goddess, swarmed like bright bees, filling the nights with glory. Out of it too came the Dark Powers, enshadowing the days. Men died in ecstasy and terror, their minds and their hearts overwhelmed. It seemed all mankind would perish. It was only when the Powers had fled away, and the first of the Guardians had contained the bones in a vault and closed up the chasm by desperate magic that the survivors could return. Each guardian tells this to his successor, but now the danger is so great that I tell you."

"Has *another* goddess fallen from the sky?" someone asked.

"No, but a similar duty is upon me."

So the Guardian went forth, dressed the half-white, half-black vestments of his office, with his staff of power in his hand and wax plugs in his ears. It was the first time in centuries that the feet of a guardian had touched the streets of the lower city which surrounds the base of Ai Hanlo Mountain. He walked past deserted shops and houses, then out the Sunrise Gate, onto the plain. So great was the crowd that it took him many hours to get within sight of the singer. He stepped over the corpses of people who had been entranced by the music of Ain Harad, but not sustained by it, and so had perished of hunger and thirst, and, as of old, of ecstasy.

When he stood before the blank-faced lyre player, he spoke a word that only the Guardian may know, and held aloft a reliquary containing a splinter of the bones of the Goddess.

Silence struck the crowd, as if the spinning world had suddenly snapped to a halt. All stood frozen in shock. For Ain, returning to himself, it was the most exquisite of agonies to be wrenched from his contemplation of the Bright Lady. But some remembrance of his former life came to him and, dazed, not sure of where he was or how he can come to be there, he stared with reverent awe into the face of the Guardian, that holiest of men, and paid heed when the Guardian leaned over and whispered a command in his ear.

Obediently he went at once, parting the crowd as he passed, and made his way in silence out of the land of Randelcainé, wandering ever northward, knowing many hardships as he grew from boy into man, never able to rest until he came to that place where he could resume his music and his song. He crossed mountain ranges on the backs of wild beasts. Though the oceans would no longer bear him up; he couldn't walk on water anymore; he crossed them on the backs of whales, taming and commanding each with that single word the Guardian had spoken, until at the very last, close to death, he reached a warm valley in the middle of the ice country at the top of the world.

There he crawled to the base of a tree and sat up, his back against the tree, the warmth of the valley washing over him, bringing faint sensation into his frozen legs. He dreamed once again of the Bright Lady, and once more touched the strings of his lyre. As before, he played without ceasing, and the spirits and the Powers swarmed around him like bright bees.

In Randelcainé, those who had heard him could not return to their lives after having known such beauty. Some retired to monasteries and caves, where they worshipped little sounds and shadows and the rustlings of leaves and conversed with the silence. The streets of the city were quiet for a generation. Those who did not shut themselves away lived out their lives in longing, wishing only to travel beyond death so that they could hear that song again. Thereafter, all those who died were dressed in traveling cloaks and shoes, and staves were put into their hands, that they might rise from their funeral biers and walk the long road into paradise.

In time Ain Harad was united with his family, for the lord of the goats had become the lord of the dead. Those very near to death could just barely hear his song, faint and far away, growing louder as they sank out of this life. First his father came to him, then his mother, then his brother Zadain, who was slain in battle.

Thus, by the wisdom of the Guardian, the world came a little closer to order amid the chaos that followed the death of the Goddess.

THE STORY OF A DADAR

It was in the time of the death of the Goddess that the thing happened, when the Earth rolled wildly in the dark spaces without any hand to guide it, or so the poets tell us, when Dark Powers and Bright drifted across the land, and all things were in disorder.

It was also in the open grasslands that it happened, beyond the end of the forests, where you can walk for three days due south and come to the frontier of Randelcainé. All was strange to me. I had never been there before, where not a tree was to be seen, anymore than I had been to a place where there are no stars. All that afternoon, my wife Tamda and I drove our wagon through the familiar woods. Slowly the trees began to seem farther apart, and there was more underbrush. I remember how the heat of the day faded quite quickly, and the long, red rays of the setting sun filtered between the trunks, almost parallel to the ground, giving the undersides of the leaves a final burst of color before twilight came on. The trees ahead of us stood in silhouette like black pillars, those behind us, in glory. Above, little birds and winged lizards fluttered in the branches. I reflected that these things had always been thus, even in the earliest times, when the great cities of the Earth's mightier days stood new and shining, and other gods and goddesses, the predecessors of the one which had just died, ruled the sky. Those ancients could just as well have been seeing this sunset and this forest through my eyes.

Then a wagon wheel sank axle-deep in mud, and I didn't

have time to reflect on anything. The two of us struggled and gasped in pained breaths that we weren't young anymore. If only our son were still with us.... But he had gone away to serve the Religion. What is religion when your wheel is stuck?

When at last the wagon rolled free, stars peered down between the branches. The night air seemed very cold. We sat still, panting, until Tamda had the good sense to get our cloaks, lest the chill get into us.

So it was that we emerged from the forest in darkness. At first I was hardly aware that there were no more trees. It seemed merely that there were more stars, but then the moon came up and revealed the vast dark carpet of the plain rising and falling before us. Imagine a fish, which had always inhabited the dark and narrow crags among the rocks at the bottom of the sea, suddenly rising up, into the open wonder of the sea itself. So it was. Overhead the Autumn Hunter was high in the sky. The Polar Dragon turned behind us, and the Harpist was rising. By these signs we knew our way. Neither of us wanted to stop for the night. I suppose plainsmen feel the same way, their first night in the forest. So we pushed on and shortly before dawn reached our destination.

The village glowed on the plain like a beast with a thousand eyes, reclining there, alive with torches. We would never have found it otherwise. The houses were all curving humps of sod, hollowed out and walled with logs. Had they not been lit, we would have passed them in the night, thinking them little hills.

We were expected. Everyone was awake and waiting. A man in a plumed helmet took our horse by the bridle and led us to a building larger than all the others.

"Are you Pandiphar Nen?" asked the chieftain who stood at the door.

"Yes. You sent for me," I said. "You understand, then, that I do not heal broken bones, or cure any sickness which can be cured with a herb or a little spell?"

"Yes, I do, or I would not have sent for you."

"The price is high."

"Please, bargain later. It is my daughter, sore afflicted. She has...left us. Her mind is in darkness, far underground."

Tamda and I climbed down from the wagon seat. I got my bag out of the back. We were shown inside. The house had but one room, and a fire burned in the middle floor. The smoke hole wasn't large enough, and the air was thick. On a pile of hides to one side a maiden lay, her eyes open, but her gaze distracted. She did not seem aware of us. She rolled her head and muttered to herself. I listened for a moment, catching a few words, but most of it was strange to me.

"Put the fire—out," I said to those who had come in with us.

"And leave us alone." This was done. I waited for the smoke to clear.

Then I made a mixture of the ground root of the death tree, the water of life, common flour to hold it all together, plus other ingredients, including something called Agda's Toe. Agda was my master, to whom I had been apprenticed when I was fifteen, some thirty years before. Then I had believed he had an infinite supply of toes, which could be regrown whenever he cut them off and sold them to pharmacies all over the world, but of late I had had my doubts. He never took off his shoes in public.

I ate a spoonful of the mixture and washed it down with wine. I sang the song of the false death, with Tamda at my side to make sure that I did not truly die. She would hold my wrist and take my pulse, counting one heartbeat a minute, and listen for a shallow breath about as often. If I got into trouble she would shout my name and call me back. She alone had this power.

I departed. At once my awareness was out of my body, sharing that of the girl. I saw through her eyes. Tamda and I stood absolutely still, distorted out of shape, like tall sculptures of glowing jade. The room was full of a white mist, and in it swam things like the luminous skeletons of fishes, and some, like impossible herons made of coral sticks, walked on a surface below the floor, wading in the earth. They sang to me, trying to lull me into sleep within a sleep, but I paid them no heed. They were common spirits of the air. I had seen them many times before.

I turned inward. Indeed, the girl's soul was far beneath the earth. I had a sensation of sinking a long way in thick, muddy darkness before I had an impression of a hunched shape, like something carven out of rough, dirty stone, embedded in her.

I began to draw the spirit out. Literally, I drew it. By a trick known only to healers, I was both deep inside the girl's soul and in my own body. I was aware as my hands took up drawing paper and charcoal and began to sketch the image of the spirit. When I was a child I had always had an urge to draw things in the dirt, on walls, hides, scraps of paper, any thing, and my father always boxed my ears and told me not to waste my time. But when I began to draw things he had seen in his dreams, and things others saw in theirs, he understood my talent. Everything after that, even my apprenticeship to Agda, was a refinement of technique and nothing more.

I knew what to do from much experience. As my hand moved over the paper, I wrestled with the thing inside the girl. Soon I saw it more clearly, a frog-like king clad in robes of living marble. He had long, webbed claws like a beast, but his face bespoke vast intelligence and age. I understood him to be a creature from some earlier age of the Earth, trying to return now that the Goddess was dead. His eyes seemed to speak to me, saying, "Why should I not have this girl, and walk beneath the sky again?"

"You shall not have her," I said in the language of the dream, and as I spoke, my hand completed the drawing. Then my body got to its feet, stood over the girl, and with a pair of tongs reached into her mouth, pulling out first my spirit, then the other. It was like flying up out of a mountain through a little hole in the top, into my own hand.

"Pandiphar Nen," said my wife, and with the sound I came into myself. I was whole and fully awake. The white mist and the things in it were gone. The task should have been over. The second spirit I'd extracted should have melted into the air now that I had captured its image.

But the stone king was standing before us. Tamda screamed. It turned to stare into my eyes, and its gaze caught me as surely as any prey is ever charmed by a snake. I was helpless.

"Dadar," it said. "Know that I was placed here to bring this message to you from worlds beyond the world. I am sent by your creator. Know that you are a *dadar*, a wizard's shadow and not a man, a hollow thing like a serpent's skin filled with wind, pretending to be a serpent, deluding itself. The master shall make himself known shortly, and then you shall be sent on the task for which he made you, his dadar."

Then, howling, the creature went through the closed door of the house like a battering ram, scattering wood and screaming at the villagers outside.

I was in a daze, only half aware of anything.

"Let us get away from here," Tamda was saying. "They'll think we're witches. Hurry, before they regain their courage. Forget about the payment."

"I don't understand," was all I could say. "It wasn't supposed to happen like that."

She gathered our things and bundled me into the back of the wagon. No one interfered as she drove away from the village.

* * * *

The wagon rattled around me. Sunlight burned through the canvas cover. I lay in the stuffy heat, thinking.

The problem, and the reason I felt so much dread, was that I *did* understand what had happened. My spotty education was more than enough to include everything I needed to know. Some wizard had directed me, his dadar, into that village for his own ends. I knew full well what a dadar was. The world has never been thick with them, but they have been around since the very beginning. They are projections, like a shadow cast by a man standing before a campfire at night, but somehow the shadow is given flesh and breath and a semblance of consciousness. Hamdo, the First Man, made one. He had shaped with his hands the egg from which all mankind was to be born, but while he slept by the River of Life, a toad came along and swallowed it. Then a serpent swallowed the toad and a fox swallowed the serpent, and was in turn devoured by a lion, which fell prey to a bull, which was eaten by a dragon, which in turn was swallowed by an Earth Thing for which there is no name, which before long found itself residing in the belly of a Sky Thing which remained similarly nameless. Therefore Hamdo climbed the mountain on which the sky turns, charmed the Sky Thing to sleep with his singing—for he was the greatest of all singers—and then, on the mountaintop, he made a dadar of himself, and put a feather in one of its hands and a burning torch in the other. He sent it inside the Sky Thing to make it regurgitate the Earth Thing, the dragon, the bull, the lion, and so forth. From inside the toad it cut itself free, rescuing the egg. Things were different in those days, I suspect. Animals don't eat like that now. But the dadar was still a dadar, a reflection in the mirror of Hamdo.

More recently, the philosopher Telechronos spent so much time brooding among the ruins of the Old Places that he nearly went mad. He made a dadar for company. It became his leading disciple.

And a king of the Heshites was found to be a dadar. The priests gathered to break the link between the dadar and its master, lest some unseen, malevolent wizard lead the country to doom. The link was broken and the king crumbled into dust. A dadar is an unstable, insubstantial thing, like a collection of dust motes blown into shape by the wind.

Thus I feared every sound, every movement, every change in the direction of the wind, lest these be enough to unmake me. All the confidence I had gained in the years of my life ran away like water. I was nothing. An illusion, even to *myself*. A speck of dust drifting between the years.

I wept like a child abandoned in the cold and the dark.

And I argued: can an illusion weep? Can its tears make a blanket wet? But then, how could I, with the senses of a dadar, know the blanket to be real, or the wagon, or the tears?

I looked up front and saw only the horse nodding as it walked, and Tamda huddled at the reins. I did not speak to her, nor did she turn to speak to me. I think she was nearly as afraid as was I.

And I argued: But I have sired two sons. Two? One died when the cold of winter settled into him and spring did not drive it forth, but even in death he was real. He did not vanish like a burst bubble. And the other—he lives yet. Just this year he was called by a voice within him to journey south to the holy city of Ai Hanlo. I walked with him a long way, then wept when he passed from sight around a bend in the forest path. Does this not make me a man?

I was back to weeping. All roads of thought seemed to lead there.

I looked up again and saw that the sky was beginning to darken.

"Stop," I said to Tamda, and she reined the horse. She was trembling as we made camp. We went through the motions of settling down to supper, but suddenly she was in my arms and sobbing.

"Please…don't go away. Don't leave me. I'm too old to learn to be without you."

I was sobbing too. "I love you. Does that not make me a man? How can I prove it? Can a shadow feel such a thing?"

"I don't know. What is going on? Are we both mad?"

"No, it isn't that. I'm sure."

"I wish it were. To be mad is to be filled with passion, and at least that's real."

Although both of us were tired and hungry, we made love there on the ground as the stars came out. But even as I did I was haunted by the thought that a shadow may make a shadow's love and know nothing better.

Later, it was Tamda who put into words what I was groping for. She gave me a plan for action.

"You must find this wizard whose dadar you are," she said, "and kill him. Then you'll be free. You won't fade away. I'm sure of it. We must go to him when he summons you." She took a sheathed knife and put it inside my shirt. "When the time comes, surprise him."

Then I got up and fetched my folio of drawing paper. I sat down beside her and paged through the book. I stopped to stare at the image of the frog king. I couldn't help but admire the artistry. It was good work. When I wasn't practicing my more esoteric skill, I simply drew. Sometimes I sold the pictures in towns we passed through. Sometimes I even sold the ones I'd made while healing, after the spirits were dispersed and we didn't need them anymore.

I began to draw. I closed my eyes and let my hand drift. It didn't seem to want to make any marks. I felt my hand slide along the page, the charcoal only touching paper seven— eight?—nine times?

Then I opened my eyes and saw that I'd made a fair outline of the Autumn Hunter, which vanishes from the southern sky as the year ends.

"We travel south," I said.

* * * *

When first I looked over the plain by day, I thought of the fish from the deep ocean crags—now bursting out of the water altogether, into the air. As far as I could see, green and brown grasses rippled beneath the sun. Here and there stood a scrubby tree. A herd of antelopes grazed far away. Once we passed quite near to a green-scaled thing walking upright on thin legs, fluttering useless wings in annoyance at our presence. It stood twice as tall as a man, but looked harmless, even comical. I had heard of such creatures, half-shaped, still forming. They are said to emerge whenever one age ends and another begins. I had heard they were commoner in the south, as if the strangeness radiated from the holy city of Ai Hanlo, where the actual bones of the Goddess lay.

The journey was comforting. I relished every new experience more than I had any since I was a boy. But then the melancholy thought arose that it was only because I was about to lose these things, all sensations, all perception, even my very self, that they seemed more rare and exquisite.

Tamda slept in the back of the wagon while I drove. Horses are supposed to be able to detect supernatural creatures pretending to be men, but ours behaved normally for me.

The plain was divided by a winding silver line, which I knew to be the Endless River. It was said to engirdle the world. My son said he would follow it on the way to the holy city. I stopped by the bank to water the horse and to bathe. Tamda awoke and prepared a soup with river water. Later, I took up pen and paper and began to draw.

She watched me intently.

"Is it a message from our enemy?"

It wasn't. A bird bobbing on a reed had caught my fancy, and I made a picture of it. It was a charming little sketch, the sort some rich lady would pay well for.

Later, in a town called Toradesh, by a bend in the river, a man came to us, begging that we rid his father of the spirit which possessed him. There were many people around, and I could not refuse. Tamda and I were shown into a basement room, where an old man was kept tied to a bed. His eyes were wide with his madness. He did not blink. There was foam at the corners of his mouth. He stank of filth.

The picture I drew was of a long flight of stairs, winding down into the darkness. Once I had departed from my body, I was on those sodden, wooden stairs, descending into a region of dampness and decay. At the bottom I waded knee-deep in mud until I came to a slime-covered door. I pulled on an iron ring to open it, but the wood was so soft that the metal came away in my hand. I kicked the hole thus begun until it was big enough for me to wriggle through.

On the other side something massive and hunched over, dark with glowing eyes, sat nearly buried in the muck.

"Begone!" I said. "I command you, leave this place. Be

vomited up and leave this man."

The thing turned to me and laughed. Its voice was that of a child, but hideous, as if the child had never grown up, but lost all innocence and wallowed in cruelty for a thousand years.

"Gladly would I leave, *dadar*, for the soul of this man is rotten and there is not much left of it. But you have no soul, so where would I go?"

"If I have no soul, what is this standing before you?"

"It is the dadar of a dadar, the image of an image, the rippling of water made by another wave. *Dadar*, Etash Wesa made you, and sends you as a present to his brother, Emdo Wesa. There is enmity between them, which you shall consummate. More than that you need not know. Your actions are his, your thoughts his. From now on, he shall guide you."

In the blinking of an eye I was back in the basement room, and the old man was mad as ever. Tamda let out a startled cry. She had not called me. The townspeople scowled and muttered something about "theatrical fake." Tamda tried to calm them. We had failed, she told them, and thus would demand no payment. We left the town at once. It may have only been the subtle and remote workings of Etash Wesa, directing my fate, which prevented us from being smeared with dung and driven out with rods. Someone mentioned that as the traditional punishment for frauds.

* * * *

I was drifting. Sometimes in a dream I would see a hill or a bend in the road or men poling a raft along the river. Sometimes I would draw pictures of these things or awaken to find that I had drawn them. Especially in these cases, when the image was firmly in my mind, I could be sure that sooner or later I would behold those things while waking. I drove the wagon when I could, letting instinct which I knew to be the instructions of my maker be my guide.

I didn't have any doubt now that I truly was a dadar, a thing like dust carried in the wind. I was going to confront Emdo Wesa. Then what? Would some other secret of my nature be revealed?

Once I fancied that in the presence of Emdo Wesa I would explode into flame, consuming both of us. For this purpose alone I had been created. The rest was random happenstance.

Tamda said little as the miles went by. She knew she was losing me. Sometimes when she did speak she mentioned things I could not recall at all, as if I were slipping away from myself, becoming two, real and unreal, a reflection again reflected.

* * * *

I awoke in the middle of the day, the reins at my feet. The horse had wandered to the side of the road to graze, pulling the wagon askew. How had I gotten there? I didn't remember any morning. Last I remembered, we were travelling nearly into the sunset. Tamda was asleep in the back.

I had a vision of a man in an iridescent robe, bent over a steaming pot. I could not see his face. His back was toward me. He was missing the last three fingers of his right hand. With thumb and forefinger only he reached into the pot, immersing his arm all the way to the shoulder—and yet the pot wasn't a third that deep—and as he did there was a scratching inside my chest, as if a huge spider within me began to stir. I gagged. It was coming up my throat, into my mouth.

Then it retreated back inside me and there was a sudden, intense pain. It had wrapped its legs around my heart, and was squeezing, until blood rushed to my temples and my head and chest were about to—

* * * *

I awoke with a scream. A flock of startled birds rose all around me, wheeling in the twilight of early dawn.

I was sitting by a campfire in the middle of the grassland.

There was no sign of Tamda or the wagon.

Flames crackled. There was no other sound except that of the birds. I let out a grunt of surprise.

"What's the matter? Don't you know where you are?"

I looked up, regarding the speaker, saying nothing. He stood opposite me, a spear with a rabbit impaled on it in his gloved hands. He had a long beard, black hair streaked with grey, and he wore a long robe alternately striped blue and red. For an instant I feared he was the man from my vision, but by the way his hands worked, spitting the rabbit over the fire, I was sure he had all his fingers. I guessed him to be slightly younger than myself, and by his speech, a foreigner. He seemed to take my presence for granted, as if we had met before this instant. Carefully, trying not to reveal the gaps in my memory, I got him to tell me what I wanted to know.

"You may have heard of my country," he said. "Here in the north the people say the air is so thick in Zabortash that men carry it around in buckets, into which they dunk their heads when they want to breathe. They blame our foul dispositions on this. But these things are slanderous lies. Am I not a man, like any other?" He smiled when he spoke, and I felt sure he was deliberately mocking me. This was a new terror, but I forced myself to remain calm. I allowed that he seemed a man, like any other.

"Now you, on the other hand," he went on, "seem strange. Last night when you came upon my humble camp, you were like one walking in his sleep. 'Who are you?' you asked, and I said 'I am Kabor Asha,' but a few minutes later you asked again, and again I answered, and it seemed that your mind wandered even farther than your body did. Most strange."

He offered me some of the rabbit. When we were done eating, he noticed that I was watching him as he wiped his gloves clean, without removing them.

"You are wondering why I don't take them off and wash them, of course. I can't, you see, because I am not alone. In my country no magician bares his hands in public. It's obscene."

"You are…a magician?"

"That's another rumor they have here in the north, that everyone in Zabortash is a magician. It's not true, but they are so numerous that there is no work for many. That is why I wander, you see, to practice my art."

And again I wondered if he were mocking me, but I made no sign. An idea came to me. Another magician could help me against my enemy. At the very least, it would complicate Etash Wesa's plans. So words poured out of me in a torrent. I was well into my story before I realized what I was doing. Then there was nothing to do but finish. I told him all.

"I know of Emdo Wesa," he said when I had finished. "I can take you to him. Then the whole unpleasant business will be over and you'll be free."

"Wait! What business? What am I supposed to do? Who are you? How do you know—?"

Before I could do anything he stood over me. He had opened his robe. Beneath he wore some sort of armor. The scales glittered blue and black, close against his skin. I had a sudden fear that it wasn't armor at all, that he was some kind of reptile—

The cloak closed over me, covering my head as he knelt to embrace me, hugging me to his chest.

His flesh was cold and hard as iron. I couldn't feel any heart beating.

"Help! Wait! Where is my wife? What have you done—?"

"You didn't tell me you had a wife," he said as he pushed me over backwards and tumbled onto me.

The ground did not catch us. We were falling off a precipice, tumbling over and over in the air, the wind roaring by us, for a long time. I screamed and struggled, and then all the strength went out of me and I hung limp. He straightened out from our hunched position and stopped somersaulting. I could see nothing but darkness beneath his cloak, but somehow I had the impression that he bore me in his arms like a bird of prey carrying off a fish.

The fish, from out of the crag, wandering into the wide ocean, bursting into the air, snatched away by a sea hawk—

—falling among faint lights, false images behind my eyelids, but then stars, as pure and clear as any seen by night over the open plain, as if Kabor Asha had all the universe inside him.

We stopped falling without any impact or even a cessation of motion. My vertigo simply faded slowly away, and after a time I felt solid ground beneath my feet.

He took his robe off me, and I saw that we stood on a little hill before a vast city which rose up tier upon tier, like something carven out of a mountain. Every stone, every wall, every rooftop of it was of dull black stone, and it stood silent and empty against a steel grey sky. As far as I could see the ground was bare and dusty grey. Every color, every trace of life seemed drained out of this place.

"Behold the holy city of Ai Hanlo," said my guide and captor, "where lie the bones of the Goddess. But this is not the Ai Hanlo to which pilgrims flock, where the Guardian rules over half a million citizens. No, this is one of the shadows of the city, in a world of shadows. Where the bones of the Goddess lie all magic intersects, all powers are centered. All shadows come together here, branching out into separate worlds. Thus, in a sense, all practitioners of deepest magic, not that petty and shallow stuff you yourself use, the sort you can see on any street corner in Zabortash, but the deepest, most secret magic, which partakes of the inner nature of things; all who know this and immerse themselves into it—all these dwell in Ai Hanlo, alone, in some shadow or other, where ordinary men cannot follow. In this particular shadow Emdo Wesa dwells. You must go to him."

I looked up at the city in dread. It was no city, but some monster, waiting to devour me in the labyrinths of its mouth, to dissolve me utterly.

Dadar though I was, if I had any will, I would resist.

I ran down the hill, away from the city, away from the one who called himself Kabor Asha.

"Stop! Fool!"

The spider in my chest scurried to my heart and squeezed

and sank its fangs deep. I screamed once, but the sound broke into gurgling, and the pain filled me.

The next thing I knew the Zaborman was helping me to my feet. I was numb and weak. I could not fight him.

"Don't try to run away," he said. "Listen to me. I can still help you. I can be your friend."

"Who are you really? You didn't find me just by chance."

"No, I did not. Let me merely say that I am one who wants to see you complete your mission and go free. I want to help you do what Etash Wesa has sent you to do, and get it over with."

"You seem to know what I must do."

"Yes, I do. It is quite simple. You will find Emdo sleeping. Reach beneath his pillow and take out the jeweled dagger you find there. With it, cut his throat from ear to ear."

"Why should I murder a man I do not know, with whom I have no quarrel?"

"Because you were created for that very reason. Be comforted. You have no more guilt in this than does the dagger."

"That's very comforting," I said bitterly. "What happens to me afterwards?"

"In all honesty, I do not know. You could go on for a while, the way ripples do in a pool, even after the stone that made them comes to rest on the bottom. If so, take that as reward for services rendered."

So, filled with helpless dread, like a victim led to slaughter, even though I was supposed to do the slaughtering, I let him guide me through the dark gate of this shadow Ai Hanlo, through the wide squares, up streets so steep that steps were cut in them, below gaping empty windows, to that gate beyond which, in the real city, no common man was allowed to go. But no guards stopped us, and we entered the inner city, the vast complex containing the palace of the Guardian and—in all the shadows too?—the bones of the Goddess resting in holy splendor. All the while the air was still and dry, not warm, not cold, giving no sensation at all. There was an overwhelming odor of must, like that of a tomb which had not been opened for a dozen centuries.

We came to the topmost part of the palace, the very summit of the mountain, to a great chamber beneath a black dome. In the true city the dome was golden, and was said to glow with the sunset hours after the rest of the world was dark.

In that vast, empty room, by the faint light of the grey sky coming in through a skylight, I could make out two mosaics on the floor, one of a lady dressed in black, with stars in her hair, and another, of the lady's twin, in flowing white, with a tree in one hand and the blazing sun in the other. The Goddess, in her bright and dark aspects, as she was before she fell from the heavens and shattered into a million pieces, which we know as the Powers.

Where the feet of the two images came together, there was a dais, and on it a throne. A man sat there asleep, his head on an armrest. I had expected him in a bed, the pillow beneath his head. But, no, he was sitting on it.

We crept closer, climbing the few steps until we stood by the throne. We stood over the sleeping man. He was very thin. I could not make out his features.

"Take the dagger, and do what you must," said Kabor Asha, and as he spoke he stepped down from the dais. "Do it!" he whispered to me. "Hurry! Fear not; it is a magic weapon, the only one which can pierce him. Now carefully draw it out."

The hilt was sticking out from beneath the pillow. Delicately, I took hold of it and inched it away. The task was easier than I had expected. The thing slid out of a scabbard, which remained beneath the pillow. Once I froze in abject terror as my victim's eyelids fluttered, but he did not wake.

"Do what you must!"

I felt as if I were about to slay myself, as if the first prick of the blade would burst me like a bubble. But then I told myself, well, I had been created for this. What years I had lived, I had lived. What man can avoid his appointed doom? My life is done, I thought. There are more painful ways to die than merely winking out of existence.

I took the sleeping man firmly by the hair, and quickly,

savagely, before he could react, I slashed his throat so deeply that I felt the blade touch his neck bone.

I winced, and braced myself for oblivion, but nothing happened.

Nothing.

There was no blood from the open throat. Only a little dust dribbled from the wound, and the body deflated, like a punctured waterbag, until it was no more than a crumpled mass.

The one who had brought me here ascended the dais again.

"What does this mean?" I asked. "Why doesn't he die like a man?"

"I can explain. Give me the knife." Without thinking, I gave it to him.

He slammed it hilt-deep into my heart. There was—

—I—

—the beginning of pain; a scream, my knees like running sand—

—stood still. He held me up, impaled on the blade, frozen forever in an impossible dance of death.

"Dadar," he said. "I can explain. He does not die like a man because he is not a man. He is a thing like a dadar, like you. A reflection of a reflection. You have killed one of your own number. Dadar, it should be all clear to you when you understand that I am Emdo Wesa, the one my brother sent you to murder."

* * * *

Hearing came first. Footsteps. The sound of a small metal instrument being dropped into a glass jar. Breathing. Slowly, images coalesced out of the air. Bright areas became torches set in a wall. A drifting smear became a more unified shape, and wore the face of Emdo Wesa, whom I had known as Kabor Asha the Zaborman.

Was he with me, even beyond death?

I shook my head to clear it, and was aware of my body. I was bound spread-eagled to a table, and was stripped to the waist. Emdo Wesa, holding a sharp knife, bent over me. Impossibly, because I felt no pain, there was an immense gaping hole in my chest. I felt sure he could have ducked his head into it. And yet, I was numb, and blood did not spurt out. I watched almost with disinterest, as if all were part of a remote pageant performed by spirits in some other plane of existence. In the shadows.

"You know," laughed the wizard, seeing that I was awake, "you could say it was obvious from the beginning that my brother had a hand in this."

He put down the knife and reached into the cavity. His gloves were off and I could see that he indeed lacked three fingers. In their place light flickered.

He drew out a severed hand, totally covered with blood. From out of my chest. He took a ring off one of the fingers, then threw the hand away like so much garbage.

"Yes," he said, examining the ring. "It is my brother's hand. His last one. He used the other to make another dadar. How long ago was that? I don't remember. Oh, I should tell you something. To make a dadar, the wizard must cut off a piece of his living flesh. You have to amputate something. Dadars are not made frivolously. So far I have had but three enemies I could not otherwise deal with, and each cost me a finger to make a dadar. But my brother, I believe, is more quarrelsome. He has lots of enemies. He has changed himself hideously. I won't tell you the cause of our feud, because it would go on an on, and I don't care to spend that much time doing so, but I will say this. The world, all the worlds, would be better off without him. He is a monster."

"M—monster…"

Emdo Wesa smiled and said softly. "Don't strain yourself, my friend. Don't try to speak."

"Who…? Friend…?"

"Now you have a good mind, for a dadar. I must compliment my brother on his workmanship. Or you shall, when you see him. You are so full of questions. Let me set your mind at rest and answer a few. First, know that sorcery changes the sorcerer. Every act makes him a little less a part of the human world. It has to be done with moderation. Otherwise, like my brother, one will drift like an anchorless ship, far, far into strangeness. He has. I don't think his mind works at all like a human one anymore. But he is still clever. Why did he create you, and let you live unsuspecting for forty-five years before using you? It is because I have long journeyed outside of time, and forty-five years in this world has no duration outside. When I looked back into time, to see how things were going, at a point years ahead of where I departed, I saw you killing me in my sleep. It was no illusion, but a true thing. So I had to arrange for another to die in my place. *That* was what I had seen. Then I was able to come back some days before the event, encounter you, and make sure things occurred as planned. Thus my brother was thwarted."

Fear, nausea, and delirium washed over me. I felt like I would vomit out my insides, but nothing came. I screamed my wife's name.

"Tamda is not with you anymore," said Emdo Wesa. "It is useless to call her."

He reached somewhere beyond the range of vision and came back with a still beating heart in his hands.

"No...Tamda! You—monster!"

"Calm yourself. Calm yourself. I didn't say where I got this. It is for you, that you might live." He placed it in my chest. "You don't think I...no, how could you? I am not some inhuman fiend like my brother. I am a man, like anyone else. I am human. I have feelings. I can perceive beauty, know sorrow and joy. I haven't lost that. I am moved by compassion. I know what love is, even the love of a dadar."

His breath came out like smoke. By the light of the torches I could see that what I had taken to be tight-fitting scale armor was really his flesh. His three ghostly fingers flickered as he sewed up the wound.

I screamed again.

He walked along the table, toward my face, the knife in hand once more.

* * * *

I thought that my being on the hill outside the shadow city, with Emdo Wesa beside me, was all a dream, something conjured by my desperate mind in my last moments of life. But the scene had duration, and I felt hard ground beneath me, and I touched my body and found that it was real. I groped under my shirt and encountered a tender spot, where the wound had been closed and still had a thread holding it. Much to my surprise I also encountered the dagger my wife had given me. Obviously my new master had nothing to fear from ordinary blades.

One side of my face tingled. There was something subtly wrong with my vision, as if one eye perceived things more intensely than did the other.

I looked at Emdo Wesa. He had a bandage over one side of his face, covering an eye.

Again I was a dadar.

"I am returning you to my brother," he said. "I shall see everything you see and do. When the time comes, I shall direct you. When your task is completed, I promise you, I shall release you."

"How can I ever believe that?"

"Why, you have my word, as a human being."

* * * *

There is another gap in my memory here. I made to answer, when I looked up I saw a clear, blue sky. Surf crashed nearby, the air was filled with spray. I was no longer in the shadow, but on a beach somewhere in the real world, on a bright, day, and the wizard was no longer with me.

I had come to the ocean. I had looked upon lakes before, and but never the ocean. I had only heard of it, from those who had travelled far. Water stretched to the horizon, a vast array of whitecapped waves marching toward me like the ranks of endless army, only to break into foam at my feet. The wonder of it almost overcame the terror of what had gone before. For this, it was almost worth what I had endured. Perhaps, I thought, I had gone mad, and had imagined all that had gone before in my madness, and in my distracted state wandered over the world until at last I came to the shore of the sea. That was how I had come here.

But then I saw that there were no footsteps in the sand. I walked forward a step, and then there was a single set. I was not wet, so I had not come out of the waves, to have my tracks washed away behind me. No, I had been deposited here, out of the air.

When I pulled up my shirt, I saw the closed wound on my chest, red and swollen, the end of the black thread sticking out of it. It hurt when I breathed deeply.

Everything was true. I could not weep. All the salt water in creation was before me, so what would my tears amount to? Besides, I had expended them all before.

Anyway, a dadar is not a man, and his tears are all illusions.

I prayed to the bones of the Goddess, wherever they might be, and I called on the Bright Powers, repeating the names of them that I knew. But what are the prayers of a dadar?

Then I knelt down and began to draw in the wet sand. My hand moved by itself. Only when I realized what I was doing did I take out my dagger and use it as a stylus.

* * * *

I made a crude outline. It was only a suggestion of a shape, and there were no colors to it, of course, but somehow this act set my senses spreading like smoke over the land and sea. I felt every wave in its rising, every grain of sand pressing against the rest, here concealing a shell, there a stone. I felt the chill of the great depths and the crushing currents beyond the reach of the sun. I heard the long and ancient song of the whales, a fragment of that single, endless poem which the leviathans have called out to one another since the beginning of the world. I seemed to pass out of my body for a while. There was no sensation. Then came a vague sense of direction, as if I were being led by invisible hands to the edge of an abyss.

I became aware of the drawing again. It had grown far more elaborate. My gaze drifted from it to the sky, and I saw that the sky was no longer blue, but a vivid, burning red, and I looked out over the ocean, which was now an ocean of blood, new and thick and spurting from some torn artery as huge as creation.

An object broke the surface near the horizon. It was little more than a speck, but it grew larger as it neared me, moving like a ship even though it had no sail or oarsmen to propel it. It was a rectangular box, rising and falling in the waves of blood, drawing ever nearer the shore, until I could discern quite clearly that it was a coffin of intricate and antique workmanship, embossed in gold and covered with strange hieroglyphs.

My will was not my own. Of its own volition my body rose and waded into the sea, till blood rose above my waist. My mind wanted to flee, but remained there, helpless, until the coffin was within arm's reach. Then it ceased to rise and fall; but remained perfectly still, oblivious to the movement of the waves around it.

I watched with the terror of inevitability, like some prey cornered by the hunter when there is no further place to run, as the lid silently rose. Within was darkness, not merely an absence of light, but a living, substantial thing.

And slowly this darkness faded, and my new eye penetrated it. I saw Etash Wesa, the enemy against whom I had been sent, the one who had remained on earth for so long, never venturing out of time, the one who had fought so many feuds with so many enemies.

Indeed, by the look of him, Etash Wesa had made many, many dadars. His almost shapeless pink bulk floated inside the coffin, awash in blood, slowly turning over. In the gouged-out bulk which had been a head, there was an opening—I couldn't call it a mouth—which mewed and babbled and spat blood when it rose above the surface. One stubby remnant of an arm twitched like a useless flipper. And yet, this was no helpless thing. Somehow I knew it was almost infinitely aware and powerful, and that it had grown far, far away from the humanity that spawned it, until it no longer saw or felt as men did. I think it touched my mind and its presence was an intense, exquisite torture beyond the ability of words to describe or the mind to conceive. No one thought can encompass the mind of Etash Wesa.

In its twisted way, with something other than a voice, it seemed to be saying, "My dadar? Where is my dadar? I have been separated from it, and yet I shall find it."

The greatest terror of all those I had known was that Etash Wesa would indeed find me. I could look on him no more. Somehow I could move again. Screaming, I stumbled onto the beach. I obliterated the drawing. I covered my eyes with my hands. I pounded my head to drive out the memory of what I had seen, but still the red sky looked down on me, the sea of blood washed at my feet, and the thing in the coffin murmured.

I picked up my knife out of the sand. If I lived not another instant it would be preferable to living in the sight of Etash Wesa. What did I care of my promised freedom? What did I care of strange wars between wizards? What did I care, even if the world would be better off rid of Etash Wesa?

I did what I had to. I gouged out the eye Emdo had given me. Had I burst like a bubble then, it would have been a blessed escape.

I heard Emdo's voice for an instant: "No! Stop!" Then he was gone. The pain was real. The blood ran down my face. I gasped, fell onto the sand, and lay there, panting, bleeding, waiting for the end to come.

I waited for a long time. The sun set and the stars came out. The salt tide went out and came back in again, nudging seaweed against my feet.

The rest is a muddle, a fever dream within a dream within a dream. I think someone found me. I remember walking along a road for a time. There was a bandage over my empty socket.

There were a few words, a song, a carriage wheel creaking and rustling through dry leaves. I think I lay for a day beneath the hot sun in the middle of a harvested field. A boy and several dogs came upon me, then ran away in fright when I sat up.

Somehow I came to Ai Hanlo, the real city, where the Guardian rules, where the bones of the Goddess lie in holy splendor at the core of Ai Hanlo Mountain. I remembered slowly—my mind was clouded, my thoughts like pale blossoms drifting to the surface—that my son was here, that he had come to serve the Religion. I went to the square of the mendicants, beneath the wall where the Guardian comes all draped in gold and silver to bless the crowds. I slept with the sick and the lame. Somebody stole my boots. So, barefoot, tattered, stinking, my face a running sore, I went to the gate of the inner city and demanded to see my son. But the soldiers laughed and sent me away. I begged, but they would not call for him.

But what is the begging of a dadar?

I prayed to whatever Forces or Powers there might be, to the remaining wisps of holiness that might linger over the bones of the Goddess, but what good are the prayers of a dadar?

What good? At the very end, when I sat in a doorway, very near to death, a gate opened and a procession of priests came out, and I saw a face I knew, and I pushed through the crowd with the last of my strength. I called my son's name and he stopped, and recognized me, and wept at my wretchedness. He took me to his rooms and comforted me, and later I told him that above all else I wanted to rejoin Tamda, his mother, my beloved, if she would have me, knowing me to be a dadar, without a soul, an uncertain thing.

"But Father," my son said, "consider what uncertain things all men are. What is a man, but a bubble in the foam, a speck of dust on the wind? Can any man know that his next breath will not be his last? Can he know how fortune will treat him, even tomorrow? What of the calamities that carry him off, or the diseases, or even that one, faint· breath of damp midnight air which touches his old bones and makes an end to him? Then what? Do we walk a long road till at last we come to the paradise at the top of the world, there to hear forever the blessed music of the Singer? Or do we merely lie in the ground? You think these are strange words, coming from me? But the Goddess is dead, and the last remnants of her holiness quickly drain away. All things are uncertain. The world is uncertain. Will the sun rise tomorrow? Father, you are weeping. How can a mere projection, an empty thing like a skin filled with wind—how can such a thing weep? It may deceive itself, but not others. I see your tears. I know that you are more than a sudden, random, fleeting shape, as much as any man is. Yes, a man. If you were not always a man, I think you have become one over the years through your living and your love."

Which brings me back to weeping.

When at last I was able to travel from Ai Hanlo, my son went with me. We followed the way Tamda's wagon was said to have gone, asking after her in every town. She made a few coins singing, people said, or selling sketches or doing sleight of hand. She looked thin and worn, they said.

At last we found her at a crossroads. It had to be more than just chance. She leapt down from the wagon and ran to me. Again we all three wept.

Later she said to me, "We are always uncertain. If you fade away, so shall I, when we are old. It may be very sudden. How are you unlike any man in this? Stay with me. Let the days pass one at a time, and live them one at a time. You can love. How are you unlike any man in this?"

Which brings me back to weeping.

THE DIMINISHING MAN

Regard the city as it blankets the whole of Ai Hanlo Mountain, that axis on which the world turns in this time of darkness and transition. From the heart of the mountain the fading power of the Goddess still flows in a trickle.

In holiness hear this.

In the time of the death of the Goddess hear this.

Blessed prince of cities, hear this.

Regard Ai Hanlo, The City, where dwells the Guardian of the Bones of the Goddess. From the summit, from a skylight in the golden dome of the palace of the Guardian, the signs are first seen, and the seasons, and the days, and the years.

It is said that from that vantage point the Guardian observed the life of the magician Emdo Wesa, and was troubled by it, but later approved.

Such things are said. Such things are rumors. Who can know what the truth is, in the time of the death of the Goddess, when even the Guardian is troubled?

In holiness hear this. In the end it comes to holiness.

Now the tale is of Emdo Wesa.

I.

It was in Ai Hanlo that Emdo Wesa dwelt, both in an empty city by himself, in a gray world of another plane, dusty and still, and in the city of jostling crowds, with his days filled with the cries of peddlers, the rumble of carts on the cobbled streets, the shouting of children, and the drawn-out, dirge-like chanting of pilgrims as they made their way in long lines up the steep side of the mountain to the inner city where once a day the Guardian would come forth to bless them, and touch the sick with a reliquary containing a fragment of a bone of the Goddess.

Emdo Wesa lived in two places at once because he was both a mighty magician and a wretched old man. Both aspects were masks, concealing one another. He was tall. He was thin. His pointed beard had been black, but was graying. One of his eyes was gone, the socket covered with a leather patch. He wore the long blue-and-red-striped robe, the cylindrical cap, and the heavy boots of a wandering magician of Zabortash, and he would never remove his gloves in public, as no Zaborman would, thinking the showing of hands obscene. But he was no common conjurer. Nor was he any common old man. He lived in a wide, heavy, covered wagon of Heshite make, which was kept parked in a particularly stinking alley. When he needed to go somewhere, so the urchins said, he would carve the shapes of horses out of the air with a special knife, one at noon, the other at midnight. One horse was yellow-white in color, the other inky black. You could tell when he was preparing for a journey, because he would have one horse standing around for twelve hours before it was time to carve the other.

He made love potions and broths to drive out the ague. He spoke to the stars on behalf of those who gave him a coin. He sold dried human tongues which he had gotten from wrestling from sundown to dawn with revived corpses. At the last instant, each corpse would try to give him the kiss of death, thrusting its tongue into his mouth, and he would bite it off. These tongues made talismans of awesome potency.

For all this, Emdo Wesa had a harried look about him, like that of a man who fears his death the next instant, the next hour, the next day, but does not know which it will be. He once let slip that he had a brother who was a monster, who hated him, and waxed stronger inexorably.

* * * *

One evening, while reading in the back of his wagon by the light of an oil lamp, the smoke of which further discolored the wagon's canopy, Emdo Wesa fell asleep over the book and had a vision.

He found himself standing on a plain of smooth, cold, black glass before a city made of flickering panes of light. Within he saw the ghosts of the builders, skeletons glowing faintly, drifting up and down like fish in a still pond. He walked toward the place. The Sun rose. The Sun set. Three days seemed to pass, and still, with no way to measure his progress on the featureless plain, the city seemed no nearer.

Then he sat down, waiting until he was wholly calm, until his body no longer felt the frigid glass beneath him, and he performed the rite of *psadeu-ma*, which he had learned as a boy, when studying to be a priest of the Guardian of the Bones, before magic beguiled him. He opened his soul, not to feel the lingering echo of the death of the Goddess, as only the holiest of men can do, but to be touched by the city.

And yet, as he did, he felt the power of the Goddess more clearly than he ever had before. It ran through his body like a fever. It shook him like a rag in the wind, so awesome, so vast it was, even as it faded, even in death.

This power was his. He had been drawn to it. He knew, as certainly as he knew anything, that his destiny was within that city.

He came out of the trance of *psadeu-ma* and began walking toward it once again, but almost at once, by a trick of perspective, like a mirage viewed from a differing angle, the city vanished. So did the plain of glass. He was standing on a hill, overlooking a rolling prairie. A herd of *katas*, the upright, spiketailed lizards ridden by the cavalrymen of the Holy Empire, grazed in the distance.

He cried out in anger and despair.

Suddenly there was a man beside him, tall like himself, but

clad in black, pacing back and forth, oblivious to his presence. He took advantage of this to steal away, for the very sight of that one filled him with unreasoning dread. But his legs were like half-melted wax. He moved very, very slowly down the side of the hill, his heart pounding, his breath ragged. He tried to think of some magical way to convey himself away, but nothing came. His thoughts were scattered. Then he looked over his shoulder and saw that the other had finally spotted him, and was following. He screamed and ran all the harder.

When the other was almost upon him, he looked back and saw that the dark man's face was a blank oval, wholly featureless.

The other reached out, but just as he was about to touch him, Emdo Wesa saw a door hanging suspended in the air. He opened it and stumbled through. There was no time to wonder where it came from.

Now he was on a familiar street in Ai Hanlo. Above him near to the mountain's peak, a soldier blew on a silver horn, signifying the third hour of the night watch. He walked a ways, his heart thumping. He came upon a guardsman of the lower city making his rounds.

"What are you doing out this late, old man?" The guardsman lowered his pike.

"Just taking the night air."

The guard looked at him strangely, but let him pass.

He came to a square with a fountain in the middle, around which beggars slept. Above the square was a lighted window. Within, a woman sang a love song.

He tried to weep, remembering what it was to be young and in love, so long ago, but he could not. He had no tears, having sacrificed them in a magical experiment once. Besides, he was not sure he had ever been in love. His memory played tricks on him sometimes.

Wearily he sat on the edge of the fountain. Some beggars shuffled away from him, looking up uneasily. He cupped his hands, dipped them into the water, washed his face, then cupped them again and drank.

There was a light flickering at the bottom of the fountain. His eye was caught by it, and he was charmed, as a rat is by the gaze of a snake. The fountain seemed as deep as any sea. Shimmering, far, far below was a white oval. It reminded him of an egg. Then it was a new sun being born in the cloudy darkness between the worlds, rising to glory.

Then again he knew helpless terror, as the thing became a pale, swimming monster, glimpsed through the impossibly clear water, so far down that it looked tiny, but rushing up to devour him.

Finally the oval became a face. It was the black-clad man, ascending an invisible, spiraling staircase. He heard footsteps far away and below, muffled by the water. Every time the figure went around the spiral, it changed. Once, and it was without a right arm. Again, it lacked a left. Further, a leg was gone, and then another, but the dark man kept on coming, his footfalls louder and louder, for all that his limbs were gone and his trunk was beginning to disappear.

All this while the face slowly assumed features, like clay being molded by unseen fingers. First there were vague indentations for the eye sockets, and a swelling where the nose was to be, but when it paused, only a hand's breadth below the surface, it was entirely clear. The graying beard spread out on the water like a tangled weed. One eye was covered with a patch.

The face was his own.

"Even the greatest of magicians knows fear when his death is upon him," it said.

Abstractly, removed from the situation, one part of his paralyzed mind pondered: Where had he heard those words before? Who had spoken them?

In a flash, he knew: He had said them, many years before, when announcing to his master that he was no longer an apprentice. He had killed his master after a long duel, to prove the point, as was expected of him.

Somehow this recollection freed him, and he ran breathlessly away from the fountain. He thought he heard the water splashing behind him.

He came to his wagon at last, in the alley, and crawled in the back. There he found the book left open on a mat, and the lamp burned out. He slumped down by the book, asleep.

And awoke with a shriek, the head of the diminishing man in his lap.

"Even the greatest of magicians knows fear," it said.

He scrambled out the front of the wagon, over the driver's seat, tripped, and fell headlong into mud. There he lay panting, unable to get up, for all he was sure each breath would be his last.

Nothing happened.

Eventually, he caught hold of the wagon and dragged himself to his feet. He picked up a board from the ground and spoke a word, transforming it into a battleaxe with a flaming blade. This in hand, he crept around to the rear. Over the tailgate he saw a figure in a blue-and-red-striped robe asleep by a book and a burned-out lamp.

Then Emdo Wesa awoke with a start and crawled to the back of the wagon, looking this way and that for someone he thought he'd seen peering in at him. There was no one. The alleyway was empty.

Above, near to the dome of the Guardian, a soldier blew on a golden horn, heralding the dawn.

* * * *

Therefore Emdo Wesa took the smallest and sharpest of his knives and, mirror in hand, cut a tiny piece out of the flesh of his remaining eye. With it he made a *dadar*, a living projection of himself, spreading it first into an inchoate black mass, more like a hole in the air than a solid thing, then shaping it into the dark silhouette of an eagle. Since so little flesh had been used, it would not live long. It was a thing of the moment.

"Go and see as I would see," he commanded it. "Fetch me a

dreamer who can dream this dream of mine more fully than I."

Then he launched the bird, and it departed in the muted thunder of its wings. An hour later it returned, holding a boy in its claws by the hair, setting him down gently just before it dissipated.

At first the magician was startled. Then he was dismayed. The boy was naked, trembling and weeping, his eyes wide with fear and pain, his back and thighs criss-crossed with the bloody marks of a whip. But still he knew that this was his dreamer, so he took him into the wagon, put oil on his wounds, and wrapped him in a blanket.

For a while, the boy was so befuddled that he could not speak. His teeth chattered, and he stared about warily, like a caged animal. But when he seemed more at ease, Emdo Wesa questioned him.

"How many years have you?" he said.

"Thir—thirteen, and a few months—I don't know, exactly. I've forgotten. Since I was small, I—"

"The number is best forgotten. I have more years than you could probably count with all the numbers you know. I don't worry about it. But tell me, have you a name?"

"I am called Tamliade, Master."

"Tamliade, are you truly a great dreamer?"

"Yes—I mean, that was why my owner punished me. A dream came to me and I stood up to walk into it and the chain around my ankle tripped me and I fell flat on my face and woke up and all the others were laughing and the man said I was an idiot and he would not buy me and—"

"You were a slave, then?"

"Yes, Master, I am."

"You do not have to call me Master. When I am done with you, I shall set you free."

Tamliade only looked at him dully, then bowed his head.

"Tell me of your dreams," Emdo Wesa commanded him.

"When I was little—I think I was five—I was playing in a puddle, making boats out of leaves and sticks. Suddenly I forgot what I was doing, where I was, who I was, everything. The sky was dark and I was in a strange place. I saw, far away, a city made out of flames. It was pale red, and the towers were almost frozen in place. But they flickered. I thought it was the famous holy city of Ai Hanlo that everybody was always going to. I am from Hesh, in the forest country. I had never seen the city, you understand. I told my parents about it. My father said I was mad. My mother wept. I promised her I would stop seeing the place if it would make her happy, and she tried to smile, but I couldn't help it. I saw the place many more times: Any time, no matter what I was doing, suddenly I would be in a dream. I saw many other things. I tried to keep it all a secret, but everyone knew. I almost got run over by a cart that way once. Then, one night, when I was eleven—my mother had died by then—I suddenly found myself in that other place as I was, wearing my night tunic. It was not like a dream at all. All around me, all around the city of fire, the ground was smooth and hard and cold, like glass. I was barefoot and it was like walking on ice. My feet stuck to it. I could feel the air blowing against my legs. There was a little wind and it blew from behind me, toward the city, stirring up clouds of sparkling black dust. I got so close that time that I could almost reach out and touch the walls. They were not flames, but a kind of glass, and faintly warm. The tops of the towers were so high that I could not see them above me. I looked up and saw them disappearing into the sky, and I noticed that all the stars were out of place. They didn't make any of the usual patterns. Then the sun rose suddenly, blinding me, and the city was gone, and I stumbled into the branches of a soft hair-needle tree. When I could see again, I found myself in a forest. There were men crashing through the bushes all around me. The whole village had come to search for me. They were glad to find me. But my father was angry. He dragged me home by the ear. Then he said I was stupid and useless and he threw me out of the house. Later, bandits caught me and sold me as a slave."

"So your dreams have not done you much good, have they?"

"No, Master."

"Do you know what they are?"

"No, Master."

"I have an idea," said Emdo Wesa. "I think they are manifestations of the Goddess, the most powerful to have touched anyone in many years. They are echoes in a cave from the shout of her passing."

All along, the boy had merely recited the tale of his life as if it were an abstract thing about people who had lived long ago. But suddenly there was a frightened tone in his voice. He had been shocked into the present.

"But why me? I'm nobody important. Why should it come to me? I don't want it."

"Tamliade, listen. When I was your age—and that was long and long ago—I had a master, by which I mean a teacher, who told me that I was filled up with magic, even as you are filled with dreams, that this magic whirled inside me like a storm building in fury. I was frightened. I said what you have said: *Why me?* And he told me that there is no *why*. When a river cuts a new channel, he said, the water flows through. Does the part of the bank which gave way ask, *Why me? Why not six yards further downstream?* No, the thing merely happens. Thus it did not matter that I was frightened. That affected nothing. My teacher next told me that I would be a great magician one day, greater than he. I was no longer frightened. I was proud. So he told me the story of Nordec Ta Haincé, the great singer who lost his songs on account of pride and wandered the world in despair for three hundred years, kept alive by his own emptiness, searching for an echo of his own voice. And hearing that I was humbled. Finally, my teacher laughed, and said it was a silly story, and I was silly to believe it. Nordec Ta Haincé would have lost his songs at the same time whether he was proud or humble, since it was his destiny to do so, pre-ordained as all things are. This was a very difficult lesson, but when I came to understand it, I knew it to be a great one. There is no *why*."

Once more the boy sat passively, silent. Emdo Wesa sat

beside him, also silent. Then he got out of the wagon, made a fire in the alleyway, and set a pot of tea on it.

After a while, Tamliade looked out, still wrapped in the blanket.

"What are you doing, Master?"

The magician handed him a steaming cup.

"Drink this. It will make you sleep. When you wake you will be healed and the pain will be gone."

Tamliade hesitated, then drank slowly.

Emdo Wesa took him in his arms, asleep, wrapped in the blanket, to a tailor shop and laid him out on the counter. The tailor gaped in terror, but obeyed, barely able to control his hands, when the magician bade him take the boy's measurements and make him a suit of clothing like his own, only without ornamentation.

Then he left, taking Tamliade with him. The tailor would know where to deliver.

That day at noon, he carved a horse out of air. Toward evening the clothing arrived. At midnight, he carved another horse. Shortly after dawn the next day, he left the city through the Sunrise Gate, which was firmly locked. The guards did not see him. He made the wagon so thin it slipped through the crack.

The street urchins had a lot to talk about.

* * * *

Near mid-morning, Emdo Wesa pulled the wagon over to the side of the road, got down, went around to the back, and looked in over the tailgate. The interior of the wagon was divided into two compartments by leather curtains tied firmly shut. The boy was sitting with his back to them, surrounded by wicker crates.

"Are you awake?"

Tamliade stirred.

"Then get out of there."

The boy climbed down, walking unsteadily, looking down at his clothing. He felt himself gingerly, unsure he was really healed. The magician led him a few yards back the way they had come, to a bend in the road.

Far away, across tilled fields, the golden dome of Ai Hanlo shone on the horizon like a sunset.

"It is a custom of travelers," said Emdo Wesa, "to take one last look and pray that they might one day see this sight again."

"Master, when I was little I heard of the holy city, and like everyone else I wanted to visit it, but when I was brought there in chains to be sold, I saw it differently. I don't know if I want to see it again, ever."

"Either you will pray or you will not, as the river flows and the bank gives way."

Tamliade did not pray.

* * * *

A week passed. To Emdo Wesa, Tamliade was more puzzling than many of the mysteries of magic. He observed the boy as he would some new creature kept in a cage. In the end, he confessed to himself that he simply did not understand him. And yet, he had been young once, too, and had been alone in the world more often than not, and he knew what it was to be frightened, to be mistreated. More than that, he knew what it was to have a vision so overpowering that it drives away all other concerns. Yet he had been isolated so long, with his art for lover, for kin, for master, that he felt nothing. He knew this was not good, but there wasn't even a struggle toward emotion. He was hollow inside. Therefore he merely noted things:

Tamliade was always eager to please, and distinctly unhappy when there was nothing for him to do. So the magician let him prepare the camp at night and perform whatever chores he could, whether necessary or not.

When they came to a town, he bought the boy a book, a long romance "filled with magicians, wizards, heroes, monsters, and all sorts of extravagant things," the storekeeper had said. Tamliade read it slowly, with apparent difficulty, but without asking for help. He seldom spoke.

In another town, he left the boy to mind the wagon while he went for supplies. When he came back, he found him cowering in the seat, surrounded by a flock of young girls who would reach out to touch him, then dart away in a storm of giggles. One of them stood a distance away, blew several kisses, and began to unlace her blouse. The boy gaped and blushed, frozen where he sat. All of them shrieked in merriment.

When they saw the magician, they ran off.

Wesa noted all this. It occurred to him upon reflection that it was very sad how the boy did not seem to know how to express himself, to feel, to reach out and touch the world. Perhaps his spirit was broken. Or else it was the dreaming. Still he did not understand.

* * * *

"Tamliade, do you like music?" the magician asked one night as they made camp.

"Yes…I suppose so."

"Then play this." He gave the boy a flute.

Tamliade played, every third or fourth note a false one, and the magician danced, awkwardly. He laughed and clapped his hands. His laughter was coarse, grating. He tried to sing, but this, like his laughter, was more like something he had forgotten and was trying to imitate than like real song.

The boy only stared at him.

* * * *

"Master, where are we going?" Tamliade finally asked one night.

An image flashed into Emdo Wesa's mind, of a tortoise coming out of its shell, very slowly. He made a smile, remembering how to do it. Then he grew grim.

"We are going to that city you have seen in your dream. We

must find this manifestation of the Goddess and gain the power of it. Has that not been obvious all along?"

"But how can we go into a dream by riding on a road?" Then the boy put his hand over his mouth and looked down, afraid he'd said too much. "I mean—Master—I know you can do much magic—"

"Ah—well asked. I will tell you this much about the art. We do not move because we will come to the city that way, but so that my brother cannot see us. Did I ever tell you about my brother? No, because you did not ask. But now I shall. His name is Etash Wesa. He is a monster. He does not see as men do. He can reach out and know where everyone is, but his vision is like a fog and it takes time to settle. So when I move around, it takes him time to find me again. He is my enemy and seeks to destroy me. Do not ask the cause of our enmity. It is long and deep and more than you could understand. Not even I can comprehend all that he has become, but believe this: the world would be better off without him. He has drifted far, far into strangeness. Magic has that effect, changing the magician slowly, subtly, but inevitably. Often he must take parts of his own body and make *dadars*, living beings which are extensions of his will. This must be done with great care and a minimum of times, or the magician loses all that he once was. My brother has not remembered to be humane and compassionate, and the strangeness has devoured him. It has cost me much to fight him, all this time. You may wonder how you figure into all this, why you should be a part of our deadly quarrel. Yes, you are a part. Almost certainly the overseer who beat you was one of his *dadars*, perhaps the bandits who sold you also. I am sure that his design was to kill you before I could find you, so I would not be led to this thing we seek. I am sure the man would have beaten you to death had I not snatched you away suddenly."

"He looked surprised."

"Even my brother can be surprised. That is why I am still alive. I have eluded him many times. But he grows stronger, and I think that he could cover up the whole world like a cancer if left to himself. Therefore I must have you with me when this dream comes again."

The boy was silent. They sat down and ate an evening meal together. Then, as they were ready to go to sleep, he asked another question, unbidden. It was a curious thing. Emdo Wesa noted it.

"Master, if magic changes the magician, but you are not the way your brother is, then what has it done to you?"

"Ah...again, well asked. You grow bolder—"

"I didn't mean to—"

"No, be still. It was well asked, and I shall answer. I have remembered to be humane and compassionate, unlike my brother. Therefore I have not changed as he has. But I have paid a great price. Look."

He took off his gloves for the first time in Tamliade's presence, revealing that he had no hands, but instead flickering lights, like soft, sculpted flames, replacing flesh and bone up to the elbows.

The boy let out a scream of terror, got up, and ran.

"Tamliade! Where are you going?"

He stopped running and came sheepishly back to the campfire.

"I don't know."

The hands glowed like paper lanterns.

* * * *

The dream came to Tamliade again among the hills, on the borderlands of Hesh. It was in the autumn of the year. They had been travelling for more than a month, and had left the plains behind. The forested slopes around them were filled with brilliant colors by day. But night, leaves rustled, the wind chanting the dry litanies of the death of summer. Among the stars, the Stag fled across the sky, the Winter Dogs at its heels.

The magician and the boy sat in a clearing on a cloudless, brisk night, waiting for a pot of stew to come to a boil. Suddenly

Wesa was aware that the boy was staring up, but not at the stars. His eyes were unfocused.

"Tamliade?"

There was no response.

He snapped his fingers in front of Tamliade's face. Again, nothing.

He knew what to do. At once he carried the boy to the back of the wagon, then went around to the front and got in, huddling in the compartment behind the leather curtain. There he preformed *psadeu-ma*, opening his soul to Tamliade's vision, becoming one with him.

Through the eyes of the boy and with his feelings and memories, he first sat in a puddle of rainwater, viewing things there which were not reflected, his leaf boats drifting forgotten across the image. Then darkness, drifting, and finally sharp sensation. He was cold all over. He felt the night air on his bare shoulders and back. His knees were sunk in mud. A stick figure moved before him on a gray field, then fleshed out into a puffy-faced man dressed in a dirty smock and round skullcap.

Naked, the boy knelt before the tethering post to which his wrists were bound.

"A good slave," the man was saying, "obeys and obeys and obeys. He does not question. He has no will of his own, no feelings. He may only anticipate his master's wishes, and never displease him. His mind is inferior. Remember that. You are stupid! You are scum!"

The overseer's cap was that of a freedman. He hadn't had it long. He waved his hand to signal someone standing behind the boy. A whip cracked across Tamliade's back, again, again, again. He screamed. He tried to stand up. The whip caught him around the legs and yanked him down into the mud. He let himself sink there, trying to escape the pain, the shouting, the screaming. He curled around the post, glancing up one last time to see the overseer begin to fade, to darken, to melt into a black mass, more of a silhouette cut out of the air than a living man.

Then Tamliade's spirit was drifting from his body. It was

someone else who whimpered, far away. He felt nothing. The sound of the whip reminded him of a village tanner beating hide.

Another sensation: Again, the night was cold, and his bare feet sank ankle-deep in mud, but this time a soft, long-needled branch brushed against his face. It was the branch of a ledbya, the hair-needle tree. Little winged lizards fluttered higher up, invisible but noisy.

He emerged into a clearing where the forest floor was made of smooth, black glass. He turned to look back the way he had come, and the trees were gone. There was only the black glass, vanishing into the murky distance. The sky overhead was dark, with less than a dozen stars in it.

He walked a long way, and with every step the glass grew colder. The soles of his feet stuck to it. He was afraid that all his body's warmth would be drawn out and he would freeze solid, standing there forever. He skipped and jumped, and shivered with the cold.

Then something glowed red on the horizon, a flickering, like distant flames. He ran toward it.

A dome of pale light rose, and there were towers around it, a half-seen reflection of a ghost of the city of Ai Hanlo.

Somehow, next, he was *there*, inside the city, among the towers, in a kind of maze. He wandered for hours through corridors and courtyards, through galleries and narrow streets. The transition between indoors and outdoors was more subtle than he could fathom. He crossed a wide square and suddenly found himself in a room no larger than a closet and hung with draperies in which luminous threads seemed to shift and form ever-changing patterns as he watched. For a time he stood there, hypnotized, but a feeling of excitement came over him, of dread and expectation and indefinable longing. He pushed the curtains aside and forced his way into a vast hall filled with incomprehensible machines, some of them only made of flickering fields of light, others of multi-colored, glistening metals. There was a transparent column in which spheres the size of houses drifted up and down, passing through one another again and again, like no solid thing. A dark hemisphere of rough metal occupied much of the middle of the floor. It remind him of a turtle shell, but this would have to be a turtle large enough to devour horses. Inside it, hammers beat. In time they found a rhythm, which became a harmony, which became a kind of song.

Then he was in a corridor again, long and dark, with light at the far end. Up ahead, he heard the faint sound of weeping. He hurried toward it, toward the light.

Something he had taken for drapery suddenly turned around, and for an instant he beheld a beautiful lady veiled in blue the color of dawn, clad in a robe streaked with purple and dark orange like the last moments of sunset; and the horned Moon gleamed in her hair and the stars trailed behind her like a cloak. The scene was all a jumble. He was with this lady in the corridor. From a clearing in the forest of ledbya trees he saw her drifting across the sky, silent as a cloud. He felt in her presence the vivid, unmistakable nearness of the power of the Goddess. His body shook with it. In this realization, the minds of Emdo Wesa and Tamliade began to separate. The magician understood. The boy did not.

The lady wept. Rain fell down on Tamliade. He lay naked and whimpering in the mud, his wrists tied to the post. Men were crashing through the bushes all around.

Emdo Wesa felt his hold on the dream slipping. He struggled to submerge himself again. Once more he became Tamliade.

His father had him by the ear. They were in the smithy.

"You are mad. You are an imbecile," his father shouted, his face only inches away, spittle flying. "You wander off after whatever drips into your hollow head."

His father pinched his arm hard. "Look at that. Scrawny. No muscles. Useless. You'll never be anything but a tramp. Away with you. Wander the roads and follow your vision. And starve for all I care."

His mother wept.

He sat in the hot dust at a crossroads beneath the glaring sun, rattling a begging bowl.

An old woman led her blind husband up to him, saying, "Holy One, you have been touched by some fragment of the Goddess. Have you the power to heal?"

A bird alighted on the lip of the bowl and began to sing, in words and a voice like that of a little child, of Ai Hanlo the holy city. He had a vision of Ai Hanlo rising against the horizon, its golden dome aflame with sunset when all the plains were dark. He saw himself walking the long and winding road to Ai Hanlo, where lay the bones of the Goddess in holy splendor, where the Guardian, the priest-king who watched over them, would surely be able to explain his vision to him.

But the bird stopped singing and grew into an enormous black eagle and seized him by the hair, carrying him high into the air. He looked down on the city, the road, on the Endless River flowing past like a glittering serpent in the starlight. The sunset was gone. The sky was wholly dark. With a thunder of wings, the eagle shut out the stars, filling the sky. There were mountains below, passing like great whales beneath the sea. Then the land was black and smooth, and before him was the city of lights, ghost of Ai Hanlo, flickering in and out of existence like a mirage seen from different angles.

The bird did not take him there. It alighted in a tree and let go of him. He fell with a bump onto soft loam and ledbya needles. The winged lizards chittered at him.

An old, blind slave, whose face was criss-crossed with the scars of the lash that had taken his eyes, sat beside him, saying, "A man's fate is a man's fate, and life is but an illusion. There is no why. Therefore, be comforted."

Emdo Wesa felt himself failing out of the dream again. Tamliade seemed further and further removed, only a half-remembered echo, like the ringing that lingers in the air long after a gong has become silent.

A bird dropped out of the tree onto the wizard's knee, followed by another, and another. More landed on his shoulders. In his old body, with his flaming hands, he was naked. The claws of the birds dug into his flesh. The blind slave melted like wax and slowly became a huge, black bird with a beak the color of blood.

"Brother, I have found you," it said.

"Even the greatest of magicians knows fear when his death is upon him."

II.

In holiness hear this.
It ends in holiness.
Now the tale is of Tamliade.

* * * *

The boy heard the old, blind slave droning on and on. The voice faded to a whisper, the individual words slowly submerging. Then there was only wind.

Another sound came. The lady was weeping. No, she was singing, and in thousands of voices, fragmented like a statue dashed to pieces. The voices became shriller, harsher, like a million birds crammed into a tiny space and shrieking all at once.

He rose out of his dream, and awoke in the back of the wagon, among the wicker crates.

The million birds still shrieked. The wagon, massive as it was, shook like a toy in the fist of a child.

Countless tiny bodies slammed against the other side of the leather partition. From within, over the thundering cacophony, came the voice of Emdo Wesa shouting, "No, Brother, you haven't got me yet! And you shall not!" Then the voice cracked in desperation, and there were high screams, almost like those of a woman, interspersed with strange words.

The wagon shook all the more. The birds shrieked louder. Emdo Wesa's voice was gone.

Tamliade was over the tailgate in an instant, but his foot

caught on something in the baggage, and he tumbled down onto the ground. He recovered quickly, but stood there trembling, taking one step this way, another that. He wanted to rescue Emdo Wesa. He wanted to get away. His mind was in confusion, fighting with itself.

Before he knew what he was doing he was off and running. He leapt over the remains of the campfire and the forgotten stewpot and kept going, but when he was a short distance away, he heard the magician call out in a voice louder than anything human, like thunder, shaking the earth, repeating a formula three times. The cries of the birds were drowned out.

Then there was only silence.

The boy stopped and turned around. It was morning, he noticed for the first time. The sky was growing light. But the wagon was glowing more brightly than the sun. It drove off the last of twilight. The glare of it was blinding. He covered his eyes and fell to his knees.

Emdo Wesa spoke clearly, in a voice scarcely louder than ordinary conversation, *"Lady. I give you my hand. Take me now into your dwelling place."*

The light faded. Tamliade uncovered his eyes and was astonished to see that the wagon had not been wholly consumed. It stood as it always did. The horses were hitched to it, impassive as statues.

He rose slowly. His greatest fear now was that the magician had gone off somewhere, leaving him alone, unable to cope with what was happening. He approached the wagon slowly.

"Master?"

The front flap opened and Emdo Wesa crawled wearily out. His clothing was in rags, and he bled from countless cuts. He stumbled, seemed about to fall, and Tamliade ran forward to catch him. But he caught himself, and slid down to the ground, sitting with his head against the front wheel.

"Master?"

Wesa looked at him almost as if he didn't recognize him. After a time he spoke.

"Oh there you are. I knew you wouldn't run away again."

"What happened?"

"My brother. He came through the dream. I've driven him away for now."

* * * *

Tamliade and Emdo Wesa fled from Etash Wesa thereafter, never spending more than a few hours in the same place. It was too dangerous to camp. They would stop for a meal sometimes, then drive all night, one relieving the other at the reins. The horses, fortunately, were tireless.

"I do not think we can elude my brother for long," magician said. "He has altered himself too much. He moves outside the physical spaces, without regard to distances, and somehow he can sense our presence even if we stop long enough to piss. Do not ask me more. I cannot put a description of him fully into words."

"Master, is there anything I can do?"

"Only one thing. You must behold the vision clearly one more time, long enough for the two of us to pass into it and gain whatever power is to be had from it. We must hope that my brother will stay away long enough for us to do this much."

"But the dream just comes. How can I control it?"

"You can't. Imagine yourself creeping up on a sleeping giant. His hair is long and blowing in the wind, whirling all around. He has one silver hair, his dream hair. Eventually it will blow within your reach. When it does, you must seize it and climb into the great dream. You can't know when. Just be ready."

Days turned into weeks, and autumn into winter. They were heading north. The cold came earlier in this part of the world. The hills of Hesh were long behind them. There were rolling plains again for a while, brown and gray and covered endlessly with mud and dead weed stalks, and then the faces of two kings rose up out of the earth, carven out of huge rocks, with sharp features and pointed, towering crowns worn dull by the winds of years. Trees grew on their eyebrows. Tamliade looked back, and saw four low hills behind him, the knees of the kings as they slept beneath a blanket of soil.

Emdo Wesa paid them no heed. He drove the wagon on a straight path between them, and almost at once the ground rose into high, sharp ridges, into cliffs, and there were mountains all around, revealed as they drove through curtain after curtain of low-lying clouds. The air was damp and so cold it was almost painful to breathe.

Out of the grey sky rain whipped into their faces, then sleet, then snow, and the world was white and pale grey and the blue of ice, and everything faded into sameness a short distance away. Only a slight darkening betokened nightfall. Once, when the way was wholly obscured, Emdo Wesa stood up on the wagon seat, took off his gloves, and parted the storm with his flaming hands.

The boy was filled with fear. He was exhausted. He was cold. They hadn't eaten anything but scraps of cold meat for days. The wizard went on like a thing of clockwork, oblivious to all, his mind caught up entirely, Tamliade was sure, with formulae, stratagems, and enchantments. He wondered if he would be noticed if he froze to death and fell off into the snow.

For a time the storm eased a little, and the wagon crawled up the side of a huge, rolling slope like an insect on the body of a beached whale.

"I think my brother has sent us this storm," said Emdo Wesa when the tempest returned. "I am sure he has."

Once, suddenly—Tamliade was not sure if it was day or night—he drew the wagon to a halt and left the boy behind as he stepped off the seat onto an invisible stairway, and climbed into the sky. Lightning flashed for hours amidst the blizzard, and a thunder like the tread of giants shook the land. When the magician came back down all he said was, "My brother is close behind us now."

In the end they came to a high mountain pass blocked with enough snow to entomb a city. The magician reached out with his burning hands to melt the snow, but it refroze almost immediately. An hour's worth of trying left a long trail of strangely sculpted ice shapes, but the pass was as blocked as ever. They could not go on. Emdo Wesa spied a cave and drove the wagon into it, leaving the howling storm behind. Tamliade found the darkness comforting, but still it was intensely cold inside. He sat still on the wagon seat, passively awaiting whatever was to happen.

The magician got down and lit a fire with his hand, burning only air for fuel.

"Now we must wait," he said. "Here, perhaps, shall be our battleground."

Tamliade got down and walked around. He waved his arms, trying to bring feeling into his numb extremities. But he was too tired to keep it up for long.

Then he stood still, and the flash of a vision came over him, but almost immediately he was back in the cold cave. He had to think back to sort out the images and sensations. He looked up, and saw that the magician was gazing at him with intense interest.

"Yes.... What was it?"

"I don't know, really. I was in darkness. It felt stuffy, close, as if I were buried in a coffin near to the surface of the ground. It sounds funny, but it was very hot. I was in great pain. I burned all over. I think...I think all my limbs had been cut off, and bleeding stumps banged against the sides of the box. I couldn't see anything. I smelled blood, but it was rotten, putrid, and thick as cold grease. It was washing all over me. I was floating. There was water running outside. I heard the cries of strange birds. Master, it was a terrible thing I saw. What is it?"

Emdo Wesa forced a grotesque smile, as if someone else had yanked the ends of his mouth up with two fingers. It only disturbed the boy even more.

"Ah yes," the magician said. "The swamps of Zabortash. My brother is there. He touched you with his mind."

The boy tried to sound cheerful, but deep inside he knew

only despair.

"If he is there…what have we got to worry about? So far away."

"So far away. But so near. He is almost upon us."

"If only the vision would come."

Wesa paused. He stood regarding the boy. He held his hand to his chin and scratched his beard. This gesture somehow comforted the boy. Any ordinary man with a beard did it.

"Tamliade, I think there is a way to bring on the vision right now. But you must be very brave."

"Yes, Master. What must I do?" He spoke like one being led to execution.

"You must think back to what you saw and felt. You must reach out to my brother. He will draw you out of yourself, into dreams. He is more a dream than a real thing now. Most of him is no longer in the world you live in."

"Then what happens?"

"Here is the peril: he will try to take you over, to seize you and your vision, to gain the power of this thing you have seen. If I can hold him off, we can escape into the dream he has opened. Then there is hope. If not, it is the end. Do you understand?"

"Yes, I understand. I will do whatever you say."

Emdo Wesa sat. He motioned Tamliade to sit beside him on the rough, frigid cave floor. He reached for the boy's hand. Tamliade drew away.

"You said you would do anything."

"Please, Master. I didn't think. But I am afraid to touch your hand."

"Even when gloved? Oh, very well." The magician got up and fetched a cord from the wagon. He tied one end around Tamliade's wrist, and held the other. Then he said down, closed his eyes, and began to chant, *"Psadeu-ma te, psadeu-ma hae, psadeu-ma—"* His voice faded away into grey distance. Tamliade was drifting. Deliberately, with all his strength of mind, he forced his thoughts back to the sounds of the swamp of Zabortash, the close, filthy air inside the coffin, the pain—

Suddenly he felt it again, and he was *there*. He wanted to scream, but it seemed he had no voice.

He felt something else. It wasn't a sensation. It was more something intruding on his consciousness, at first raw, unimaginable power, then intense hatred, overwhelming all thought, all feeling, all awareness. He forgot about his promise to Emdo Wesa. He wanted to get out, to escape this thing. He didn't care about his vision, about what happened to his master, or even what happened to the world. He had to get out. It was like climbing up the side of a sand pit, the sand falling down, down, faster and faster, burying—

Etash Wesa had him. Etash Wesa was snuffing out his very self.

Deep, deep, beyond the hatred, another mind worked and turned in incomprehensible, alien ways. Tamliade was without any means to grasp what it felt, what it thought.

Something yanked his wrist hard. He tumbled forward, face down into foul-smelling muck, then through it, out of darkness, into red haze, then white light like the burst from the wagon that morning. He tumbled over and over, falling forever. Somehow he was aware that his master was with him.

He stopped. There was no impact, just a cessation of falling. The light shrank to spots before his eyes, then faded entirely, and he saw that he was inside the city of lights, the city of his vision.

Emdo Wesa let go of the cord. With both his flaming hands, he seemed to be tying up invisible strings in the air. Tamliade thought of the partition in the wagon.

"That should keep him away for a short time," the magician said when he had finished. "But we have only a short time."

Wesa led him through the courtyards and galleries, past the towers, the tapestries, the strange machines, along the twisting alleyways.

The boy craned his neck back. The tops of the towers above him shifted like clouds. Long, thin walkways seemed to trail like spiderwebs in a breeze. He forgot himself for a moment and stopped to stare.

The magician took up the cord and yanked.

"Don't stray from me. The angles here will deceive you. So can the distances. You'd never find your way out."

"This place…is it real?"

"Yes. You have dreamed it. No, no, I don't mean that. You did not create it. It is objectively here, but *here* is not on the same Earth you and I know. I think it is something out of a past age, overlooked by time, left behind to gutter out like a candle flame."

They walked along a marble corridor. The walls didn't quite seem solid. The whole place seemed to flicker on the verge of transparency.

"Is this place like the Old Places, the ruins?"

"Yes, like those. There are ruins everywhere, as one age piles atop the next. But, this one does not decay into dust and rubble. Consider: before the Goddess there lived another, a god or goddess or some similar thing, and before that one another, and before another. Each presided over a period of time, an age, and when each died, there was a confused interval before another was born. We live in one such. Some of these ages are dark, some glittering and glorious, and they stretch out like the scales of a snake, into eternity. This place is one of the scales broken loose or a fragment of one, or a reflection, or dust, or, in a way, a *dadar* of the past."

"I do not understand."

"Nor do I. Nor does anyone. It is a thing which can only be half-grasped. Therefore we have no time to discuss it. Hurry. Come along. My brother will be through eventually, and in any case, unless we are successful, and I gain the power to fight him, we cannot leave this place."

They came to a broad gallery in which the floor looked solid but gave no sensation at all. Tamliade's knees buckled, his unconscious mind sure he had just stepped off a cliff, but he did not fall. Uneasily, he walked on. The magician dragged him by the cord. His hand was going numb. He walked a little faster until there was slack, then loosened the loop.

An animate skeleton floated before them in the air, clad in garments of smoke, with a crown of crystal on its head, its bones glowing like old coals.

"Fellow," cried the magician. "Take us to the lady of this place. I know she is here. I have seen her in dreams."

The thing drifted like a leaf on a stream, and they followed.

Gradually their surroundings became more substantial. The walls were smooth and cold to the touch. Their footfalls echoed as they walked. Tamliade gazed down at his own reflection in the polished pavement, and that of his master. The skeleton gave no reflection at all. He looked back to see the way they had come slowly suffusing into panes of light, into flickering shapes, into a soft glow. Emdo Wesa gazed steadily ahead, undistracted.

The way grew narrower and darker. Soon there was only a faint light, from no discernable source. Their guide glowed ahead of them like a beacon, casting huge, distorted shadows on the walls.

A double door opened before them, and they faced another corridor, this one filled with mirrors.

The spirit rose up and vanished into the gloom. Tamliade wasn't sure if there was a ceiling up there or not. He looked ahead, at the mirrors. Wesa was studying them intently. Each was perfectly circular, about five feet across; they were held out from the walls on either side by enormous hands, which grasped them between thumb and forefinger. The hands were alternately purest white and darkest black. Tamliade thought they were only carved mounts, but as Wesa dragged him forward and they approached one, the thing turned, angling the mirror for them to see. The hands were alive.

The magician did not seem to be startled, or even to care.

They stood before the first mirror. At first it revealed only themselves. Then the scene changed. Beyond was a forest, in the full bloom of summer. The trees had long blue-gray needles. Far away, between the trunks, sunlight glimmered off the surface of a lake. Tamliade knew the place. He had played by that lake many times when he was small. Now he could smell the resinous scent of the trees, and the warm breeze ruffled his hair.

He gaped in wonder, but Emdo Wesa yanked him away.

"No, not that one."

As he was dragged away he reached out, and touched only cold glass.

Through other mirrors, as they passed, he saw scenes of cities, deserts, forests, ships at sea, some of them familiar, some of them not. There was a place underground, where water ran down the side of a cavern, and a stone ship lay beached. On its decks crouched creatures half like frogs, half like men, frozen, clad in gowns of flowing stone. Their eyes seemed to follow him. He looked into another mirror and saw himself naked, bound to the post, writhing under the lash. In the next, he was being carried off by the eagle, Emdo Wesa's *dadar*. Then he lay on the counter before the astonished tailor. He saw Emdo Wesa's wagon become thin and slip out through the crack in the Sunrise Gate. Ai Hanlo fell away beneath the horizon. The girls in the town teased him and laughed. The intervals between each mirror decreased. There were three in which he and his master sat beside the same fire. It was the last camp they had made.

Still Emdo Wesa walked steadily on, dragging Tamliade like a mechanical thing.

The way was not straight. It twisted and lurched sickeningly at times, turning at impossible angles, up, down, sideways, otherways. The mirrors were always there, turning to be seen, following them.

He saw the city of lights from the outside, as it had appeared in dreams. Yes, it did look like a ghost of Ai Hanlo. Its dome at the top was a pale red.

And he saw the apparition before them, leading them to the corridor of mirrors, and he looked into a mirror and saw himself and Emdo Wesa looking into a mirror in which sunlight sparkled off a lake behind some trees. Emdo Wesa dragged him on. They seemed to walk forever. At last they came to a halt, looking into a mirror at an image of themselves looking into a mirror at themselves looking into mirrors, until the images were too small to make out. All the images were of the present time.

"I think we have found what we want," said Emdo Wesa. "Behold."

The magician pointed, not at a mirror, but to the end of the corridor. Tamliade looked. Far away from them, as he had seen in dreams, a bit of drapery turned in the gloom, and was not drapery at all. Either in a vaster mirror or truly there, the lady stood, veiled in the dawn, clad in a gown of sunset, with the horned Moon in her hair and the stars trailing behind her like a cloak.

Emdo Wesa began to run, dragging Tamliade. He had never seen the old man move like that. But as they ran, the lady only seemed farther away.

All the mirrors they passed were dark.

She was not fleeing from them. It was a trick of distance. She stood, rigid as a statue, and they seemed to be running on a treadmill, the floor ever growing longer before them.

Then, in the blinking of an eye, she was gone, and they came to a halt at the end of the corridor, Tamliade gasping for breath, his master standing silently.

There was another mirror before them, far larger than the others, held up by two hands, one dark, one pale and softly glowing. There was no image. The circle of glass was dark at first. But slowly it filled with stars. The outline of a hill appeared. The horned Moon rose over it.

"Ah, yes," said the wizard. He removed the glove from his right hand, holding Tamliade's cord with his left. He reached out to touch the glass surface and it rippled like water. The flaming hand passed through. He stepped into the mirror, pulling the boy after him.

Tamliade felt another lurch, again as if he had stepped off a cliff, but he did not fall. There was a wash of cold, as if he had been immersed in an icy pool. The night air was frigid. The stars were sharp and bright. They did not twinkle. A stiff wind blew.

He and the magician climbed the hill. He looked back and saw the city of lights flickering behind them. Once more it looked insubstantial, a thing of sculpted vapors.

The stars overhead formed no constellations he had ever seen before.

At last, when the Moon was overhead, they came to the opening of a cave near the top of the hill. Within was a pool of clear, still water, beneath the surface of which lay the lady, asleep, her dark hair spread out in the water like a gently swaying weed.

Tamliade was afraid, not of danger, but out of awe. He trembled. Emdo Wesa did not seem to react at all.

"Who is she? What is she?"

The magician ignored him, let go of the cord, and knelt by the water's edge. Tamliade took the opportunity to back a few steps away. He waited and listened as the magician, chanting a litany in a strange tongue, reached down into the water with his fiery hand and raised the lady up, She rose like a ghost, like smoke, like a cloud driven across the sky. Her eyes opened. She spoke in a voice that was gentle, distant, dry, like the rustling of leaves in an autumn wind.

"Thou, rescuer, my salvation, know that I am a reflection, an image, an echo of the Goddess. Yes, as you would say, a *dadar* of she who has died."

"You know my thoughts…" said Emdo Wesa.

"Indeed, I summoned thee. I dreamed thee into being. I dreamed all the years of thy life, making thee my *dadar*, so that in the fullness of time my hand would be touched, I would be raised up as thou hast done…to give me the gift of death, for I have lived long, long beyond my time, when she who created me by gazing into a mirror has ceased to be. No, do not seek understanding. You cannot. With her passing, all things created of her became powerless, frozen outside of time. Now with another touch of your hand, your power will pass into me, your magic, and I shall have the strength to sleep the sleep without dreams."

"But—but, my lady," gasped Emdo Wesa, showing more emotion than Tamliade had ever seen in him, "you must give me *your* power to be added to mine, that I might defeat my enemy. Everything depends on this. Everything. The whole world. You must. That is what I have come for, to get it before he does."

"What care I for your world? I live in it no longer. What care I for your quarrels? That is not what I created you for so long ago, my *dadar*. Did you really not know? Everything you have ever done has been orchestrated toward this end, my end, not yours."

Emdo Wesa stood helpless, hands at his side, wheezing and heaving. Tamliade guessed that he was trying to weep, but could not find it within himself to do so.

The lady gently removed the glove from his left hand, then folded both of his hands between hers. When she let them go, they were the color of dirty smoke, grey and black. They longer glowed.

Like a mote of light, the lady drifted out of the cave, past Tamliade, apparently unaware of his presence. He turned and saw her rising slowly into the sky, drifting among the stars. For an instant he saw her huge, more awesome, more beautiful, more terrible than anything he could comprehend, stretched across the heavens, clad in the night, holding the Moon, scattering the stars like seed. Then she faded. Briefly, the sky was dark. Then, at the place where she had disappeared, a luminious speck appeared. It grew and quavered, flowing at the edges like a liquid thing pouring into the universe, becoming ever brighter.

The whole sky exploded in brilliance, and, just before his eyes were dazzled utterly, he saw the lady again cloaked in flame, her gown of purest white, astride a dolphin with the Sun in one hand and a tree in the other.

He fainted to the ground at the mouth of the cave.

* * * *

Tamliade was next aware of something warm and fluid

washing over him. He opened his eyes. It was day. The sky was a dull grey above him.

He brought a wet hand up to his face and screamed aloud when he saw that it was covered with blood.

He scrambled to his feet and ran back into the cave, sick with the dread of utter disorientation. The blood flowed after him. He and the magician came out again, and climbed to the top of the hill as the cave filled up. The summit alone stood a few feet above the surface of an ocean of blood, which stretched to the horizon in all directions. The city of lights was gone. Everywhere, only the waveless, dark surface. The stench was overwhelming.

Emdo Wesa stood silently. He pointed. The boy looked and saw something floating far away. It was only a speck at first. He strained to see it. Slowly it drew nearer, carried by some inexorable current. He felt mounting terror as it approached. He ran around in futile circles like a headless chicken. He fell to his knees and covered his eyes.

"Get up," said Emdo Wesa sharply. "Look. Have dignity."

Startled, he obeyed. The panic left him.

The thing was nearby now. He could see quite clearly that it was a coffin, bobbing up and down gently on the sea of blood.

A voice thundered from all directions at once. He felt his bones vibrate with it.

"Brother, I have found you. I am here."

Tamliade looked at his master's brother. Etash Wesa was pink, wormlike, the ruined bulk of his body twisting around and around inside the lidless coffin, awash in blood. There was an empty-socketed protuberance which might have once been a head, but it seemed smashed and pushed to one side. All three openings alternately spewed gore and babbled as the thing rolled over. He couldn't tell which had been the mouth. One stubby remnant of an arm thumped against the wooden sides.

"My brother has made many, many *dadars*," Emdo Wesa explained. "Do not think he is helpless because of his appearance. He is far more advanced in magic than I, and almost infinitely powerful."

"Brother, the boy touches dreams. He was your instrument once. Now he shall be mine. Give him to me and I shall spare you, Your power is gone. I do not fear you. There can be no further rivalry between us."

Tamliade began to weep softly.

"Are you afraid?" his master asked, as if merely curious.

"No. I am not afraid anymore. It is my fate and there is nothing I can do about it. I understand that much. I have never been free, even before I was a slave. *No.* My tears are for *you.* Out of pity. You have been kind to me in your way. You have been more of a father than my father was. You awakened me to being a person again, not a thing. I don't know…it just came out like that and in *my* way, as best I could, I came to love you. Even when you frightened me. And now…and now I see your future clearly. Call it a vision. I see what will happen if you survive this day. I see you eaten up and changed by your magic, more enslaved by it than ever I was. I do not think he means to kill you now. No, you will be like your brother someday, wretched and pathetic for all that you are terrible. So I am not afraid. I weep for you."

Then Tamliade walked to the very edge of the blood sea. The coffin moved in closer. Blood washed over his boots.

"Master," he said, "if I give myself up to him, and you will be able to turn aside from your magic and become a man again, then I will gladly do it, because I am nothing and you are great and wise."

"No, my loyal servant, that will not necessary," said Emdo Wesa. "I know a better way. Even my brother will be surprised."

The thing in the coffin began to thrash about. Tamliade leapt back.

He watched in horrified fascination as Emdo Wesa produced a long knife from out of his clothing and stabbed himself full in the chest with it, sinking it in to the hilt. The magician cut out his own living, beating heart. The wound did not bleed. There was fire within, the gaping hole like the mouth of a furnace.

Once again, holding the heart high over his head, Emdo Wesa's hands flared to life. He was transfigured, enshrouded in light. With a mighty heave he hurled the heart into the coffin.

Etash Wesa screamed.

From horizon to horizon, the ocean of blood exploded into a raging inferno of red flame.

* * * *

Tamliade found himself lying face down in deep snow. The cold was a shock. Sputtering, startled, disoriented, he raised himself to his hands and knees.

His master stood with his back to him, absolutely still.

Snow had been accumulating on him for some time.

"Master? Emdo Wesa? Are you all right? What happened? Was it real?"

There was no reply. He stood unsteadily on frozen legs and staggered through knee-deep snow, circling the stiff figure.

Emdo Wesa stared blankly ahead. His eyepatch was gone. Both of his sockets were empty. His mouth hung open. A pale light flickered within, as if his head were a lantern with a single candle inside. The hole in the front of his coat had somehow become glued shut.

"Master? Do you know me? *Speak to me!*"

The magician spoke without moving his lips. The voice was hollow, grating, without inflection, like that of a bronze head enchanted into an imitation of life.

"There are many things for me to do. I am weak. I must become strong again. So many projects to undertake, so many spells to master, worlds to explore. I will gather all knowledge and power to myself in the end. My brother is not dead. In the end, I shall conquer him."

Again Tamliade wept.

"I would have…instead you did this for me. *Why?* You gave up everything you were."

Emdo Wesa did not answer. Tamliade recalled what his

master had told him once: *There is no why.*

He was standing on a sloping hillside. He looked up. Through the falling snow he dimly made out the mouth of the cave. He climbed up, gasping from the exertion, and stumbled inside. His master did not follow.

When next he slept—he did not know if it were night or day—he saw Emdo Wesa's death in a dream. It was not at all like that of Etash Wesa. He had been wrong. He saw the magician dissipating, drifting apart like a storm whose strength is spent, like dust and ashes on the wind.

* * * *

He spent all that winter in the cave. The horses were gone for want of conjuring, and there was no way he could leave. He lived precariously off the supplies in the wagon, and grew very thin.

He spent his time trying to understand what he had experienced. He remembered Emdo Wesa. He learned to put his body aside and open his spirit in a manner akin to *psadeu-ma*, although he was ignorant of the term. He had many visions. He spoke with many spirits, and with the Dark and Bright Powers, the fragments of the Goddess which still wandered across the world. And he heard the fading echo of her death more clearly than had even the holiest of men for many generations.

In the spring he made his way to Ai Hanlo, entered the service of the Guardian, and became a priest.

A LANTERN MAKER OF AI HANLO

In Zabortash, all men are magicians. The air is so thick with magic that you can catch a spirit or a spell with a net on any street corner. Women wear their hair short, lest they find ghosts tangled in it. Still, they find them in their hats.

In Zabortash, even the lantern makers work wonders: the present moon is not the first to shine upon the Earth. The old one went out when the Goddess died, but a Zabortashi lantern maker consulted with a magus, and was directed to that hidden stairway which leads into the sky. He hung his finest lantern in the darkness, in the night, that the stars might not grow overproud of their brilliance, that men might know the duration of the month again.

In Zabortash, a land far to the south and filled with sluggish rivers, with swamps and steaming jungles, the air is so thick that in the darkness, in the night, the face of the moon ripples.

So it is said.

In Zabortash, further, for all that the folk are magicians, there are men who love their wives, who look on their children with pride when they are young· and wistfulness when they are old enough to remind the parents what they were like in their youth.

In Zabortash, people know beauty and feel joy, and know and feel also hurt and hunger and sorrow.

So it is said.

* * * *

In the time of the death of the Goddess, there dwelt a lantern maker in Zabortash named Talnaco Ramat who was skilled in his art. He was a young man, and wholly in love with the maiden Mirithemne, but she would not have him, being of a higher caste than he, and he would not be satisfied with any other. Therefore he labored long on a lantern of special design. He cut intricate shapes into the shell of it, making holes for light to shine through. The lantern was like a metal box, as tall as an outstretched hand, rectangular with a domed top and a metal ring hinged onto the dome to serve as a handle. At the outset, it was like any other lantern Talnaco Ramat might make, but he inlaid it with precious stones and plated it with gold. He carved schools of fish into it, swimming around the base, and those winged lizards called *kwisi*, which hop from branch to branch and are supposed to bring constancy and long life. He carved hills and villages, the winding river which is called Endless, and he fashioned the top half of the lantern into the shape of Ai Hanlo, the holiest of cities and center of the world, where the bones of the Goddess lie in blessed splendor. That city is built on a mountain; at the summit stands a golden dome, beneath which the Guardian of the Bones of the Goddess holds court. In this likeness was the dome of the lantern made, complete with tiny windows and ringed with battlements and towers.

Finally, Talnaco Ramat carved his own image and that of his beloved into the metal. He depicted the two of them walking hand in hand along the bank of the river, going up to the city.

Then he lit a candle inside the lantern and carried it into a darkened loft. Light streamed through the carven metal, and all his creations were outlined by it. As he watched, the river seemed to flow. The images were projected onto the walls and roof of the loft. Then he was not in the loft at all, but beside Mirithemne. All around them lizards hopped from branch to branch, wings buzzing, fleshy tails dangling.

Mirithemne smiled. The day was bright and clear. Rivermen sang as they poled a barge along. A great *drontha*, a warship of the Holy Empire, crawled against the current like a centipede on its banks of oars.

They came to the holy city, entering through the Sunrise Gate, mingling with the crowds. They passed through the square where mendicants waited below the wall that shut them out of the Guardian's palace. Once a week, he explained to Mirithemne, priests came to the top of that wall, and, holding aloft reliquaries containing splinters of the bones of the Goddess, blessed the people below. Miraculous cures still happened, but they were not as common as they had once been. The power of the Goddess was fading.

He led Mirithemne to a house at the end of a narrow lane. A wooden sign with a lantern painted on it hung over the door. He got out a key.

"This will be our home," he said.

He unlocked the door and went in, only to find himself alone in the loft, with the candle of the lantern sputtering out.

He was satisfied. The lantern was adequate.

That night, in the darkness, after the moon had set, he spoke a spell into the open door of the lantern and it filled with a light softer than candle flame, with vapors excited by the ardor of his love.

He climbed onto the roof of his shop and set the lantern down on a ledge. He spoke the name of his beloved three times, and he spoke other words. Then he gently pushed the lantern off the ledge.

It hung suspended in air, and drifted off like a lazy, glowing moth on a gentle breeze. He sat for a time, watching it disappear over the rooftops of the town.

But the next morning he found the lantern on his doorstep. Its light had gone out and its shell was tarnished. He knew then for a certainty that his suit was hopeless. A sorrow lodged in his heart, which never left him.

The sign was very clear.

* * * *

So Talnaco Ramat transported himself to Ai Hanlo by some means which comes as easily to a Zaborman as breathing. The great distance was traversed, the tangled way made straight, dangers avoided, and the lantern maker come to the Sunrise Gate, dragging a two-wheeled cart filled with his belongings.

For a moment he had the idea that he would become rich here in Ai Hanlo, since the folk there had surely never seen anything as wondrous as a finely-wrought Zabortashi lantern.

He was wrong. There was no novelty. In fact, there are so many magicians in Zabortash that many of them go abroad in search of work. A number of them had settled in Ai Hanlo. Some of those made lanterns. He had to join a guild and pay a share of his earnings, but it was a comfort to be surrounded by men and women who spoke his own language. They found a place for him to live and work.

It was a house at the end of a narrow lane, with a wooden sign over the door.

He prospered in his new life and seemed to forget his old. In time he married a woman of the city called Kachelle, and she bore him three daughters, and, later, a son, whom he named Venda. His life passed peacefully as his family grew. He made lanterns of great complexity and beauty and sold them to nobles of the city, even to the Guardian himself. For all that, he was never too proud to turn out a simple oil lamp, or even to mold candlesticks.

So his years were filled. Then his daughters married, and went to live with their husbands. Later, his wife Kachelle died, and he had only Venda, his youngest, for company. He taught the boy every facet of his craft, all the secrets of magic that he knew. He knew only little spells and shallow magic—he was not a magus who could make the world tremble at his gaze—but to Venda it was impressive.

In time Venda married, and brought his wife to live with his father. As his sisters had done before him, he made his father a grandfather, and the house was filled with the shouts of children, and the sounds of their running feet, not to mention the clangor and crash when one of them blundered into a pile of lanterns.

All these children were of the city. They spoke without the accent of Zabortash, as did Venda's wife, who never seemed quite convinced that Zabortash was a real place, and that the stories about it were other than fables. Venda himself had never been there.

So Talnaco Ramat began to feel alone, a stranger once more in a strange country. For the first time in decades he began to long for his homeland and the places of his youth.

One day, while rummaging in the loft above his shop, he found something wrapped in an oily rag. He unwrapped it, and beheld the tarnished lantern he had made for Mirithemne, so long ago. He had forgotten about it all these years. Now memories flooded back.

Once again he saw himself on the rooftop, watching the lantern float above the town. He remembered the songs he had composed for Mirithemne, and the letters he had labored over with uncertain penmanship. He remembered the great fairs of Zabortash, where grand magi and lesser magicians and craftsmen of all sorts came together to conjoin their magic, that the Earth might continue to follow the sun through the universe, now that the Goddess was dead, and not be lost in the darkness, in the night. There were wares displayed, feats performed. The high born women of the land were in attendance, among them Mirithemne. He smiled at her, and waved, and even spoke with her when she mingled with the crowd of common folk. She smiled back—was it out of politeness, or something more?

Talnaco Ramat remembered what it is like to be young.

Therefore he took up the lantern and carefully polished it, until it shone as it had on the day of its completion. He oiled the hinges of its door.

He waited for evening with barely controlled excitement, speaking to his son and his son's family about trifling things, his mind far removed in time and space.

High up Ai Hanlo Mountain, a soldier blew a curving horn

that hung from an arch, announcing that the sun had set.

Talnaco Ramat went out into the cool evening air, bearing the lantern. The dome of the Guardian's palace still glowed with the last light of day. He came to a courtyard he knew, which was filled with trees. It was the autumn of the year, and dead leaves rustled underfoot. He sat down on a stone bench and looked up at the dome, waiting for it to grow dark.

He was alone. The night was quiet, but for occasional distant noises of the city.

When the time came, he did not hesitate. He lit a candle and placed it inside the lantern with a steady hand, speaking as he did the most powerful spells he knew. The candle burned more brightly than it would have with mere flame. He closed the door of the lantern and at once the intricate carvings in the metal shell were outlined in fire. He set the lantern down on the bench and knelt before it, entranced by the shifting shapes. The glowing fishes swam in the air before his eyes. The Endless River flowed around him, its fiery waters splashing over the walls of the courtyard, swirling between the tree trunks. Everywhere, spirits of the air were suddenly visible in the magic light: glowing, stick-legged things wading in the earth like impossible herons; an immense serpent beneath the ground, engirdling the world, its gold and silver scales polished bright as mirrors. He saw turning at the world's core that great rose, half of fire, half of darkness, where dwell the Bright and Dark Powers, the fragments of the godhead.

He turned away from all this, drawing his awareness back into himself, into the courtyard. He concentrated on the lantern before him. It seemed to float in the air. The light grew brighter, brighter; the door opened and he was blinded.

When he could see again, he was by the side of the river called Endless, at a spot he knew well. Mirithemne was with him. He could not see her; but he sensed her presence. She was just beyond the periphery of his vision. He spoke; she did not answer; but he knew she heard.

He was still kneeling, as he had been in the courtyard. He got to his feet, expecting every joint to ache with the strain, but he found that, although he still wore the clothes he had as an old man, and his tools were still in the pockets of his apron, he was young again. He got up easily. He looked at his beard and saw that it was no longer white.

When he walked, he heard Mirithemne's footsteps beside him, but when he turned, she was not there. He continued walking. The sky was clear and the day warm.

He came to the mouth of a cave in the side of a hill which sloped down to meet the river. From within he heard a voice crying, "I am burning!"

He rushed inside and there found an anchorite writhing on the floor of the cave. The man was dressed in rags. His beard and hair were matted with dirt. His skin was brown and wrinkled, like old leather, but there was no fire.

"I prayed for it. Long I prayed for it. Now I have it, and I am burning," the anchorite said, his voice frenzied.

"What have you prayed for? You don't seem to be burning," Talnaco said, puzzled. He turned to Mirithemne, sure that she would understand, but she was not there.

"I prayed," said the anchorite. "I prayed that a fragment of the Goddess would settle on me, that I might be made as holy as she. Oh, it was an arrogant wish! But now it is fulfilled, and I am burning with the spirit. Soon I will be completely consumed."

Before the lantern maker could reply, the other began to babble. He prophesied in tongues, but there was no one to understand his prophecies, except perhaps Mirithemne. He spoke the thousand names of the Goddess, first the common ones, then those known to sages, then those which only the greatest of Guardians may apprehend but dimly, and finally all the rest, which never before had been spoken.

Talnaco waited patiently while he was doing all this.

At last the holy man sat up, and stared at the lantern maker in a distracted way.

"You too are burning," he said. "No, it's not like that at all."

The holy man fell down once more, writhing. He babbled.

Then he was calm and lay with his eyes closed, as if he were sleeping. Slowly, with apparent deliberation, he spoke the name of Mirithemne.

Talnaco fled. For a time he lost his way in a dark forest, but still his beloved seemed to be with him. For days and nights he travelled, resting little. When he finally emerged from the forest, the river was before him again. Once more an imperial *drontha* crawled against the current on the legs of its oars. Once more the rivermen sang as they poled their barge.

He made his way to Ai Hanlo, entering through the Sunrise Gate. He followed streets he knew until he stood before his own door. The key was in the pocket of his apron. He went inside. The place was filled with dust and cobwebs. At once he set to work cleaning it, making it ready for the practice of his craft.

So again a young Zabortashi lantern maker established himself in Ai Hanlo, He labored long and hard, selling excellent lanterns to the best clients. In each lantern, somewhere among the intricacies of the design, he carved the image of Mirithemne, all the while sensing her nearness. She became more evident every day. He found his bed rumpled when he had not slept in it. His cupboard was left open when he had closed it. He heard footsteps. He heard shutters and doors opening and closing, but when he went to see, no one was there.

One day he found a woman's comb on a chair. There were long, yellow hairs in it. Mirithemne's hair was like that. Then he found her mirror, and when he looked into it, he saw someone staring over his shoulder.

He turned. The carpet on the floor moved slightly, but he was alone in the room.

At last, as he sat in his workshop in the upper room of the house, just below the loft, there were gentle footsteps on the stairway outside, followed by a light rapping at the door.

"Enter," he said.

The door opened slowly, but no one entered: He got up, and found Mirithemne's lantern on the threshold.

The sign was very clear.

Therefore Talnaco Ramat bore the lantern into a courtyard he knew. It was sunset, in the autumn of the year. High above the city, a soldier blew on a curving horn. The light of the golden dome faded, while the light of the lantern grew brighter.

The door of the lantern opened. His eyes were dazzled. He fell to his knees.

And when he could see again, Mirithemne stood before him, holding the lantern, as graceful and as beautiful as he had remembered her. She smiled at him, and, reaching down, took his hand in hers and lifted him to his feet. Then she danced to music he could not hear, her long dress whirling, the leaves whirling, the golden shapes projected by the lantern whirling over the walls, the trees, the ground, over Talnaco himself as she danced, the lantern in hand.

He could never imagine her more perfect than she was at that moment.

Later, she was in his arms and they spoke words of love. Later still he sat with his memories, and it seemed he had lived out his life with her, in the shop at the end of the narrow lane, in the city, and that he had grown old. Still Mirithemne was with him. He vaguely remembered how it had been otherwise, but he was not sure of it, and this troubled him.

He vaguely remembered that he had a son called Venda. He was old. He was getting confused. He would ask Mirithemne.

* * * *

In the darkness, in the night, Venda made his way up a narrow, sloping street that ended in a stairway, climbed the stairway, and came to the wall which separates the lower, or outer part of Ai Hanlo from the inner city, where dwell the Guardian of the Bones of the Goddess, his priests, his courtiers, and his soldiers. Venda could not go beyond the wall, but he could open a certain door, and slide into an unlighted room no larger than a closet, closing the door behind him.

He dropped a coin into a bowl and rang a bell. A window slid open in front of him. He could see nothing, but he heard a priest breathing.

"The power of the Goddess fades like an echo in a cave," the priest said, "but perhaps enough lingers to comfort you."

"I don't come for myself," Venda said, and he explained how he had watched his father go into a courtyard with an old lantern and vanish in a flash of light.

The priest came out and went with him. He saw that the priest was very young, little more than a boy, and he wondered if he would be able to do anything. But he said nothing, out of respect. Then he realized that this was a certain Tamliade, something of a prodigy, already renowned for his visions.

They came to the courtyard and found the lantern, still glowing brightly. The priest opened its door. The light was dazzling. For a time Venda could see nothing. For a time they seemed to walk on pathways of light, through forests of frozen fire.

They found Talnaco Ramat sitting in the mouth of a cave, with the lantern before him, its door open, the light from within brilliant.

"Father, return with us," Venda said.

"Go away. I am with my beloved."

Venda saw no one but himself, his father, and the priest, but before he could say anything, his father reached out and snapped the door of the lantern shut.

The scene vanished, like a reflection in a pool shattered by a stone.

* * * *

They found themselves in the courtyard, standing before the lantern, which rested on the bench. Again the priest opened the little door, and the light was blinding. The priest led Venda by the hand. When he could see again, they were walking after his father, up the road to the Sunrise Gate of Ai Hanlo. His father hurried with long strides, bearing the lantern. Its door was open. The light was less brilliant than before.

"Father—"

"Sir," said the boy priest. "Come away."

Talnaco stopped suddenly and turned to the priest. "What do you know of the ways of love, young man?"

"Why—why, nothing."

"Then you will not understand why I won't go with you."

"Father," said Venda softly.

Talnaco snapped the door of the lantern shut.

* * * *

"If you want to get another priest, do so, but it won't do any good," the boy Tamliade said.

They stood in the courtyard, in the darkness, in the night. "It's not that," Venda said. "What do we do now?"

"We merely follow him to where he is going. He has gone far already."

The priest opened the door of the lantern. The light was dim. It seemed to flow out, like the waters of the river, splashing over the ground and between the trees.

Again they stood by the riverbank. An imperial *drontha* went by. Boatmen poled a barge.

Venda followed the priest. They came to a cave, where lay the blackened, shriveled corpse of an anchorite. They passed through the dark forest and eventually into Ai Hanlo, along a narrow street, until they came to the shop with the wooden sign over its door.

The door was unlocked. The two of them went quietly inside, then up the stairs until they stood before the door to Talnaco Ramat's workroom.

Venda rapped gently.

"Enter," came the voice from within. They entered, and saw Talnaco seated at his workbench, polishing a lantern. He looked older and more tired than Venda had ever seen him before.

"Father, you are in a dream."

His father smiled and said gently, "You are a true son. I am glad that you care about me."

"None of this is real," the priest said, gesturing with a sweep of his hand.

"Do you think I don't know that? I have lived out my life suspended in a single, golden moment of time. It doesn't make any difference. Mirithemne is with me."

He glanced at the empty air as if he were looking at someone.

"This thing you think is your beloved," the priest said, "is in truth some spirit or Power, some fragment of the Goddess which has entered your mind through the lantern, like a moth drawn to a random flame. It is without form or intelligence. Your longing gives it a certain semblance of a shape, but it loves you no more than do the wind and the rain."

"Perhaps I am in love with the mere memory of being in love. Perhaps…in my memory now, I remember two lives. In one my wife was called Kachelle, in the other Mirithemne. In both, I had a son, Venda. Both are in my memory now. How shall I weigh them and know which is the more true?"

Venda looked helplessly at the priest, whose face was expressionless.

"I am tired," said Talnaco Ramat. He rose, taking the lantern, and walked slowly out of the room. The light was very faint now. They followed him to the courtyard. By the time he set the lantern down on the bench, the light had gone out.

The priest snapped the metal door shut. Then he and Venda led Talnaco home. He was delirious with fever.

"He is burned by the spirit," the priest said. "There is little we can do."

They sat by Talnaco's bedside, as he lay dying. Venda wept. Toward the very end, the old man was lucid.

"Do not weep, son," he said. "I have known great happiness in both of my lives."

"Father, was there ever someone called Mirithemne, or did you imagine her?"

"She is real enough. She's probably old and ugly now. I don't think she ever knew my name."

Venda wept.

At the very end, his father said, "I have found the greatest treasure. It was worth the struggle."

Venda did not answer, but the priest leaned forward, and whispered, "What is it?"

"A smile. A touch. Whirling leaves. A single moment frozen in time."

HOLY FIRE

The master said: "What is the nature of a vision?"

The student said: "As you have taught us, it is an opening of a window, through which we see things that are hidden."

The master said: "When that window is open, what may come in out of the darkness? What if you can't shut the window?"

—Telechronos of Hesh,
The Wind from the Grave of the Goddess

I.

The door opened slowly. His father came in. Tamliade sat up in bed, peering into the darkness. He was five years old that summer.

His father was a big man, broad-shouldered, his arms muscled, his hands gnarled. As he crossed the room, a shaft of moonlight caught his face through an unshuttered window, and his beard seemed to be made of gold.

The boy slid to the floor, his bare feet rustling straw.

"Sh-sh. Don't wake your mother."

Tamliade glanced across the room to where his mother slept, a mere mound against a wall where the moonlight did not touch.

"What is it?"

"Be quiet and come with me."

He groped around for a robe, didn't find one, and went

outside with his father, wearing only his nightgown. He stood by his father's side, shivering beneath the bright stars. He could make out the rooftops of the houses of the village, his father's smithy gaping black and empty, and moonlight gleaming on the Endless River. To the north, there was a line of trees that looked like a ridge in the darkness, where the forests of Hesh ended and the grasslands began. To the west, the moon nearly touched the horizon. To the east, there was a faint glow, presaging dawn, and above it a plume of light swept across the sky.

His father pointed.

"I wanted you to see that. Do you know what it is?"

"A feathered star."

"I met a…a wise man today. He came from Zabortash. That's a country where everyone is learned, and most of them are magicians. He said, the wise man, that this thing is a fragment of the Goddess, who has died. It drifts across the sky, burning with holiness. Finally it settles, and touches someone, and burns them too, but inside, with holiness. That's what he said. I didn't understand all of it."

Tamliade didn't understand either. He didn't understand why his father was showing him this. But there was something in his father's manner which made him pay close attention. His father stood there, staring at the feathered star, or whatever it was, his mouth half open, as if there were something he wanted to say but could not find the words. He could tell that his father was a little bit afraid, and he was too. He could tell that to his father this was a premonition of something, and his father was groping for the shape of the thing, but it always eluded him.

And Tamliade wondered if it meant that he would die soon. It was the first time he had ever thought of death. It was very strange.

Then he felt a little ashamed, as if his father were trying to show him something rare and beautiful, and it was his own fault that he couldn't appreciate it.

He felt very close to his father that night, as they stood beneath the stars. It was a rare thing that his father had any time for him. This was a special night.

They stood there for what seemed a long time, until the sky brightened and the fragment of the Goddess was no longer visible.

"Let's go in," his father said.

* * * *

He tried to cling to the memory of that night, in later years. It was a delicate treasure, as fragile as a perfect image reflected in an unrippled pool. But visions drove him away. He saw cities of fire and crystal in waking dreams. Spirits spoke to him, and entered him, wrenching and twisting. He shrieked in his dreams as the spirits filled him, as he felt his soul moving in the frigid depths beyond the world, far, far from his body, from his own time, from everything he had ever known or cared about.

Once a caravan passed through their village. In addition to the usual pack animals and wagons, there was a long line of slaves linked together with chains attached to their collars.

He stood with his mother in the market place, watching. He was ten years old then.

"Who are they?"

"Captives in some war. It doesn't matter."

He looked at them closely. Some of them were very strange, their skins dark, their faces flat and round, their hair tied in little braids. Some wore the remnants of costumes like nothing he had seen before. Some had tattooed faces. But others could have been men and women and children from his own village. They could have been people he knew. All of them had one thing in common: he saw in their faces a longing for their scattered homes, for the lives they had been dragged away from.

"It's like that with me," he said suddenly. "I'm like them."

"You say such strange things sometimes," his mother said, leading him away.

* * * *

He struggled to get back, to be himself, to keep his life for himself. But the visions drove him on.

He was useless as a helper to his father. He would fall into fits of distraction while working the bellows, or let an iron drop in the dirt and wander off, following things no one else could see. His father's temper was short, and repeated attempts to "beat some sense" into him only frightened him.

Then a prophet came, a wild-looking, half-naked man who wore a headband from which tiny icons dangled. He proclaimed to all who would listen how the Goddess who had died, in the aftermath of whose death signs and wonders multiplied, had been a mortal woman once. She had not asked for what had happened to her. Divinity had settled in her like a drifting spark, then flared into a raging fire, consuming whatever she might have originally been. She was helpless to stop it.

This would happen again, the prophet said, very soon.

Tamliade's terror mounted.

Still the visions possessed him. His mother wept. His father cursed. After his mother had died, when he was eleven, his father turned him out of the house to wander the world in pursuit of his vision, or find his fortune, or perish, or whatever. And the spirits dragged him and pulled him, like herdboys with a reluctant cow; and voices howled in his ears at night, and he saw things invisible to those around him, and wandered, and worked wonders, and begged at roadsides. People came to him to be touched and healed of their afflictions.

"What good is my touch?" he would say, "when I cannot heal myself."

But still they came, and there were those who fell down and worshipped him as the divinity reborn, which can be either male or female, a god or a goddess. But every time they gathered around him, he eluded them, led by flickering shapes into desolate places, sometimes seeming to remember in dreams regions he had not yet come to.

He only wanted to be himself, to live his own life, but the choice was not his. In time he fell among bandits and was sold as a slave, and an old slave he met explained to him that the remark he'd made to his mother in the market place was a prophecy, a sure manifestation of the divine.

Later, he was apprenticed to Emdo Wesa, a mighty magician and maker of dadars, whose flesh diminished each time he created another projection of himself. Tamliade saw himself as a kind of dadar, no more able to fathom the purpose to which he was directed than could one of Emdo Wesa's creations. Indeed, at first, the magician saw him only as a useful instrument, like a perspective glass or a forceps, but humanity grew within him, and, very briefly, he became the kind of father Tamliade could barely preserve in his memory.

Then Emdo Wesa diminished, and Tamliade was free to wander again.

* * * *

A ragged man came to him once, as he lay awake by a campfire in the ruin of a city a million years old. The man stood in the middle of the fire, taking shape out of the smoke. His eyes were two stars.

"Tamliade," he said. "I speak to you because you alone can hear me. Listen: I was Tueset anil-Gitan, which means Master of the Bowl of Night. I was the greatest magician of my time. I could bind the moon to my will. But I had an enemy, who, through cunning and treachery, gained power over me. So I thought to trick him. It was a splendid stratagem: I seemed to bow to his spells. Each year, on an appointed day, I fell into a certain stream, floated against the current, until I came to the place where my enemy was waiting. There he made a banquet of my flesh in darkest holiness. In the last years I went into seclusion, for I was hideous to behold. At last, when he made a soup from my ground bones, and drank it, I spoke to him out of a reflection in the bottom of the pot. 'You are conquered from within,' I told him. 'My flesh is the substance of your body.' 'Yes,' he said, 'but I have long since been consumed by my magic. There is nothing left of me. You are master of an empty house.' And it was so. Here I am, the ghost of a ghost.

"Tamliade, I have come to you because I am real only to you, because there is no other person in the world who is as sensitive to things of the spirit as you. I had hoped to possess you, to walk in your flesh beneath the sun again. But you are nearly consumed. You are like a tattered flag in the wind that blows from the grave of the Goddess. We are already too much alike. What am I to do?"

The spirit sank down into the fire. The flames crackled. The night was still.

* * * *

In time the boy came to Ai Hanlo, the famous city at the center of the world, where lie the bones of the Goddess in holy splendor. He was sixteen then, his face darkened by the sun, his body hardened to many privations, but still the spirits roared within him. For long periods he could not even remember who he was.

He climbed the narrow streets, up Ai Hanlo Mountain, to the gate of the inner city, where dwelt the Guardian of the Bones of the Goddess with his priests and his court, presiding over the Holy Empire. He stood before the gate for twelve days and nights, shouting in strange languages, thundering with the voice of the powers within him, helpless and invincible, agonized, afraid, filled with strange ecstasies. In the darkness, spheres of light like tiny suns flickered around his head.

At last the gate was opened and the Guardian summoned him into his own household.

II.

Because he had had so many visions, because he had heard the echo of the death of the Goddess more clearly than had anyone for generations, because he was the conduit through which holy manifestations poured into the world, Tamliade was made a priest at once. He went through no novitiate, for all he was not learned, for all he could barely read and write his own Heshite tongue and spoke the Language of the City awkwardly; for all he knew nothing of the lore of cultures long since vanished and could pronounce none of the secret names of the Goddess.

Every day he came before the Guardian and his advisors, and told them of his dreams. When a vision came by daylight, he went and reported that, too, as soon as he had recovered.

Scribes recorded everything he said in elegant script. Scholars came from many lands to marvel, to read, and to listen. All the while he was cared for. He ate more regularly than he had in years. He wore fine clothing. Tutors filled his empty hours. He learned of epochs before his own, how each period of history has a god or goddess, by whose dreams it is shaped; how the present was a chaotic interregnum between the death of one divinity and the birth of the next.

The new god would be discovered soon, he was assured, and his terror mounted.

The Guardian himself instructed him in certain facets of holy lore, words of power and, as he passed certain thresholds of understanding, the secret names of the Goddess, one by one.

He was allowed nearly complete access to the ancient library of the guardians, encouraged to read anything he wanted, from history to romance poetry to hagiography. Once he overheard one librarian whisper to another that the future could be foretold by what books he chose. It was a more reliable method than casting painted stones, the man said. The other nodded.

So his days passed, frequently interrupted by visions. Autumn approached. The sky turned a sullen grey as rains threatened. He had not been beyond the wall of the inner city in nearly a year.

* * * *

It was a rare afternoon in that season when the sky was clear, and the sun sank into the west in a splash of purples and reds.

Tamliade stood before an open window, looking out over the land, watching the sun set, when suddenly he felt the familiar dislocation of the onset of a vision, and it seemed that the sun rose again, in the west, searing the sky, and came hurtling toward him. The room he stood in filled with light. He felt heat through the open window. He reached to close the shutters, but the glare was too painful. He fell to his knees, covering his face with his hands.

Then it was dark. He looked up, and saw that stars shone in the night sky.

The sun, diminished to a dimly glowing disc, hung in the air before him, just inside the windowsill.

It had a face on it like a mask. Behind the eyes, embers burned.

There came a voice like something shouted through a long metal horn.

"Come to me."

He rose and followed the thing as it drifted out of the room, along a corridor where huge tapestries billowed in a draft. He came to a massive double door of wood and iron. The apparition hesitated, passed through in a way his eye could not follow, its light shining through from the other side where the two doors met. He pressed with all his might against cold iron and damp wood, and slowly the door creaked open enough for him to slip through. He found himself at the top of a curving staircase cut into the rock of Ai Hanlo Mountain. Down, down, he followed the glowing face. At first the stairs and walls were dry. Then they became wet, covered with nitre and mold. The stairway opened out into a cavern piled high in rotting crates. Rusting, unlighted lanterns hung from beams overhead. At the bottom of the stairs, he walked across an irregular, rock-strewn floor. The light that led him grew less. Darkness and cold closed in. In places the floor was ankle-deep in mud. His shoes a sucking sound as he walked.

He came to another door, just as massive as the first, but so rotted that pieces of it came away in his hand. The sun face drifted through. He broke away enough wood and followed.

The light was very dim. He thought he saw tall grasses growing around him. He thought he saw trees of immense height, vanishing overhead into darkness, and vines overladen with moss that hung like matted hair.

He thought the way narrowed, that he was again in a small space, an underground room.

The disc came to rest against a far wall.

"Do you not know me?" it said.

"No, I do not know you."

The light went out. Below it, something began to glow a dull red, like old embers someone has blown upon. Flames flickered in the mud. By their light he saw a dark, rectangular object. The flames rose higher. He saw that it was a coffin, intricately carven. Slowly the lid rose. There was a red light within.

Blood poured out of the coffin, like water from a fountain, sizzling through the flames, splashing over him.

Within the coffin floated something that had once been a man, something without any limbs but one quivering stump of an arm, without a face, with only a lipless hole for a mouth, vomiting blood.

"Tamliade," came the voice again. *"Do you not know me? I am Etash Wesa."*

He screamed, covered his face, fell over backwards, splashing blood.

He was still screaming when soldiers found him writhing on the floor of a long-disused storeroom, his clothing dripping scarlet. They knew who he was. As soon as they saw that he was not bleeding from any grievous wound, they took him by either arm and hauled him in front of the Guardian as fast as they could run.

Tamliade knelt, exhausted, sobbing, in the throne room of the Guardian, beneath the great golden dome of Ai Hanlo.

The Guardian dismissed his retainers, then bade the boy to

rise. But he did not. He merely babbled of what he had seen.

"It is Etash Wesa. He is the brother of my master, Emdo Wesa. He is a monster, a thing wholly changed by magic. He is a cancer, my master said. He will destroy the world if he isn't stopped. It isn't possible to understand him. It isn't possible to know how powerful he is, what he can do. Emdo Wesa was afraid of him. He fought him. With the magic that ate him away, he fought him. He wanted to save me. But now he's gone, and Etash Wesa has found me!'"

"I know about Etash Wesa," the Guardian said quietly. "He exists beyond the material world. You, Tamliade, are on a precipice. Above, a glorious summit. Below, an abyss, in which lurks Etash Wesa. The great danger of dreaming, the danger which is greatest to you of all people, is that you will fall into that abyss, into the power of Etash Wesa."

"He has found me. What can I do?"

The Guardian was silent. Tamliade looked up, and saw that he had been kneeling on a floor mosaic of the Goddess in both her aspects, dark and bright, with the moon in her hair and the sun in her hand.

"You must think on the Goddess," said the Guardian, "When Etash Wesa reaches for you, direct yourself away from the abyss, toward the summit. Otherwise it will be the malevolence of Etash Wesa, rather than holiness, which flows through you into the world."

* * * *

Several nights later he lit a lantern in his room, so he could sit up late reading.

The light poured out of the lantern like glowing smoke, pooled on the floor, then rose in a luminous column, which gradually took on the shape of his old master, Emdo Wesa. There was a gaping hole in his chest where his heart had once been. White flames burned in there now. His eyes were gone. Flames burned in his sockets, and in his mouth. His face was expressionless.

His magician's gloves were worn or burned through. His hands were made, not of flesh, but of pale, flickering light.

Still, Tamliade was overjoyed to see him. "Have you come to help me? I need you."

"I am lost," said Emdo Wesa, his voice a distant whisper, like the wind. "I have seen the road that the dead walk on, when they journey away from life, but I cannot follow it. It…shifts from my gaze…because I have never truly died and yet do not live…"

"I have seen Etash Wesa. Help me."

"You of all would be the first to glimpse him. Yours is the sight. You cannot comprehend the evil of him, or the enmity that exists between us. These things are vaster than the dark sea between the worlds."

"How can I get away? What can I do?"

"I am lost…I cannot follow the road…I thought I would learn so much, discover, explore…. There's nothing out there."

At draft blew through the room. The candle flame inside Tamliade's lantern flickered. Emdo Wesa was gone.

* * * *

Still the visions came with greater intensity, at any hour of day or night, overwhelming his every sense. Often as he sat at lessons or meals, or as he walked alone with his thoughts, he would suddenly fall to the ground and writhe like a rag doll shaken by an invisible hand. He shrieked, and babbled holy names. He crashed into walls, overturned tables, and dug with his hands, casting up dirt and stones, all the while screaming, "Help me! I don't want any of this! Take it away!"

But more often than not his words were not intelligible, and those who came to restrain him would glance at one another and say, "He is in the ecstasy of his vision. Who knows what he really sees and hears?" All knew how the pangs of divinity had come upon the girl who had become the Goddess, millennia before, and they wondered aloud, "Could this be the one?"

All others who beheld him dropped to their knees, their faces pale with awe.

At last, when he could bear it no longer, he came to a decision. In all the hagiographies, and also in the romances and even the sober histories, when someone was touched by the wind from the grave of the Goddess, which is alternately called holiness or fate, it was never any good to run or to hide. There was no place to go. The wind sought one out. It was a hot wind, igniting holy fire which consumed or transformed or molded anew. The only thing to do, Tamliade concluded, was to turn and face the wind, to walk into it, to force whatever was going to happen to him to happen now, simply to get it over with.

He was filled with a dread which nearly froze his resolve, but also, for all he tried to deny it, with anticipation. Already his mind was being filled with thoughts he could not describe even to himself, any more than one born blind and raised entirely among the blind could describe sudden and overwhelming sight. He felt the lure of the transcendent, the unknown and unknowable, which could mold him as a modeler shapes clay, into something beyond his power to imagine.

He decided on a journey. He told no one about it. The Guardian, he knew, would never let him go. He had no friends. People were unfailingly polite to him. They answered when he addressed them, but he knew that to the priests he was a prize exhibit, a miraculous resource, and to the novices, who were more his own age, he was a freak to be whispered about.

Then, there was Etash Wesa to be considered, Etash Wesa who waited for him at the periphery of dreams, waiting for a chance to pour into the world, to seize control.

If he turned to face his visions directly, wouldn't that draw Etash Wesa to him?

He considered. He didn't really believe the Guardian could protect him, and if Etash Wesa was to find him, he could do so just as easily in Ai Hanlo. Besides, he hoped that whatever was to happen to him would happen before Etash Wesa was aware of it, even if this meant his own dissolution.

He was willing to take every risk. He couldn't go on like this.

* * * *

Tamliade sat in his room in the middle of the night, with a single lamp burning. He looked around at all he possessed, or all that had been provided for him: a few books, a trunk with a few clothes in it, an easel where a half-finished painting stood. He had decided once that he would like to learn how to paint. So a tutor in this subject was sent for. But when he began, a dream came upon him, and when he awoke there were only smears of paint on the canvas. Some people claimed to find meaning in it.

He looked around at these things. There was nothing. This was the closest thing he had had to a home in a long time, and he would not miss it.

So he rose and put on travelling clothes: baggy trousers, boots, and a many-pocketed jacket that reached to his knees. He stuffed a hooded cloak into a bag. He could use it as a blanket. Into the bag also went spare clothing, a tiny lamp and a bottle of oil, and one book, beautifully illuminated, filled with the offices of the priesthood and tales of famous adepts designed to guide the reader through the journey of this life.

Then he peered into the corridor outside his room to see that no one was about, and left. His heart was beating rapidly. Every sound seemed exaggerated, sure to betray him. But he came undiscovered to the kitchen. There cooks snored on benches. He tiptoed among them with desperate care, and took bread, cheese, dried meat, and a bottle of wine. As an afterthought, he took a long knife. He couldn't find a scabbard for it, so he wrapped it in a towel.

From a cloakroom beyond the kitchen he took a staff and a broad-brimmed hat.

He slipped from the Guardian's palace out a window. He came to a place he knew, where a tree grew against a wall of the inner city. So long had Ai Hanlo been secure that no one had bothered to cut it down. The tree embraced the wall. The wall supported the tree. Stones and twisted branches intermingled. It was easy to climb down from the top of the wall into the tree.

The branches enclosed a little world, where birds had nested for centuries. He saw them asleep, perched in rows or gathered in clusters. He climbed more carefully than ever, struggling to be silent, but one bird awoke, and another, and another, and soon they burst into the air in a cacophony of shrieks and a muffled thunder of wings.

He froze, sure that someone would come running.

But no one came. So he continued his descent, came to a rooftop, and dropped into a street.

He wandered in the dark, muddy labyrinth of the lower city. Once someone called to him from a doorway and made a lewd suggestion. Another time he heard footsteps all around him, and stood perfectly still in almost total darkness until they were gone. At last he found a secluded niche between two tall, shuttered buildings, and sat down to await the dawn.

He awoke in twilight and began walking, always downhill. Sunlight touched the roofs and reached into the alleys. Shutters banged open. He followed the earliest risers until he came to one of the city's great gates. He didn't know which one it was. He hesitated, for he knew that the guards at the gate often questioned those who left the city at odd hours, or charged them a toll. He didn't have any money.

But luck was with him. It was a market day. During the night ships had come to the docks, and already trading stalls were set up all along the road that led from the river to the gate. Inside the city, shopkeepers swept their doorsteps, lowered canopies, and set up goods. Soon the square before the gate was filled with people. It was an easy enough matter for him to go out.

Then he ducked under a rope, went between two stalls, and turned away from the road, coming after a while to the edge of the cultivated fields beyond the city, and onto the broad plain to the south.

III.

He travelled for three days and nights. The autumn rains hadn't quite started, so the sky was filled with clouds, while the plains were still dry with the dust of summer. The days were pleasant, the nights cold. Always Ai Hanlo Mountain remained visible behind him, the golden dome of the Guardian's palace like a sun setting in the blue-grey mist of the mountain.

He slept in hollows or in occasional groves of gnarled trees, and ate of the food he had brought with him, also roots and a fat, flightless bird he struck down with his staff. In his years as a wanderer he had learned to survive in places far more desolate than this.

On the fourth day he came to the site of a city far more ancient than Ai Hanlo, perhaps even older than Ai Hanlo Mountain itself. All he saw at first were mounds of stone and earth. It was hard to tell that they were not natural formations. Grass and stunted trees grew over them. Wild goats scampered away as he approached, and a lizard, walking upright on its hind legs, stood on a mound and hissed, then jumped, and glided a short distance away on stubby wings.

But in the evening, as the sun set and the shadows shifted, the city manifested itself to the sound of bells, which he heard faintly at first, then more clearly. They rang, and towers and walls rose on every side, translucent as smoke, merging with the darkness of the oncoming night, becoming more solid, shutting out the sky. At last, when the clouds broke overhead, silver rooftops gleamed beneath the stars, and Tamliade's footsteps echoed down long, empty streets. Every once in a while he would catch a glimpse of the dome of Ai Hanlo, still glowing with the light of the vanished sun.

The windows of the city began to glow softly. He hurried on his way. Still the unseen bells rang. Then the people of the city were all around him, bearing lanterns, ringing hand bells—tall, slender folk with long golden hair and pale faces, clad in golden gowns.

He came to a square where there was a statue of some hero grappling with a giant.

Overhead, silver ships detached themselves from rooftops, drifting like clouds.

A great multitude gathered around him, whispering, "He can see us! For the first time since the death of our god, there is one who can see us!"

They asked him for news of the world. Their speech was strange. He could barely make out what they were saying, but he tried to answer as well as he could. Soon he could tell by their puzzlement that too much time had passed, and the names and nations and places meant nothing to them.

Some of them, losing interest, turned away. They pulled off their gowns, leaving them where they fell, and stood naked, men and women. Delicate, translucent wings unfolded from their backs. They took to the air, drifting, some of them still bearing lanterns. Against the dark sky, they looked like huge butterflies.

Still the crowd pressed him.

"Your goddess is dead too. Another shall come soon after. The fire of divinity never goes out. It may burn low for an age, but soon it flares up again. Sighted one, are you the one in which it burns?"

Tamliade was afraid. "No," he said, nearly weeping. "I'm not."

He pushed through them and ran through the streets of the city.

"Please take no offense," his questioners called after him. "It was wrong to speak of such holy things. Forgive us."

As he ran, the walls, the houses, the strangely fashioned arches all rippled like water, then filled with a lurid orange light, like molten metal. He ran breathlessly, looking for a way out. He was lost in the maze of streets. Those people he passed merely watched him go.

Then they screamed. The city burst into flame. The people

burned like paper cutouts, fragments of them rising and tumbling in the hot air.

Tamliade couldn't find his way out. He came to a courtyard and cowered in the middle of it. The ground shook. The pavement cracked. All around him, the city died.

Wading through the ruin, a giant came before him clad in armor of molten bronze which flowed and changed shape constantly.

"Where is this one who sees?" the giant thundered from behind its visor. "I am master here. He belongs to me."

The giant reached down and picked him up. He screamed as the armored fingers burned into his sides. He was lifted to the giant's face. The visor rose of its own accord, and there was a blast of heat, as if a furnace door had been opened. Within was only blinding flame at first, but then a face formed. He had seen it before, on the statue in the square.

The giant's gaze penetrated his dreams. The visions came again, every one he had ever had, all at once. The pain of this was greater than the burning. Still the giant probed, beyond his visions, into worlds he had but glimpsed, using him as a mere eyepiece.

In time he felt and knew nothing more than an eyepiece would.

* * * *

It was mid-morning when he-awoke, face down in the dust. Stiffly, he got to his feet. There was no city around him, only low mounds. He touched his sides gingerly. He was not burned.

The contents of his bag were spilled over the ground. He gathered them up. The wine bottle had broken. He couldn't find his staff, and realized he must have flung it away in the paroxysm of his vision.

He left the ruin, and in another day's walking came to the crest of a low hill. Beyond. that, he knew, the dome of Ai Hanlo would no longer be visible. So he knelt and said the common prayer of travelers, expressing the hope that what holiness still lingered over the grave of the Goddess would be enough to guide him back within sight of the city.

In truth, if he could somehow be free of his visions, he would have been content never to look on the city again. But still he said the prayer. Then he walked down the far side of the hill, and did not look back.

Two more days passed. He was truly alone now. For so long he had been a wanderer, but during his residence in Ai Hanlo his world had seemed to contract, until all he knew were a few corridors, and rooms filled with dust and shadows, and the universe was shut in by the wall of the inner city. Now it was strange, and a little frightening, to cross this almost featureless land beyond the limits of all he had known.

It was a quiet time, and he savored each moment.

He came to no more ruins. No more ghosts appeared to him. There were only occasional flights of birds far away, and a few animals that fled his approach. He had no visions. His mind cleared. He knew that he clung to his existence precariously, and without warning the wind from the grave of the Goddess might sweep him away to be consumed in holy fire, but a fancy came to him: perhaps if he continued thinking only of immediate things, he could go on forever.

The threatening sky brought him out of his reverie. He came to a series of low, craggy hills. Where two joined, there was a narrow valley, and at the end of the valley, a cave. As soon as he saw the cave, the winter rains began in a thundering torrent. He knew it was a sign. He ran for the cave, arriving drenched and breathless. He sat in its mouth for a while, watching the rain weave shimmering curtains against the grey sky.

He wanted to start a fire, but there was no kindling. He got his cloak out of his bag. It was reasonably dry, so he wrapped it around himself and sat, hugging his knees, thinking over what he had come here to do.

Now that he was facing it, now that the time had come, he was afraid, but he knew there was no going back.

For whatever reason, perhaps because a fragment of the Goddess had fallen on him that night he saw the feathered star, he could see and hear and feel things the senses of ordinary people shut out. He had heard the echo of the death of the Goddess more clearly than had anyone in generations, even those holy men who spent decades in fasting and discipline before they could make out the faintest trace of that sound in a way that was not truly hearing.

For him, it had come without any effort.

As the years went by and the visions increased, he was losing himself. For longer and longer periods he was no one at all, just a jumble of sensations. Often, when he awoke, he could not remember who he was, and his memories came back little by little, as if he were reborn again and again after each seizure, weaker every time.

He wondered: had he always been Tamliade, or was Tamliade a haphazard construct by someone who could not recall who he really was? Was he like a drop of rain, a mere transition between the sky and earth? He had read somewhere: if the raindrop has consciousness; if it feels the passage of the air and sees the ground rushing up to meet it; this does not make it fall any less swiftly.

His plan was simple. In a remote place such as this cave, free from any distraction, he would deliberately summon up all the visions inside him. With all the concentration he could manage, he would reach out and find—he had no idea what he would find. It was as if he were tired of youth, and were forcing maturity upon himself now, rather than waiting for inevitable growth. He would make an end now. He would arrive at the cause of his visions. He would either achieve some revelation, or be transformed, or die. He could not go on as he was.

There was a little food remaining in his bag. He ate the rest of it. If he did not succeed, he didn't think he would need it. If he did, perhaps he would be beyond such considerations altogether.

The rain fell, filling the cave with the echoes of its sound.

Tamliade began to clear his mind, to concentrate according

to disciplines the priests had taught him.

He hesitated. It is one thing to be told by a magician, "You can fly." It is quite another to jump off a cliff to test this. Tamliade was at the edge of the cliff. In his case there was the further problem that he might never be able to touch ground again.

He waited, listening to the rain, shivering from the cold. Night fell. Still it rained. It was useless to wait any longer.

He began an exercise known as "the string of beads." One by one he drew "beads" out of his memory and examined them:

Standing with his father beneath the dark sky. The chill of the air. The feathered star.

His wandering. An old woman hobbled before him as he sat starving and delirious at a crossroads. She led her blind husband by the hand. "Holy one," she said. "Have you the power to heal?"

Outside, in the darkness, the rain fell.

His time as a slave, filled with pain and humiliation and weary hours as the slave dealer tried hopelessly to find a buyer for a boy who lapsed into dreams uncontrollably.

The wizard Emdo Wesa, the old man who more than anything else feared his monstrous brother, Etash Wesa, who had drifted far, far into strangeness, wholly mutilated and transformed by his magic. Tamliade most clearly remembered Emdo Wesa sitting by his wagon at evening. His gloves were off for once. His hands, made of light, glowed like paper lanterns.

Still the rain fell outside the cave mouth.

Still Tamliade drew up the "string" of his life, each memory becoming more and more vivid, drawing him more away from the immediate reality of the rain and the cave and the night.

He stood again before the gate of the inner city, spheres of light circling his head, while crowds of spirits pressed around him, whispering, "Are you the one? Are you the one?"

He saw the Goddess clearly, as he had once as a child, when his vision had lifted him up from his sleep and led him out of his father's house, into the forest of *ledbya*, the hair-needle trees. He came to a clearing, looked up, and there, with the Moon in her hair and a crowd of stars on her head—

The gate of the inner city swung wide, and blood poured forth, splashing down the carven steps, around the corners of the houses; swirling around Tamliade's legs—

The spirits, whispering, their hands groping, tugging, pinching; their hands soft and warm, like animate ash—

The Goddess reached down through the trees—

The gate of the palace swung wide, and the sun, dim and red, rose out of the pooled blood in the courtyard beyond; and the sun was a mask of metal, the mouth blubbering like flesh. Blood poured from the eyes and mouth, weaving a shimmering curtain beneath the mask, like red rain, and there was a figure there, slowly solidifying, the wearer of the mask clad in a red robe, wading through the blood that splashed around Tamliade's knees—

He heard the rain outside the cave, as loud as if it were continuous thunder, and then there was thunder, and lightning dazzled his eyes.

The rain whipped into the cave on a sudden wind. He shivered.

Then, a new sound: a footstep at the mouth of the cave, gravel rattling.

The masked one stood before him, blood streaming down the mask. He tried to get up, but his body would not obey him. The intruder reached down and took him by the shoulders, the touch of his hands burning. He screamed. Blood splashed over him like rain. He was lifted. His body felt light as smoke.

"Come with me. I shall set you free at last."

Still he screamed and struggled. His body was burning and numb at the same time. He couldn't tell what his limbs were doing.

And the other laughed, and parodying the voice of the Guardian, said, *"The great danger of dreaming, the danger which is greatest to you of all people, is that you will fall into that abyss, into the power of Etash Wesa."*

He closed his eyes as the mask drew near his face. Through his eyelids he saw red haze, swirling fire.

He remembered the other thing the Guardian had said. He thought of the Goddess. He saw her above the *ledbya* trees, reaching down—

There was darkness. He was falling. Then he was on the ground, on his hands and knees in gravel and mud, crawling, scrambling down a hillside in the driving rain, as water swirled around him and rose, frigid, over his knees, his loins, and numbed where his shoulders had been burned, and closed over his head.

* * * *

There was a discontinuity in memory and sensation, as if he had wholly ceased to exist, and was slowly returning to existence in stages. He was aware of the cold first, intense, all encompassing. Then motion: he was rising, drifting in frigid water. It was a while before he was aware that he could see nothing. His face was numb. He couldn't tell if his eyes were open or closed.

Then his lungs felt like they were bursting. The pain forced him out of passivity. He struggled upward, his arms and legs stiff, kicking, crawling in the water, and broke the surface with a shock of air and relative warmth. His hoarse gasps and splashes echoed in darkness. He bobbed in the water, looked around, almost subliminally made out a shoreline of black rocks, and swam toward it.

In a minute or so he was pulling himself onto a flat shelf of stone a few feet above the water. He sat there, taking stock of his situation.

To his back was a smooth cliff. He couldn't climb it. In front of him, the water stretched into darkness. He couldn't see the shore on the other side, but there was a curving ridge line silhouetted against a steady glow of red-orange light. The ridge was circular. He was at the bottom of a huge crater which held the lake he had just emerged from. The most remarkable thing was that the light beyond the crater's lip was the same in all directions, as if somewhere, far away, huge fires burned.

He had no idea where he was or how he had gotten here, but he knew that it was not a dream, but a physical place. The rock beneath him was cold and smooth and wet where he dripped on it. He shivered. Overhead, the sky was featureless, black without stars or clouds.

The only sound was the slight lapping of the water against the shore. He sat for a while, trying to wring his cloak out, but he couldn't get it to come dry. All the while the cold seemed to grow worse. There was another sound, the chattering of his teeth.

Then he heard someone weeping. He stopped and listened. There was no question. A woman weeping, not far away to his right.

Another survey of the situation convinced him that the only way he could get anywhere was to wade along the lake's edge, so he slid back into the water. It was waist deep. He made his way carefully over slippery stones. He bunched up his cloak and held it over his head, so that when he got to land again it would at least not be absolutely soaked.

When the source of the weeping was nearby, he slipped and fell with a splash, dropping the cloak, then groping around for it.

"Stop! You're ruining it! I can't see it anymore!"

He followed the voice and scrambled onto a pebbling beach. There he could barely make out a woman in the dim light. He couldn't tell if she was old or young. Her voice merely sounded tired and full of pain.

She knelt by the water's edge and wept.

"What can't you see? I'm sorry if I—"

She spoke with a strange accent, explaining between sobs that if she looked very intensely at a certain place in the water, she could see her native city, from which she had come by means she did not understand, to which, she was sure, she could return only if she never averted her gaze from it.

Tamliade looked. He saw only black water. "What city is it?"

For a time, she only wept, then she spoke a name. He knew the name. He had read of it in certain ancient books, the name of a mighty capital which had vanished into dust a thousand years before his time.

He considered that the woman might be mad, but he knew that was not the case, and hurried away from her, on the threshold of terror.

The terrain was barren and strewn with boulders. He began to climb up the slope of the crater. After a while he felt wind biting through his wet, tattered clothing. He wished he had stayed longer to search for the cloak.

The woman's weeping followed him like a beast stalking in the night. Then it slowly faded with distance, until he was hundreds of feet above the lake, climbing alone. Occasionally his passing would send rocks tumbling in small avalanches, cracking far below.

There was a small fire burning in the mouth of a cave, far off to his right, near the top of the ridge. He made his way along the curving slope, then up, until he came to a ledge before the cave.

He half expected to see himself inside, still occupied with the rite of the string of beads. It made a certain sense in the logic of a dream. Such a thing had happened to many adepts, when they sent their souls wandering. But this was not a dream. He stood, exhausted and cold, before that cave. The firelight flickered on stone, glistening where water seeped from the cave wall. He smelled smoke, and meat cooking. He realized how hungry he was, how cold. He walked into the shallow cave and stood before the fire, warming himself.

In the darkness beyond it, something stirred. He stood still.

"Spirit, be gone!" came a shrill voice.

"I'm not a spirit," he said slowly. "Please don't send me away."

"Then sit by the fire while I decide what to do with you." The tone was more irritated than threatening. He sat cautiously. On the other side of the fire he could make out a huddled form. The smell of meat was very strong. There was also the faint stench of something rotten.

A hand grabbed him by the knee. The grip was firm, the touch dry and cold. He leaned forward, peering into the gloom. The hand let go. The other shuffled back from the fire. He got an impression of tangled hair and beard.

"You're not a spirit. Not yet."

"What do you mean—?"

A snort. "That when you die, you'll become a spirit, like everyone else. What do you think I meant?"

"I don't know."

There was no response, only a long, uncomfortable silence. The flames crackled.

"You came here because you're hungry. They all do. No one has come in a long time. I've been alone for so long. Here, take this."

A stick poked his knee. He took it. There was a piece of meat on it. He tore into it, the grease running down his chin.

"You wonder why you are here. You wonder where here is. They always do. I always explain. Not that it matters. Do you want to know?"

Tamliade nodded, and mumbled, his mouth full. "There are dreamers who travel far in their dreams. There are those whose dreams are so vast they get lost in them, and never find their way back to waking. Then there are those whose dreams burn holes in the fabric of the world. They dream. They fall through, out of the world, sometimes leaving the husk of the body behind, sometimes not. You've heard of them. I know. You're one."

"Yes, I am."

Tamliade felt strangely resigned, as if he had always known that such a thing would happen to him.

The other let out a shriek. Tamliade jumped back.

"You came here to rob me!"

"No, I didn't!"

"Yes you did. You came here of your own free will, *didn't you?* Deliberately! Deliberately!"

There followed howls, incoherent babblings, snatches of chanting in some language he didn't know.

He rose to a crouch, ready to spring away. The other continued screaming, slapping the palms of his hands on the cave floor. He could see the face dimly: pale, with watery eyes, a ragged beard, matted hair.

"I don't know what you mean! I didn't do anything to you! I didn't even know you were here!"

"Lies! Lies! Lies!"

Bewildered, afraid, Tamliade scrambled back further.

Then the voice was calm. "No, forgive me. Come back. I'm so alone here. I forget how to behave."

He paused, then slowly came back and sat by the fire. He took another bite of the meat. It had a sharp, salty taste. He couldn't tell what it was.

"This is a half-created place. Their dreams...deposit them here, like debris left on shoals by waves of the sea. This place is outside of space and time, perhaps begun by some god or goddess too feeble to complete it, or else abandoned as a bad start. You must understand...I think you do...the ability to see visions, to have deep dreams—this is not an ability at all, in all but the very greatest. It's a weakness. You lose your grip on your place in the world. You tumble down, down...here. This place is downhill from all the worlds. The Goddess being dead, there is nothing to hold you, me, or anyone in place if we start to fall...."

Tamliade nodded and continued eating.

The stranger's voice became more intent, lower. "I am one of those very rare, great dreamers. In me, dreams are an active thing. I *seize* them. I seek the secret at the bottom of dreams, and when I have it—the Goddess being dead—a new divinity will arise soon; forming out of the chaos of the universe like a swirling storm—*I am the one.*"

Tamliade grunted in astonishment and dropped the meat in his lap.

"You are surprised, boy? It interferes with your own aspirations, does it? It's so simple. All I have to do is wait. It isn't possible for anyone, even for you to live here very long... Nothing lives here. Nothing grows. That stick I gave you. It's part of the staff of someone who came before you. I wait. I wait until they perish from hunger and thirst. The fire. I know a spell to make rocks burn. No one else does. The cold gets them. I wait, until the power of divinity settles on me, until it *must* settle on me, here, in this abyss: where gods and goddesses are formed and have their beginnings. These others have all come—you have come—to find what is beyond the reach of your inner vision, the dream beyond the dream. The beauty of my plan is this: I alone survive. When you die. When the rest of them die, there is only me. In the end I shall rise from this place, transfigured in my glory."

Tamliade held the stick up to the fire and turned it slowly, filled with a dreadful suspicion. There was still a bit of meat on it.

He had to know. He put down the stick. He took off his jacket.

"What are you doing, boy?"

He put the corner of the jacket into the fire. The cloth burned. The fire flared up, lighting the cave.

The wild-haired man screamed and lurched forward.

"Come to me! You're mine!" His voice broke, became a grating squeal.

Tamliade screamed—

—Stumps, legs gone below the knees, ragged, putrid flesh, bones sticking out like white twigs—

The other lurched forward, scattering the fire—behind him, the cave floor littered with bones, with shattered skulls, scraps of clothing, jewels, swords, shoes—

The fire flared up again, as the old man's clothing caught fire, and Tamliade could see, very clearly, that he had teeth like those of a shark, filed down to points.

He froze for just a second, and the monster had him by the ankles, pulling him toward the fire, scattering the burning stones. He kicked and wriggled, clinging to outcroppings of rock, but he was pulled relentlessly back. He vomited up all he had eaten. The other had him like an enormous spider, crawling over his body, smothering him with stench. His shirt ripped. Teeth sank into his back. He screamed and rolled over, but the thing rolled with him, arms locked around his chest, squeezing the breath from him. He reached back, caught a handful of greasy hair, yanked, twisted, but still the teeth tore at him.

A rock came away in his other hand. Without thinking, he swung it around, slammed hard, and the grip was gone. He kicked furiously, felt the other fall away—surprisingly light— and he was free, crawling, stumbling out of the mouth of the cave, up the slope the rest of the way, until he was out of the crater, and he stood, swaying, looking over a landscape of dark hills and a featureless plain. In the distance, in every direction, there was a glowing barrier. The horizon burned, as if with a multiple sunrise that never came in this timeless half-world.

He was too weak to go on. He sat down where he was, trembling, his shirt in tatters, his bleeding back exposed to the frigid air. The cold sank into his lungs. It was hard to breathe. He sat there gasping.

He was safe here. He knew the madman couldn't follow. It was so cold. He thought of returning to the cave, retrieving what was left of his jacket.

No, he realized. He wasn't thinking right. He couldn't go there again.

He tried to understand what the madman had told him. He didn't know what was true, what was happening. He tried to get up, but fell forward and lay face down. He wondered: would he turn out like the old man, like Etash Wesa, consumed by his vision? The fear of this drove him on. He tried to get up again, crawled a little ways, and lay still. He felt pebbles and sand against his face, the blood drying on his wounds, the cold. In his delirium, spirits came to him like tall, thin, wavering flames. He rolled onto his side and looked up at them. Only their faces were distinct, like wrinkled, intricately-lined masks of old age and death, their eyes burning with holy fire. Only one of them spoke, but all mouthed the words.

"He shall join us soon. His vision has ended, like the others."

A wind blew through the valley, numbing Tamliade, carrying the spirits away.

He slept, resigned to his end. He was like a taper, cast into the darkness, into the night, flickering, dying.

When he slept, he did not dream. Here, where the ashes of dreams settled, it was not possible to dream further.

* * * *

When he awoke, a hooded figure sat on a stone with a glowing skull in his lap. Tamliade saw every detail clearly, as if he were already close to death and his senses were changing into those of a ghost.

Veined, wrinkled hands held the skull, the hands of an old man. The skull itself was almost translucent. It glowed like a paper lantern. There were six holes drilled in it, forming a line across the top.

"Behold," the hooded one said in a gentle voice, a filled with contented calm. "I have found the treasure I sought in my dreams. It was here all along, within my own skull. My spirit ventured even to this bare and barren place, but I had it with me the while. I yearned for it. I could not perceive it, until now. Listen, stranger, and know the peace that does not end."

Curiously unafraid, Tamliade sat up, and waited.

The hooded one raised the skull to unseen lips and blew through one of the holes, covering and uncovering the rest with his fingers. The eye sockets lit up, and the skull sang, and the sound was more than music. Tamliade had developed a new sense, a hearing beyond hearing, and his very self was overwhelmed with something so intensely beautiful that time came to a stop for him, and he was suspended like an insect in amber in one ecstatic now. The skull sang in something other than words, and his hurts no longer bothered him. He did not feel the cold, or hunger, or exhaustion. The terrors he had known melted away, and all the sorrows and memories of sorrows were like a fading dream, almost gone now that he had, for the first time in his life, truly awoken. The skull sang, and it seemed he had always been here on this rock-strewn ridge by the lip of the crater. He basked in the glory of the song like a planet beneath the sun.

Once more spirits gathered around him, settling like mist. He could see them clearly, men and children of all races and nationalities, some familiar, some strange, some clad in outlandish costumes, some not men at all, but sexless, naked, their bodies covered with golden fur and terminating into serpent form below the waist.

He saw joy on the faces of all of them, and he felt that joy himself. There was one among them in the flesh, a man of indeterminate age with skin and scraggly hair, filthy, clad only in a loincloth. He was little more than an animate skeleton. His joints were raw and bleeding. But his look was one of absolute exaltation. Tamliade knew that this one would soon lay aside his useless body, as he himself would, and remain here forever, in the place all dreams, all quests, ended.

* * * *

It was only very slowly that he realized that the song was diminishing, and more slowly still that he could tell that he was walking down a gentle slope, led by someone. Passively, still filled with the song, he followed, until the land leveled out into a plain of mud and occasional boulders. On the horizon, fires burned, no nearer than before, no farther away.

His senses concentrated on one thing at a time: was walking; his shoulders hurt where he had been burned; something heavy pressed on his shoulders; a musty-smelling coat was draped around him, reaching down to his ankles, large enough for two of him.

It seemed forever as he sat, as the other sat beside him and proceeded to dig mud out of her ears with her little fingers, shaking her head as she did so.

The one who had led him away was a girl about his own age.

Her face was oval and pale, her hair dark and tied back. She wore what must have once been a brightly-patterned dress, now ragged and filthy. One white knee showed through a tear in it. Her feet were bare and caked with mud.

As he looked at her, it seemed she was the only person he had ever known, the only one besides himself who had ever existed. It seemed that he loved her intensely, and that she was very beautiful.

After she had cleared her ears, she grabbed him by the shoulders and shook him.

"Wake up! Say something! What's your name?"

She held him where he had been burned. He cried out and drew back. She let go. The pain brought him more into himself. His life was coming back to him. His name was just beyond reach. He could almost say it.

She put her arm around him and helped him to his feet. He winced from the pressure of the wounds on his back. He stood, dazed, swaying.

"Here," she said. "Let me help you." She got the coat off. He trembled in the cold, doubled over, but she straightened him up again, worked his arms into the coat sleeves, then arranged them so he hugged himself gently, holding the coat shut, his fingertips barely sticking out of the ends of the sleeves. She led him by one arm. "Come on. Walk. I'll tell you about myself first. Then you tell me who you are."

So they walked toward the burning horizon, and she told him that her name was Azrethemne, that she was a boatman's daughter; from the southern reaches of the Endless River, near Zabortash. She wasn't from any country. She was born on the river. He was very tired. He wanted to lie down, but still she led him, and still she spoke. In her earliest childhood strange dreams had come to her, and she had sensed a vast and strange world right at the edge of her perceptions. She had heard the whispered words of the Goddess as they drifted like ashes in the darkness. She fell into fits of vision. Her parents thought her mad. They commanded her to stop, and beat her when she did not. The other girls laughed at first. Then they shunned her. Then her mother grew more and more afraid.

"It was like that with me," said Tamliade.

Her family ferried up and down the river, taking cargo and passengers. When there were rich passengers and extra coins to be had, she would dance for them and shake her tambourine, or play upon the flute. Once, while she danced, and the boat drifted lazily on a broad expanse of the river, the sun began to dance too. It came toward her across the water, its face dimmed to a bronze mask with rays around the rim and a face in the center, worn by one in a long, scarlet robe, dancing. Then a voice spoke to her, telling of this dark place to which she would journey, of the one she would rescue, and of a further journey. For this purpose she had been born into the world. To this, her dreams led.

"I saw the masked one clearly," said Tamliade.

But her father was a greedy, clinging man, a failed magician who could only do a few tricks, for all he claimed to be as great as a Zabortashi magus.

"I knew a successful magician," said Tamliade, "No, I think, two."

Her father would not let her follow her visions.

He commanded her to foretell the future, to tell the fortunes of rich passengers who paid him. When she could not, again he beat her. Then he somehow became convinced that he was the one who had the dreams, but that she had stolen them from him, that he was the one around which the storm of divinity gathered, in whom holy fire raged. In truth he had never had a dream in his life, even a simple one, like most people have. He was dead to dreaming. Still, he was sure to be the one who would rise into the heavens, breathe new life into the sun, and shape the moon with his hands. Or so he said. At first people laughed at these delusions. Then they were afraid. All the while her visions came more intensely. Spirits gathered around her and shrieked things she could not understand. The dreams filled her. She was losing herself. Then one day her father made her drink a draught that made her dream all the more. He performed a grotesque blasphemy of a rite he had only half learned, much less understood, called *psadeu-ma*, enabling him to share her dreams. And he clung to her, wrestling with her as she writhed on the deck of the boat.

When she fell out of the world, he came with her.

Soon he was transformed horribly. She fled from him. Ever since, he dwelt in a cave, waylaying newcomers, convinced they were all thieves come to steal his dream.

"I think I met him," said Tamliade.

She made to embrace him, but paused, then took his hands in hers. They stared into each other's eyes, and wept, and there passed between them such an understanding that Tamliade knew that he had finally found someone like himself, who understood, whom he could understand. He knew that he loved Azrethemne, that the feeling was real, not just something that rose out of his delirium. More than anything else he wanted to help her, to spare her some of the suffering he had gone through.

He tried to sort things out in his mind. He was still being directed toward some end. If he was to be the one who was to come after rhe Goddess, he would raise Azrethemne into the sky with him, to be his consort. He would not be alone again, even as a god. If that was to happen. Somehow, now, he didn't think so.

He wanted to know why things had turned out this way. But an old slave had told him once: *There is no why.* Things merely happen. Either accept them or don't. It makes no difference.

Now that he had found Azrethemne, he was almost content to accept everything. But he knew he had not seen the end yet. The masked one had told her she was created for some specific task. The masked one was a sending, a manifestation of Etash Wesa. When he considered that, he was again afraid, both for himself and for Azrethemne.

First, he told her his name, which had returned, and what he could recall of his life. As he spoke, memories came like a torrent. He told her what he could, bit by bit, sometimes out of sequence. He hoped she could make sense out of it all.

Again, the two of them wept. He knew that she understood.

* * * *

Once, after they had paused to rest on a boulder, Azrethemne staggered when she stood up again. Tamliade steadied her. He could tell she was very weak. How long had it been since she had eaten? She had not gone the way of her father. How long had it taken for her father to get into his present state? He asked her. She had no idea. There was no way to measure time in this changeless land. Perhaps he had truly been transformed in a few days. Perhaps time moved at a different pace for him. She didn't want to talk about it.

So they marched on, across the nearly featureless plain. The ridge, the crater, the lake where he had emerged were all behind them now, lost in the darkness. They stopped and rested many times. Sometimes they slept, even in the mud where there were no boulders. They would lie still, both of them wrapped in his coat. Getting up again was harder each time. His body seemed heavy. He had no strength at all. Oddly, the actual pangs of hunger had long since ceased to trouble him.

Once Azrethemne fainted, and he held her up. They stood, embracing, facing the burning horizon. Her eyes were closed.

She mumbled something unintelligible.

"Is there any way *out* of here?" he asked, hardly expecting an answer.

She opened her eyes, stared for a while, and spoke slowly. "I think…in all the dreams I had of you, we walked this way. The dreams ended here…we were walking. If there is any way, this must be it. We couldn't just stay where we were."

"No," he said. "We couldn't. We might as well walk. If we're going to die anyway, we have nothing to lose."

"I don't think," she said, "it will end like this. It doesn't make any sense."

And Tamliade thought bitterly that perhaps now, the Goddess

being dead, things didn't have to make sense anymore. But he didn't believe it would end like this either. Deep within him, he feared something worse.

On they went, alone. Not even spirits inhabited this remote region. The fires on the horizon looked no nearer. From the ridge top, this world had looked small, as if one could cross it in a day or two. Now, it seemed to go on forever.

They drank from occasional brackish pools. Then the ground hardened, and there were no more pools. He showed her how to put a pebble in her mouth to allay thirst, and that seemed to help a little.

He wondered if he was walking in place. They made no visible progress. Now the plain was wholly featureless, covered with dust and pebbles, without even a few large boulders to mark the way.

A thought came to him: perhaps he had to die first before he would turn into a god. He would die, and Azrethemne would bury him, and then he would rise, transfigured in holy fire.

Perhaps. He doubted she would have the strength to do it. She was failing rapidly. He all but carried her.

The single thought reverberated in his mind until he forgot all else. Perhaps he was already dead, and he walked the long road out of the world, or, like Emdo Wesa, had lost his way and could not find the road.

He had not had a vision in a long time. His mind was still, like a rope once tied into convoluted knots, now left limp in a heap.

He tried to remember his father, his days of wandering, the city, the Guardian, the visions he had seen, but it was all slipping away, and his existence consisted entirely of walking, walking forever across the empty landscape, in the darkness, toward the sunrise that never came.

He tried to imagine what it would be like to be with Azrethemne back in the world he knew, the world of colors and sounds.

There was only cold, and exhaustion, combined into a single

sensation.

Still, Azrethemne held his hand. At times he squeezed hers, to remind himself that she was there.

When neither could go any farther, they sank down and sat for a time, staring hopelessly at the horizon. Neither spoke. She drew him to her, and they embraced, and kissed, and her lips were cracked and rough. Then they lay down side by side, wrapped in the coat, hand in hand, staring into the darkness.

He thought that he would continue to hold her hand, so that she would come with him if he were raised up into the sky. Or else he would merely lie here forever, and she would be with him.

His mind emptied out completely. He was open, utterly vulnerable to any vision that might come. He had no memory of one second passing into the next. At the very end, his awareness seemed to be reaching out, searching for something, anything, and once more he heard, faintly but distinctly, the fading echo of the death of the Goddess.

Then he slept.

IV.

The dream found Azrethemne first.

Tamliade awoke as she thrashed against him. It was still dark. He was still weak. His insides felt like shriveled leather, but his mind was clear. Azrethemne lay beside him still asleep, her eyes open, moaning softly, rolling, kicking, slapping the ground with her hands.

He understood what was happening to her. He was filled with terror and pity. It was as if he were watching himself.

She screamed, "Blood!"

He started, looked around, saw nothing, and still she screamed. He held her arms to her sides, wrestling with her, whispering into her ear, "Let me have it. Give the vision to me." He wanted to help her, even if what was within her tore him apart, even if he were lost forever inside some endless nightmare. He could not stand to see this happen to her.

She arched her back, nearly threw him off, and screamed again, "Blood! Blood!"

There was no time for *psadeu-ma*, whereby he could share her dream and perhaps take it from her. That took careful preparation.

Still she screamed. Still he held her.

"Let her go!" he shouted. "I'm the one you want!"

He shouted to the fire that ringed in the world, to the darkness.

Azrethemne went suddenly limp, and a voice from within her thundered, *"You are the one I want, Tamliade. You are the one."*

He let go of her and knelt over her, gaping.

She screamed again, broke into a liquid gurgling, and vomited out an enormous quantity of blood, splattering him. He reached for her, then recoiled as she spat out blood in impossible amounts. It covered her face. It flowed over her, across the ground, splashing at his knees, pooling around her, spreading, spreading. He stared in helpless horror as the level rose, the blood surrounding her face, covering her. He stood up, stepped back, splashing. She was gone. He stood calf-deep in a lake of blood. He felt dizzy. The current slid his feet out from under him, and for a horrible instant he was submerged, his mouth filled with blood. He got to all fours, then staggered to his feet, while it rushed around him like a tide. He saw it stretching further, covering the land, until it reached the horizon, touched the fires, and burst into flame as if it were oil.

Suddenly the sky was very bright. He stood, blinded by the light as the flames roared toward him over miles of scarlet bloodscape. The heat was unbearable. He fell to his knees again, and scalding liquid splashed over his shoulders.

But he did not cover his face. He watched as the fire came weaving toward him, towering to fill the sky.

Then he saw something else: the bronze-masked man, dancing

toward him through the flames, across the sea of blood, arms, stretched wide to embrace him. In an instant he was there. He took Tamliade by both hands and raised him, until he too stood on the surface of the sea, his boots barely awash. Tamliade's hands were burning at that touch, but the flames around him did not hurt him.

"The dream is yours, Tamliade. Take it."

His hands were lifted to the rim of the mask.

The molten metal burned as his fingers were closed around it. Globules flowed down his arm. Smoke poured out of his sleeves. He cried out, but no sound came. He could not let go. His muscles would not obey him.

The body of the dancing man fell away, and there was only the mask, its eyes dazzling with the intensity of their glare. The mask rose, lifting him above the flames. He dangled. The mask flew. He looked down once. The flames, tall as they were, looked tiny, the whole land like a caldron of burning pitch.

"Azrethemne!" he shouted, but his voice was lost in the roar of the flames and wind. He wept for her, but the heat of the mask evaporated his tears.

His hands burned.

The mask spoke, the metal rippling and flowing. *"Tamliade, only a perfect dreamer would do for my purpose. Only you. Tamliade, we have met before. Do you not know me?"*

Wind roared around him. The pain in his hands was too intense for him to concentrate, to form words.

"Tamliade, I am Etash Wesa."

Once more he screamed and struggled. He tried to let go, to fall to an easy death, but his hands would not obey him. Then he hung limp, hopeless, helpless. He was beginning to understand. Etash Wesa had made many dadars in the course of his career, living projections to which he contributed a scrap of his flesh. He had made too many. He had had too many enemies, fought too many incomprehensible battles. There wasn't much left of him. He could only act on the physical world through dreams, and for all his power, he could only seize a dreamer in such a place and in such a condition as Tamliade had been.

His whole plan had simply been stupid, he realized. He should have stayed in Ai Hanlo, and lived as he had, or he should simply have killed himself. There was no escape. To project himself into his own dreams, to follow his visions where they led, was to deliberately leap into that abyss the Guardians had spoken of, where lurks Etash Wesa.

It was his own fault that he was here now. He had dared to hope. For that, there could be no forgiveness.

The mask shrieked at him as they flew, sometimes in strange languages, sometimes wordless in maniacal hatred.

* * * *

He was no longer over the sea of burning blood.

At first, he was only aware that the pain was less. Still his hands were locked to the mask, but it no longer burned him. His hands were black and swelling.

The light from the eyes was diminishing. They glowed a dull red, like coals.

He was being lowered. There was only darkness, the mask glowing in it like a pale sun, its mouth frozen. He looked down. Gradually he could make out vast, dim shapes of treetops rising to meet him, gently rolling in every direction. Then he was among them, dropping down for hours through a forest that must have been impossibly deep, its trees miles high.

The trees were dead, leafless. The trunks of the nearer ones shone a pale white by the light of the mask, the color of corpse flesh. He could not see the ground below or the sky above, only trunks and branches, fading into distance. Slowly, huge limbs rose out of the murk, loomed close, then disappeared overhead, while trunks passed endlessly by, like vertical rivers.

He thought the descent would never end, that this was a kind of death, to be lowered forever into the corpse-forest without a bottom. But finally he made out a shape below: curving tree trunks, thick as mountains, joining together to form something vaster still, rounded, jointed, curving; the fingers of a grey, swollen hand too vast to contemplate.

The mask flickered. There was horizontal movement. The mask carried him away from the hand, until it too faded into the gloom. Far below, on the forest floor, the decaying body of a giant stretched for miles upon endless miles, half submerged in a swamp of coagulated blood. The trees were growing out of it, the entire forest like a fungus growth on this thing which in any sane universe could never, never have been alive. Curves of flesh rose like islands. The skin had collapsed between some of the ribs, leaving gaping chasms large enough to swallow cities.

It seemed to take hours for the ribs to pass beneath him, the shadows shifting, the mask weaving between tree trunks. At last the chest was gone. A long interval of darkness followed.

Then, peering down, he made out the face, or part of it, the chin, with trees growing to form a beard, then the cheekbones protruding like hilltops out of the grey flesh, and, far ahead of him, the eyes, rolled-up white, so vast he could not see over the curve of them.

The descent was rapid now. The mouth yawned wide. The air was thicker, fouler than before.

Again he struggled, trying to yank the mask from its course, but he was as helpless as an ant held in a pair of tweezers, and the cracked white lips stretched around him like the rim of a canyon, and then, in absolute darkness again, as he choked on the putrid air, the glowing mask was the only thing that was real.

* * * *

Motion had ceased long before he knew it. Sensations returned slowly. His hands throbbed dully. He no longer held the mask. As his sight came into focus, he saw it hovering, still aglow, a short distance away. He fell to his knees, breaking a crusty surface, splashing in something putrid and greasy and black. He struggled to stand again, but could not escape the repugnant touch of the stuff. It closed around him waist-deep, hardening. He stepped forward, breaking. the crust. He realized he was nearly naked. His clothing had been burned away, but for a few scraps, for all that the flames had not touched his flesh.

The mask receded, impossibly far, yet still visible, as if it grew in size as it retreated until it became as large as the sun, settling behind the corpse-flesh trees.

"Come to me, Tamliade," it said at last. *"Come into my heart."*

* * * *

The stench of congealing blood was overwhelming. He wandered aimlessly through the greasy swamp, in absolute darkness, clinging from time to time in his exhaustion against the roots of trees, which indeed felt like soft, overripe carrion.

The skin on his hands felt tight. He couldn't move his fingers. His face was dry, cracked, almost numb.

At last he saw a point of light ahead and turned toward it. It didn't seem to get any closer. He didn't care. There was nowhere else to go.

He prayed to the Goddess, who was dead.

He prayed to Emdo Wesa, his former master, the brother of Etash Wesa. Emdo Wesa had treated him kindly once. Now, perhaps, if his spirit still lingered and had any power at all, he might grant Tamliade the boon of death, settling over him like smoke and smothering him.

Emdo Wesa did not appear.

Tamliade prayed, too, to the Guardian, who might stand on a scaffold before the skylight of the golden dome of Ai Hanlo, looking out over the world, and see him struggling in the darkness.

But he was not in the world any more, and the Guardian of the Bones of the Goddess did not see him.

He wept for Azrethemne, and this time his tears flowed. It seemed that in all his life, his only happiness had come in that brief interval with her, the days, or hours, or few brief moments he had spent by her side.

She was gone, lost in the phantasmagorical darkness.

He was truly alone and without hope when the light led him to the ruined temple. He climbed up out of the slime and stood on rough, crumbling stone. Roofless walls and broken pillars surrounded him.

His boots were gone. A few strips of leather clung to his ankles. He stood on a cubical block, his toes curled over the edge. He wanted to stay there, to die there, but he could not.

The source of the light was before him. There was an opening in the ground. Fires burned within.

As he approached, he saw that blood had hardened around the edges of a rectangular doorway. He walked down a flight of stairs, into a sunken room, which was, flooded, deep in pure, red blood. Red flames flickered over the surface. In the center of the room, a coffin of ancient wood floated. He recognized the intricate carvings on its sides, the signs of power and the prolongation of life.

He had come to the lair of Etash Wesa.

The lid of the coffin rose noiselessly, then fell back. The coffin rocked slightly. Blood and flames rippled. A voice spoke from within.

"Come to me, Tamliade. Embrace me, as you would your father."

It was his father's voice. He screamed and turned away.

"Sh-sh. Don't wake your mother."

He staggered up the stairs, slowly, slowly, his legs refusing to obey him.

"Be quiet and come with me…a feathered star…it drifts across the sky, burning with holiness…settles, touches…that's what…I didn't understand it all…."

Something in that voice drained him of all will. He could not help himself as he turned back toward the coffin, and waded almost to his armpits in the blood, which was hot, but not quite scalding. The flames did not harm him. He came to the side of the coffin and looked in. There he saw the ruin of a man, a thing without limbs save the stump of one arm, without face or feature, slowly rolling over in blood. What must have been a mouth opened and closed, spewing gore, gurgling.

Tamliade spoke with resignation.

"Why am I here? What do you want of me?" Steam hissed out of the mouth of Etash Wesa, and took shape.

Tamliade saw Azrethemne standing in the coffin, clad in her ragged dress. Startled, he called her name and reached up for her, but his hand passed through her calf as if through smoke. She was a wraith. Through her, he could see flames flickering behind the coffin.

The thing spoke, thundering with the voice of Etash Wesa.

"I have made too many dadars. But where my fleshly body diminished, my other one grew. I have grown it, out of dreams, out of the fears and deaths of men of many places and times. I have reached out through dreams, seizing what I might use... Tamliade. I AM THE ONE who shall come after the Goddess. When my new body lives, stands, holds the world in its hand, there can be no other. That is what my brother feared more than anything else. He knew that I am inevitable. Tamliade, when you were born, I felt you. When your visions began, you burned like a beacon in my mind; and I knew that here, at last, I had found the gateway, the path.... So I reached out for you. So I created this one you call Azrethemne, to lead you to me."

"No," said Tamliade, trembling.

"No?"

"She is not a...thing. I love her. She is real."

"But a minor instrument in my grand design. She gathered like smoke in her mother's womb."

"No."

"Many shadows think they cast shadows. You are my instrument, Tamliade. You too."

"No...."

"Your task, the purpose for which I have directed most of your life, Tamliade, is simply to dream. Dream of the Goddess,

Tamliade. More clearly than anyone else, you can hear the echo of her death, see the reflection of her life. I shall flow through you, seizing the remnant of her power, drawing her to me, into this body which I have created. Through her, united with her, I shall live, and rise up. My brother was too much of a coward to have dared such a thing. It is a brilliant plan, fully worthy of me."

"No...."

"It no longer matters what you think or will or try to do, Tamliade."

He looked around for escape, as hopeless as that was. He looked for a way to destroy Etash Wesa, to break him with his hands, to drive a knife into the shapeless blob of his body again and again. He looked, once more, for his own death. He would fall down and drown himself in blood.

But he knew Etash Wesa would prevent him.

Think of the Goddess. The Guardian had told him that so many times. But before he had always been afraid of losing himself, like a drop of water splashing in a great wave.

Now he welcomed it. He desperately sought oblivion.

The wraith of Azrethemne settled over him, choking him. He thrashed about. The room seemed to dim, to sway. The flames roared up. Blood closed over him, hot and wet, and the consciousness of Etash Wesa touched his mind—awesome, infinite, hating; hating in a tangle of emotions, of vast currents of thoughts he could not begin to grasp, swelling with malevolence beyond any scale of comprehension.

Out of darkness the great vision came upon him, more intensely than ever before, wringing him out like a rag, burning, burning.

He tried to scream. His mouth filled with hot blood.

There was only darkness, the absence of all sensation.

* * * *

The memories of Etash Wesa were his:

He was Etash Wesa, very young, running after the other children in some muddy street of Zabortash, gasping for breath, falling behind because he was too weak, because one of his legs was crooked.

—hating.

As a youth, he watched his brother Emdo Wesa dance with the maidens of the town at the Festival of the Blood of the Goddess. Emdo Wesa, who was tall, who was straight, who was beautiful; who drew the smiles and applause of the young women with his tricks and illusions.

Etash Wesa, short, ugly, crippled within and without.

—hating.

He was Etash Wesa, creating his first dadar, carefully whispering incantations syllable by syllable by the light of a single candle in a shuttered room, then bracing himself as he raised a cleaver and cut off half the index finger of his left hand. The pain faded as his awareness passed into the dadar itself, a shape condensed from shadows, given substance by his own flesh and blood and bone. It resembled a giant beetle, with shiny black wings. It commanded, and the remote, bleeding human body rose and opened the shutters. The dadar scurried to the windowsill and peered out into the tropical night, then took flight, its wings whirring. Overhead, the moon rippled in the thick air.

The dadar sought another window, and flew in. There, on a bed, lay a maiden beloved of his brother, naked in the heat of the night. She was intensely beautiful. For this Etash Wesa hated her. There was talk of marriage. For this, too, his enmity knew no bounds. The beetle-thing crept over her, clasped her sides with its spiny legs, and penetrated her with its huge, all too human member as she woke up screaming.

She was screaming ten days later, Etash Wesa understood, when she was swollen as if after nine months, and still screaming a week after that when she gave birth to thousands of worms and maggots and carrion beetles in a torrent of blood. She was screaming twenty years later still, when she died mad, white-haired, hideous.

All the while Etash Wesa watched, hating, triumphant, as his brother came to know fear, as the two of them raced one another in their acquisition of the lore of sorcery. Emdo Wesa had not planned to spend his life this way. That was the joy of Etash Wesa's revenge. He had stolen his brother's days and nights, all of them. Now he could only battle Etash Wesa.

And Etash Wesa had no life otherwise, his hatred sustaining him. He was emptiness, a malevolent void.

Slowly this void encompassed an innocent called Tamliade, as inevitably as the incoming tide encompasses a grain of sand. And Tamliade perceived this void, this vastness of Etash Wesa, but dimly. It was more than his mind could grasp. There were centuries of memory as Etash Wesa drifted into strangeness and ceased to be even remotely human. Then Tamliade saw, sharing these memories, that everything Emdo Wesa had ever told him about his brother was true, and he understood further that even Emdo Wesa had but glimpsed the barest outline of the enormity which was Etash Wesa.

Tamliade knew one thing: this ravenous void called Etash Wesa needed him to become flesh again. Etash Wesa could not connect with the physical world. He was too far gone. He had to possess someone yet living. He was himself beyond life and death. Incarnate in the body and mind of Tamliade, he could dream Tamliade's most powerful dreams, reach back through time and touch the Goddess, binding her power to himself, animating the immense body he had made for himself, rising up, seizing the heavens and the Earth, altering the stars in their courses.

"I am the one," said Etash Wesa. "I am the one."

Tamliade's only hope was to surrender utterly to his dreams, then be swallowed utterly by them, until he too failed to connect with the physical world.

Only if he destroyed himself could Etash Wesa's power be curbed.

* * * *

He was a small child again, running in his nightgown, barefoot in the chilly night, running through the forest while the shadows called out holy names, while fragments of the feathered star rained whispering through the branches, burning as they fell, and he was burning, burning as he ran, streaming fire as he sought the clearing where he could look up in the sky and see the Goddess with the moon in her hair and the stars in her crown and—

Naked, he fell down at the feet of the Guardian of the Bones of the Goddess, beneath the golden dome of Ai Hanlo.

"Help me," he whimpered. "Save me."

The Guardian reached up and swung his own face open, like the door of a furnace. His head was hollow. Inside, flares roared.

Water and blood rushed over the floor, splashing over Tamliade, bearing him, whirling like a leaf in a flood-swollen river, down Ai Hanlo Mountain, through the labyrinthine streets of the lower city, out the Sunrise Gate, into the Endless River, whirling, whirling.

The waters parted and the mask of Etash Wesa rose, lighting the sky with the color of blood.

"You are mine now, Tamliade," said Etash Wesa.

* * * *

Tamliade stood on a narrow strip of sand. Even as he stood, he felt the sand crumbling away. Hot blood washed over his ankles. To his left he saw the mask, huge, hanging in the sky above a sea of burning blood on which bobbed the open coffin of Etash Wesa, waiting.

To his right was a void of blue mist. As he watched the blood washed away the sand, ready to pour into the void, to fill it.

"Come to me now," said the voice from within the coffin.

But he ran, splashing blood and sand, toward the blue. He felt the sandbar break up under him, the blood rush past his legs, into the abyss.

He fell suddenly into nothingness, and the mist became water at his touch. He splashed in it, face down, then instinctively struggled, gained the surface and looked up into the purest blue sky he had ever seen. In the distance a white sun hovered above the horizon.

Around him, the water darkened, mingling with blood.

He strove to concentrate, to finish what he had resolved to do. He lay face down, limp in the still sea, breathing water, forcing back the gag reflex.

Memories came: his father beside him in the night; the Guardian comforting him; Azrethemne speaking, Azrethemne walking by his side, the touch of Azrethemne as they lay together.

He dismissed them all until his mind was blank, until he sank into blueness.

The sun was down there, beneath the water, burning with holy fire. It had a face. The sun shone brilliantly in the hand of a lady clad in white, astride a leaping dolphin.

He had seen that lady before. He couldn't remember where.

His mind went blank. He tasted blood in his mouth.

She reached up, embracing him, the sun still in her hand, and there was only fire and light and no sensation at all.

* * * *

"*No!*" cried Etash Wesa. "*Come back! You must become part of me first! Then, then....*"

The voice faded, was very far away. After a while, Tamliade did not hear it.

* * * *

The blood filled the blue abyss, and the sun burned with the hue of it. The coffin floated somewhere nearby.

And Tamliade and Etash Wesa and the Goddess all were one, drifting in the light.

And Tamliade felt the power of Etash Wesa scurrying through

him, like a thousand spiders exploring his body on the inside, trying to find the muscles that moved the limbs, that opened his eyes, that made him speak.

* * * *

In the end he felt his own awareness begin to disintegrate, and the mind of Etash Wesa, linked to his own, began to disintegrate too.

In the end, detached from it all, he came to an understanding. He saw things from a new perspective, and suddenly the grand schemes of Etash Wesa seemed vain, pathetic, laughable.

Etash Wesa had built his fortress on a foundation of smoke. The Goddess was dead. Etash Wesa had embraced what remained of her, an echo, a reflection, a shape the wind creates out of airborne dust, the shadow of a ghost.

Etash Wesa and Tamliade and the Goddess were one, and they were nothing.

* * * *

The mask of Etash Wesa cracked like a broken dish and fell from the sky, and there was a great earthquake; and the sun became black as sackcloth of hair, and the moon became as blood—

And the blood on the moon drained away, and the moon was purest white—

And the stars of heaven fell into the sea, even as a fig tree casts her untimely figs, When she is shaken by a mighty wind—

And there was silence in heaven.

* * * *

Tamliade saw his old master, Emdo Wesa, standing by the shore of the sea in the darkness of the starless night. Where his heart had once been burned a brilliant light, like a beacon, shining through his clothing.

He laughed gently. "You've done well, my boy," he said. "I'm proud of you."

The beacon shone brighter still, turning a part of the night into day.

Then the echo of the Goddess stirred above the waters, and parted the waters from the waters.

* * * *

He never expected to awaken. His first emotion was merely surprise. He sat up and found himself in darkness, on a narrow strip of sand. Waves lapped on either side, slightly luminescent at their crests. This was the only light.

Then a lady stood beside him, her face glowing softly, her gown a brilliant blue. For an instant he thought she was his mother come to look in on him when he had cried out in the night. He thought that everything that had happened from the vision of the feathered star onward was a single nightmare, glimpsed in a few minutes of troubled sleep when he was five years old; that he was still five; that it was over now and he was safe—

At once he saw that she was not a woman at all.

She was translucent. He could see the waves through her.

Her voice came like the wind. "Time is not the same for me, once I became what I am. As if I have eyes on the back of my head, I see both ahead and behind, in time, beyond my own death and before my transformation from mortal life. I still feel the terror of knowing truly for the first time that I was the one, even as I feel the final fading of my death, even as I feel myself projected, as you see me, into the future, like a shout echoing in the cave of time. I have caused you to be the greatest of all dreamers. Therefore you alone can perceive me so far removed from the instant of my death, so near to the beginning of a new epoch, when a new divinity shall arise. But that is beyond my sight."

"Am I the one?" Tamliade blurted, then nearly fainted with dread at the realization that he'd interrupted.

"I saw Etash Wesa born. I saw him change and darken and drift into strangeness. I saw him seek to become as I am, and therefore I caused you, the greatest dreamer, to be born so that he might not. You have done well, if you are hearing these words now, if you look on my image after so many centuries. You are not the *one*. Your mission is over. You are free. Now I shall take from you the burden of dreams."

She reached down and touched his forehead. He felt a pleasant numbness over his whole body. She drew out of his forehead a tiny sphere of light so intense that he had to look away.

When he turned back to her, he saw that she filled the sky, huge above the sea, astride a dolphin, with the moon in her hair and a tiara of stars on her head. And the stars gave birth to stars, and the moon drifted, and then there was only the night sky, darker and more beautiful than he had ever seen it before.

He slept.

* * * *

When next he awoke, he was in a different place. Full physical sensation had returned. It was dark, the air damp and hot and foul. He was lying on his back in greasy mud, nearly naked, his clothing in burnt tatters.

He sat up. As his eyes adjusted he could make out a rectangular opening above him, a doorway at the top of a flight of steps, which were worn with age and covered with vines. He understood that he was in an underground chamber of a ruined building. To one side, an ornate coffin lay tumbled over. Something had spilled out, something pale and shriveled and dead.

There was a broken, corroded bronze mask lying in the mud behind the coffin.

He stood, unsteadily, and nausea came over him, but he managed to stagger up the stairs and out onto a grassy mound.

Huge trees towered over him, laden with vines, dangling blossoms. Brightly colored birds and winged lizards squawked and chased one another among the branches. The sun was high in the sky, but shut out by a green canopy. A swamp stretched as far as he could see in all directions.

It was a natural place, not part of a dream, vaster than anything he had ever seen, but still merely part of some tropical country. He was not afraid.

He went down to the water's edge, thinking to wash himself, but only stood among reeds and watched as two men came by, poling a shallow-bottomed boat. He called out to them and waved. They turned to him, cried out in fright, made gestures, and hurried away. He did not understand, but he was too exhausted to do anything but sit among the reeds in the cool water.

After a while they came back and took him to the house of a holy man, in another part of the swamp. They bowed low as they delivered him, speaking a language he recognized but did not understand:

Emdo Wesa's language, Zabortashi.

They holy man replied to them in the same tongue, then spoke to Tamliade in the Language of the City.

* * * *

Tamliade dwelt with the holy man for a month as his strength returned and his burns healed. The holy man sat by his bedside at first, and the two of them sat together on a bench later, speaking for long hours.

The holy man gave him a robe to wear.

After a while, he told his host all he could of his visions and adventures.

"Ah yes," the other sighed. "I think such visions come only to the very young, so that they may have the rest of their lives to work them out. It wouldn't do any good to start at my age."

It seemed to Tamliade that the man was ageless, like a

gnarled tree.

"What am I to do?" he said.

"I think the course of your life is clear. You should write down all that you have experienced into a book, then become a hermit, and spend the rest of your days trying to discover the meaning of what you have written."

"No," said Tamliade. "Maybe I'll write it all down, but I feel I have been in prison all these years. I want to get out into the world and run and keep on running."

"That may be so. Where will you go?"

"I want to find Azrethemne. I love her." The other shook his head sadly.

"She was but a dadar of Etash Wesa, who is dead. She cannot exist further."

"What am I but a dadar of the Goddess, who is dead? How can I exist further?"

"You grow in wisdom. But if you find her, what will you do?"

"Live. Like anyone else."

Again, the other shook his head sadly.

"You are not like anyone else. Not even now." Confused, a little frightened, Tamliade followed the holy man out into the night. In the distance swamp birds called. Nearby, frogs croaked and chirped.

"Look," the holy man said.

"Look at what?"

"Hold up your hands."

Tamliade did so. The loose sleeves of his robe fell back, and he saw that his hands and forearms glowed a soft red where he had been burned. He pulled up one sleeve to the shoulder and saw that the skin glowed there too, the imprint of a hand clearly visible.

Then he allowed himself to be led to the water's edge, and he knelt down to look at his reflection. A spot in the middle of his forehead shone with an intense white light.

* * * *

Later, when he departed from the house of the holy man, he wore the same loose robe, and around his head a band of cloth on which were written the names of the Goddess in Zabortashi script. He went barefoot, but at night or whenever the sky was overcast, or he entered a darkened place, he always put on the long gloves of a Zabortashi magus, which came up over his elbows.

He searched for Azrethemne.

THE STOLEN HEART

My story is about many things: about a queen who was nearly greater than the Goddess, and a maiden whose courage carried her out of the netherworld, back into the land of the living. It is about lost souls, too, thousands of them, wandering in darkness. But more than that, at its core, it is about my transformation, my redemption. It is about how I became a hero, albeit a substandard, unacceptable one. Yet a hero nonetheless.

Listen—

When my friend Kodos Vion was dying, I knew only helpless, hopeless despair, and in my self-pitying grief, I came to a place which isn't on any Ai Hanlo street map, the Inn of Sorrows, called Korevanos, "the place of holy tears," where once the Goddess herself wept and time and space were closed off around the place where her tears fell.

You cannot find Korevanos. You can only arrive there, as a stone sinking into a dark lake inevitably arrives at the bottom.

Thus, I arrived.

I must tell this story, all of it, even the parts which bring me hurt and shame.

I must tell it so that my transformation will be complete, and true.

Listen—

I don't know where to begin, really. The events swirl and blend in my mind, like different colors of paint stirred in a pot.

* * * *

I ran from Kodos Vion's bedside in terror. I remember that much. I lost myself in the maze of the city.

Then I came upon the corpse of an old man set on a bier in the middle of a street, braziers of perfumed oil sputtering around him. I let out a cry and covered my face, but I was as afraid to run away as to remain, and I approached with the utmost dread, somehow irrationally certain that this was my friend lying here, ready for his spirit to begin its long journey, though I knew him to be elsewhere, back at his house.

It was only a stranger, of course. Again I ran, weeping, then staggered, breathless, gasping, my throat hoarse. I didn't know where I was or what I was going to do. I was behaving like a complete fool. My mind was all a tangle.

And that was when I found myself in Korevanos, the Inn of Sorrows.

* * * *

When Kodos Vion's illness was upon him, a woman came to my door with the news. I followed her through the city, in the glare of the summer noon. Her dusty black robe flapped in the hot wind. Her veil streamed, so that she had to hold it in place with one hand.

All she had said to me was that Kodos Vion was dying.

I couldn't believe it. No, he was eternal, like one of those immense bronze figures in the Garden of Statues. They might turn green with age, he a silvery white. But that was all. They would go on forever.

His house I found to be filled with such black-clad women, many of them known to me, the casual lovers of that lusty old scoundrel who could have been my grandfather. Some he had shared with me. Some I had introduced to him. Some both of us had cast off. But they still loved him. I passed among them unnoticed.

I stood for a moment in the great banqueting hall, beneath the frescoed ceiling. I had been there many times, of course. It was here one night, at the height of one of his famously riotous gatherings, that Kodos Vion had directed the attention of his guests to me. Great lords and ladies were there, famous savants and poets, and even a priest or two. He commended me to them as a young man of great promise, the author of verses which would one day be ranked among the greatest of our age. I think he was laughing all the while as he said this, at them, at me, at our age. In the impossible darkness that has followed the death of the Goddess, when even signs and wonders and miracles don't make any sense anymore, what else is there for us to do? *That* he had explained to me before, laughing as he did. It was his way.

"Knock their brains in, boy," he whispered to me. "Tear out their hearts. If they have either."

So, confused, a little afraid, stuttering somewhat—it was not my best delivery—I read my verses to all these distinguished people. They applauded only politely, but after that I was *someone*. I moved in the best circles of society. I never wanted for money or women or admission to the houses of the great, for I was a friend of Kodos Vion.

"Hurry," one of the black-clad ladies said, dragging me by the arm. "Don't just stand there. He will see you now. There isn't much time."

Very much in dread, I went in to see Kodos Vion. He seemed insubstantial now somehow, a pale, frail husk sunken deep into his pillows. His white hair, thinner than before, clung to his forehead as if plastered with sweat, but his face was dry, and when I held his hand, it was cold.

His breath wheezed. He lay still, staring at the ceiling of his chamber. Even after I had been there a while, he did not turn to look at me. When he tried to speak, he only mouthed the words. No sound came.

Then suddenly he reached up and grabbed me by the collar. His grip was astonishingly strong. He yanked me down until my ear was by his mouth, and *then* he spoke very clearly indeed.

Wailing, I ran from that place, and found myself, by confused and circuitous ways, on the threshold of Korevanos, the Inn of Sorrows.

* * * *

I came to myself, as if awakening from a dream—no, as if awaking *into* a dream—at the foot of a flight of wooden stairs. Up above, in darkness, wind howled. Wood creaked.

The innkeeper merely nudged me away and led me to a table, and I sat by myself in a large, darkened room, and I knew at once that I was in Korevanos.

A woman sat on a nearby bench, screaming endlessly, rocking back and forth. Her voice wasn't loud though, more like a fierce wind blowing over the mouth of a chimney pipe. I learned to ignore her, even as one who lives beside a waterfall learns to ignore its thunder.

There were two soldiers. One of them, in a desperate attempt to drive off melancholy, danced on a tabletop, pretending to be more drunk than he really was, while singing a filthy song. With all his might he leapt into the air, as if by flapping his arms he could fly away, out of this world, out of his own despair. But he only caught hold of a chandelier, a horizontal wagon wheel with candles set around the rim. One of the spokes broke in his hand, and he tumbled down against a shelf in a crashing avalanche of candles and pots and broken crockery. He lay in a heap, sobbing. No one went to his aid.

Gradually the room filled. I didn't see anyone come in. I heard no footsteps. I merely became aware of more presences, as if they had materialized out of smoke and shadows into my dream.

But this wasn't a dream, of course. I was really there.

Meanwhile, the innkeeper brought me some wine. I drank, and my senses were heightened until I could hear the blood coursing through my veins like a rushing river. I thought how the blood in Kodos Vion's veins must now be slowing down, becoming a muddy trickle.

I felt the very air on my face, every thread of clothing against my skin, rough and almost sharp. Could Kodos Vion feel as much now? No, he could not.

My purse was a stone weight in my lap. I saw every detail of the room around me, heard the slightest sound, every rustling or exhalation, smelled the sweat and wine and dust.

I looked up from my wine cup. There was a young woman seated across from me, clad in the silks and bangles and beads of a courtesan of the Inner City. Was she someone I had known from the house of Kodos Vion?

She seemed bewildered. "Why am I here?" she asked me, as if I were the only convenient person to ask, I think, not as if she really expected a sensible answer.

"Only you know that," I said, and she covered her face and hurried away.

To my right was another woman, a bit older, draped in flowing blue from head to foot. She had not been there a moment before, but I had not been aware of her arrival or her sitting down next to me. I saw that her face was painted all over with gray ash. She wept softly, her tears streaking the ash.

So it was. I might perceive a flicker at the edge of my vision, then turn to one side or the other and discover that our company had increased. Now many people sat at tables or wandered listlessly about, people of many races and nations. Many, I was sure, had never actually set foot in Ai Hanlo or in the country around it at all, but still they were here, in Korevanos.

"I want to go home! Please, let me go home!" It was a young voice shouting. I looked down.

A boy huddled under my table, clinging to one of the legs. He was richly clad, no doubt the son of some lord or high priest. He looked totally lost, helpless. His eyes stared wide. There was madness in them.

I reached my hand down to him. He whimpered and drew away.

No one else paid any attention.

I looked up. Now there was a young girl sitting across from

me. She might have been a little older than the boy, fifteen or so, but I couldn't tell, largely because was entirely covered with blood, her hair matted, the remnants of her clothing likewise soaked. Her eyes were wide too, but in them I saw only weariness. She seemed but half alive.

I looked under the table again. The boy was gone. There was a puddle of blood by the girl's bare feet.

She stank horribly, but did not actually seem to be injured. She just sat there, staring into the air, seemingly unaware of me or of anyone around her. She rubbed her hands together slowly. After a while the innkeeper brought her wine and she drank. Then he gave her a bowl of water and towel and, very, very slowly, she seemed to recognize what these things were for, and she began to clean herself a little.

I somehow knew that she had a story to tell, that I would hear it eventually, and it would be immensely important to me. But she was not ready to speak.

So I spoke to her.

"I'll tell you why *I* am here," I said. I was only speaking to her then. If anyone overheard me, let them, but I was speaking to her. The wine must have affected my senses more than I'd thought, because soon all the room seemed to fade away into a red mist, and it was only the two of us there, closed off, as if we floated inside a bubble of blood. And I told her, haltingly at first, then in a torrent of confession, something of the actual truth, how I was actually a fraud. I had wanted to be a real poet as a boy, but I became only a liar as my youth slipped away. I became a friend of Kodos Vion. Friend, or was I his parasite? I told myself I loved him. He told me he loved me. Who was the liar then? Nevertheless I was able to flatter money out of rich men while working my way up in the world through the bedchambers of their wives, while Kodos Vion and I got drunk together and laughed at my exploits. Or was he just laughing at me, behind the façade of friendship? I went on. I did what I knew how to do, out of habit, the way a fish swims and eats other fish, because that is what fishes mindlessly do. But I was empty inside, the poet in me long dead, for all I could still contrive a pretty rhyme when there was coin or pleasure to be had in exchange. Otherwise I merely groped at my art, trying to recover what I had lost, trying to express what I could no longer say.

I don't know if the girl heard or understood any of this.

"Can you imagine how it was?" the drunken soldier shouted, the same one who had fallen off the table. He'd cut himself in his fall, crashing into the crockery. Now blood streamed down the side of his face, which floated disembodied in the red mist, where he had somehow managed to intrude into the bubble. *"Can you imagine?* I was only a little boy then. I woke up, delirious with fever in the dawn to the sound of screaming crows… everyone was dead…the plague, everyone I had ever known in the world…and all my life, ever since, I have heard those crows screaming inside my head. It never stops. It never will stop. *Can you imagine?"*

"Yes," I said. "I can imagine it very well."

He screamed, a sound of infinite rage and sorrow, but then when it had passed, like a storm, he said quietly. "I just wanted to explain. I had to explain. Excuse me." And he was gone.

The mist thinned.

A tall man sat between two soldiers, blind, his eye sockets empty. He was a Zabortashi magus by his dress, yet as he moved, his long sleeves fell back, and I saw that he did not wear the elbow-length gloves that the magi favor. He had no hands at all. Light flickered from his wrists. He leaned over to suck wine from a shallow dish. There was a light inside his mouth, like the candle inside a lantern.

"Azrethemne," the bloody girl said. "I remember that my name is Azrethemne."

The blind magus raised his head turned from side to side, as if trying to locate her. Then he went back to his wine.

Somehow it seemed to matter if I could make the girl understand. I told her how I had loved Kodos Vion. I was no mere parasite. I loved him, truly, as we drank and whored together.

He called me his little son, though I was neither little nor his son. He led me on, yes, but there was something different, something miraculous, by which he, just as truly, loved every woman he bedded and every one of the innumerable bastards he fathered. And I loved him. I was part of his huge family. We all were. That was my place in the world.

Without him, I went back to being nothing. A shadow, cast by Kodos Vion, and, when he was gone, no longer cast. I had only come to realize this recently, as he was dying. As he spoke to me for the last time.

"What did he say?" the girl Azrethemne asked.

I paused, startled, and then answered her carefully.

"He was afraid. Imagine that. *Him* afraid. But he was. His fear had given him that final burst of strength. What he said was, *'It is Black Veiada, the Night Hag. She has been at my side for a long time. You must help me. No one else can. No one else would believe. I couldn't get away from her, and now she has stolen my heart!'* And I put my ear to his chest and knew that it was so. Kodos Vion still breathed, yet he had no heartbeat."

* * * *

"That's why I am here!" I shouted to the whole room. "I am not like the rest of you! I did not stumble in here in utter despair. No, mine is a mission, something heroic, a quest. I am here to save my friend. I am looking for Kodos Vion's heart, which has been stolen, but I don't know…" My voice broke. I sobbed. I failed to convince even myself, especially myself, of my singular heroism. I felt helpless as the boy under the table. Only after a while could I speak at all, and it was like a child's confession. "I don't know what to do. How can I help him? I have no idea? Who is this Night Hag anyway? How do I confront her? My friend is *dying* and, I confess, I haven't a clue."

"You don't know that he's dead yet," said Azrethemne softly.

I reached across the table and took her hand, holding tight. I had begun by pitying her. Now I wanted her to comfort *me*.

Suddenly I was ashamed. I let go.

"But he *will* die," I said. I rested my head in my folded arms and cried like a child.

Then the innkeeper was standing over me, his hand on my shoulder. "Perhaps you will find what you seek. But now, get ready. It is time to go."

I looked up. "Who are you? *What* are you? Where are we going?"

He paused, his long, pale face expressionless. "As for who I am, I merely came here, as you did. I have no memory of anything else. Therefore I am myself, nothing more. As for what I am, I can only speculate. I remember a philosopher who was here once. He said that the Goddess created me and this place both out of her own sorrow as she died, forgetting the purpose even as she completed the act. Or else she never completed it. Maybe I was meant to be something more. But I am not."

He reached up and removed his face like a mask, revealing only formless, waxen stuff behind it.

The mask continued speaking. "As for where you are going, I do not know that either. I have seen thousands come here and thousands depart. They all go…somewhere. This is only a brief meeting place, a stopping point at the beginning of such journeys. Perhaps some of those travelers come to understand after a while. But I never go with them. They never come back and tell me. Now it is time for you to go."

Azrethemne reached over and took my hand in hers, even as the inn began to dissolve around us. Sounds from above grew louder, the wind, the creaking, the moaning of desolation and darkness. Subtly, all changed into the rhythmic surge of surf. The air was clear and very cold. The last of the walls faded away as mist, and a rolling, sandy landscape stretched away in every direction. Absurdly, the wagon-wheel chandelier hung in the air.

Then benches we sat on were gone. Azrethemne and I rose, still holding my hand in her blood-sticky fingers. Now the wheel overhead vanished too, though a couple candles had fallen from it onto the ground.

People began to wander away over the sand. One or two upright beams of the inn remained, and an occasional table or bench, half buried, vanishing even as I watched, like shapes of sand dissolved by the wind. The blind magus drifted like a cloud over an ashy-gray dune and disappeared, beneath a nearly black sky.

A courtesan stumbled beside us for a moment, saying, her hands covering her face. Then she wasn't there. My attention wandered, lost focus. The woman who had been screaming fell silent, so that the only sound was that of the surf, nearby, on a shoreline I still could not find.

There was another sound too. Azrethemne's teeth chattered with the cold.

I looked around for the innkeeper. I wanted to call out to him. But he wasn't there. I could only step forward, carefully leading the barefoot girl around the heap of broken pottery the drunken soldier had crashed into.

For a while there was still one round table in the sand, surrounded by chairs, a little group that somehow refused to fade away. But then, by some means the eye could not follow, they did.

A bent old man leaning on a stick made his way slowly along the crest of a dune, singing a dirge of some kind. But only for a moment. Then he was gone too, and there was, again, only the sound of the invisible sea.

I looked up at the sky, and saw dark clouds passing before one another. But the air felt dry. I doubted it ever rained in this place. I doubted, too, that time passed normally here or that the sun rose and set, or that there even *was* a sun in the sky behind those clouds. The sky was just suffused with faint light somehow, leaving an endless twilight.

I was about to remark on this to Azrethemne, when she whispered to me, very intently, "No. Be brave. You said you were a hero. Don't lie about it. That's all you have left."

Then it was she who was leading me. I followed her to the

top of the dune. From there we could behold the ocean, dark, almost oily, its waves smearing sluggishly onto the shoreline, never breaking into white foam. Cold wind blew.

Hundreds of people had gathered on the beach, far more than I'd seen at the inn, the mass of them spread out, scattered across the sand like the stumps of tree trunks in a drowned forest. Some stood out in the water, the waves washing between their legs or over their shoulders. I strained to see in the poor light, and could not be sure, but it seemed that thousands more stood even further out, motionless as statues, their heads black specks against the dark sky and the even darker water. The only motion was of a few newcomers, who arrived at the edge of the beach, found their places, and then stood still.

I made no attempt to understand. I was beyond understanding now.

"Look," Azrethemne said, pointing.

It took a while for my eyes to adjust, to make any sense out of what I saw. I wanted to cry out, but did not. I felt only an abstract, resigned terror.

A huge, black barge rose and fell on the slumberous waves, its sails filled with wind, a floating mountain, more vast than any vessel ever build by man, a craft for giants, surely. But now the giants had died and the vessel drifted, torn rigging and sails streaming in the wind. A groaning came from the depths of it, like a hurricane blowing over the mouth of a cave.

And yet the barge drew no nearer. It hung like a painted backdrop on the sky.

Azrethemne squeezed my hand. She trembled.

Without realizing what I was doing, I began to walk down toward the beach.

She pulled me back. "No."

Numbly, like one half-awakened from a dream, I appreciated that she had just saved me from some terrible danger, for all I didn't know what that danger was. I could only react. I could only let her lead me. I didn't know if she understood better than I, was more than merely afraid, but she had a certain strength, a direction. I could only follow.

We turned our backs on the ocean and the black barge. I looked back over my shoulder once and caught sight of what might have been either a man or a woman so tall, so immense, that the pale face rose in the sky higher than the sun at noon. Gorgeous robes flapped on the wind and covered the darkness, filling the sky. But the eyes were closed and the figure's arms were folded upon its breast like those of a corpse laid out; and this apparition stood in the sea or beyond the sea, dwarfing even the great barge; and I could not have turned away from that face, ever, if Azrethemne had not yanked me once more and said, "Come *on!*" most urgently.

We made our way back the way we had come, over the crest of the dune, out of sight of the sea, wandering for a long time between further dunes, then between hills, keeping our gaze firmly upon the ground, watching our feet, always avoiding the ridge lines, lest we glance back over the distance, and behold, and be affixed by what we saw and drawn back down to water's edge, into the oily sea.

It seemed that the great apparition, dead though it was, had begun to speak now, whispering in our minds, in my mind at least, but somehow I found the strength, the concentration to tell myself over and over again, no, no, it was only the wind blowing sand, only the blown sand rustling among the harsh grasses.

When at last neither the girl nor I could go any further, we fell down in our exhaustion into the featureless sand. Here the landscape was indeed without any variation at all, no so much as a mound or a stone, and it seemed to go on forever like that.

I realized that I was terribly thirsty. I couldn't bring myself to believe, though, that I had come all this way merely to die of thirst.

Azrethemne trembled again, with the cold, and I drew her to my side, drawing my thin, outer robe around the both of us.

She began to tell me of her life then, what scattered bits she could recall. As it had been for me, her words came haltingly at first, then in a torrent. She had been gone from the world for a long time, but she remembered growing up on a boat that plied the river trade between Ai Hanlo and Zabortash. But that was so long ago, she said, that it seemed to be the life of someone else. Then she'd begun to have visions. She fell down in a frenzy and prophesied, and managed to slip out of the world. Someone had told her once that in the time of the death of the Goddess, when all is in disorder, when the remains of divinity drift across the world like ashes, having no substance, it is particularly easy to lose one's grip and end up…somewhere. She had wandered through dim, half-created places for a long time. For a while she was in the company of a young man, a boy actually, who was as often as not more helpless and afraid than she, a prophet and priest and fellow exile named Tamliade—she kept repeating his name—whom she had somehow rescued and come to love, only to lose him again in a confusion of fire and blood, an ocean of blood which filled the world until she sank and drowned in it, and found herself washed up onto the threshold of the Inn of Sorrows, as I had first beheld her.

This tale seemed…no more fantastic than any other, but there was one striking thing about it, something I couldn't quite grasp with my mind. It had to mean something that her story was *not over yet*. She believed that she was in a labyrinth, looking for the one corridor with light at the end of it, through which she might emerge back into the waking, living, concrete world.

Now I was a wanderer like her, but I lacked her courage, and I was ashamed to hope that she might rescue me as she had this Tamliade—yet I did hope it, though I could not put the notion into words. What could I say? How does one relate thirty years of nothing? I started to repeat the tale of how Black Veiada had stolen Kodos Vion's heart.

I lost the thread of the story somewhere, and could only weep.

Azrethemne in turn told me stories of heroes, how many of them were quite ordinary men at first, even inferior, mediocrities who had never sought out any adventure, who had fled from challenge or danger or honor, but who were nevertheless propelled on to become something greater.

I wanted to believe that. I desperately wanted it to be true. After a time, I felt a little less ridiculous for my efforts.

We slept, huddled in my robe.

* * * *

Black Veiada came to me in a dream. She walked soundlessly over the sand, making no footprints, and she stood over me, staring down with the gaze of some ancient stone colossus, yet at the same time as ethereal as a cloud. Her face was wrinkled, her eyes sunken and dark. Her hair and cloak streamed in the wind.

"Friend of Kodos Vion, arise," she said.

In my dream, I got up.

She offered me a goblet of wine. I drank. My will was not my own. I recognized the taste. It was the same as the wine at the Inn of Sorrows, sweet and bitter.

"Friend of Kodos Vion, come. I want you to understand."

I thought of Kodos Vion again—as if I had ever stopped thinking of him—how he had made me what I was, out of nothing, performing a miracle which now was ending.

I turned from Black Veiada and ran, staggering, kicking up sand, hoarse from gasping in the cold air. I topped a rise—which hadn't been there a minute before—and looked down, not on the sea, but on a common tavern standing incongruously in the middle of the wasteland. Light streamed from the windows. Even at a distance, I could hear the sounds of merriment.

As I drew near, I could make out some of the words of a song:

> *"Oh, I stink to high heaven,*
> *me bed's an old coat,*
> *but if ye don't like it,*
> *well bugger the goat!"*

I ran to the door and leaned against it, gasping, listening. I *knew* that voice.

I pounded hard as I could, looking back over my shoulder in terror for any sign of Black Veiada. The door opened. I tumbled into a room filled with people. Someone grabbed me by the arm, hauled me up, yanked me around, and I was face-to-face with Kodos Vion. His breath was thick with wine, his eyes wild.

"Wake up, boy!" He shook me hard. "Don't tell me you're worn out already! Up! Up!"

They were all laughing at me. Thousands of faces, like fireflies flickering in the dim light, laughing at me.

Kodos Vion began to dance, swinging me around like a rag doll, his voice like singing thunder:

> *"Bugger the goat!*
> *Bugger the goat!*
> *There's not too much choice,*
> *so go bugger the goat!"*

I wept. I didn't understand how I'd gotten to this place. It was impossible, but I so desperately wanted it to be real.

"Oh look at him! A few drinks and he's cryin' like a baby!"

A perfumed, naked woman put her arms around me, jewelry clinking.

"Ah, poor baby. He needs cheering up."

"He needs more than that," said Kodos Vion, waving her away. He led me across the room. The crowd parted for him like a sea.

We went out through a little door into a yard. I gaped in astonishment. The night sky was clear overhead, filled with brilliant stars. Over a fence I could see rooftops and towers. We were in Ai Hanlo.

Kodos Vion relieved himself against a post. Then he took me by the arm again, gently this time, and backed me against the fence. He was alive. He was *real*.

"You're a *disgrace*, boy, blubbering like that. I don't know why I put up with you."

"I'm not a boy. I'm thirty," was all I could say.

"Well you haven't learned much in all those years. That's why I brought you out here. Someone needs to explain the facts of life to you. Brace yourself. Here's the big secret: *There are no facts of life!*" He roared with laughter, bending over, slapping his thigh. "But wait! There's more. The philosophers tell us that because the Goddess is dead there is no meaning or order to anything. Well, who's to care about that. *Shit*.... Only appearances matter. If something seems to be real, accept it. Don't ask any questions. If you act like a man instead of a blubbering boy, then you are a man. If you act like a poet, you are one. Be a hero. Be anything. What goes on *inside* that soggy little head of yours hardly matters. Only what's outside matters, what you and other people can see. That's the key to happiness. It's the one thing you can be sure about."

I wanted to tell him that I didn't believe a word he was saying, that I didn't think he did either, because somewhere in the back of my mind I hadn't forgotten this was a dream, not real, that he wasn't real, I wasn't real, as if such concepts or distinctions made any sense under the present circumstances. But the words did not come.

Suddenly a look of utmost terror came over his face. He gasped, staggered away from me, clutching his chest. Then he screamed, *"She has stolen my heart!"*

The door swung open, slamming against the wall. Wind roared. The air was filled with swirling sand.

Black Veiada stood in the doorway, holding up his beating heart for me to see.

"I need this for *my beloved*," she said intensely, her words almost like a prayer. "He has waited too long. He shall wait only a little longer now."

With impossible agility, like some huge spider, she scurried up the outside of the tavern, onto the roof, and was gone.

"Help me," Kodos Vion gasped. "You said you would help me. Why have you done nothing?"

He lay in the sand at my feet. Now there was no tavern, no yard, fence, or starry sky above. Again we were in the midst of the featureless wasteland, in that unchanging half-darkness.

"*Why?* Why? Why?" His voice faded. The wind blew sand over him, burying him, as if he were sinking in quicksand. "Help me...." His face was covered up. He was gone.

"Help! Help!" I screamed, digging frantically. I shrieked, babbled like a madman, "Helpmehelpmehelpme!"

* * * *

I came to myself, still screaming, digging with my hands, hurling sand aside.

Azrethemne put her arm around me, to restrain me, to calm me.

And I stopped, and sat down, exhausted, staring at the hole I'd dug. There was no sign of Kodos Vion.

"I *saw* her," I said. "She came to me. It was Black Veiada."

"Yes, it was Black Veiada," came a voice. "That's how you know—"

The two of us jumped to either side, then stared into the hole. What had been a rounded lump of sand opened its eyes. The features became clearer: a man, buried to his neck, his face drawn, as if in great pain. His skin was almost blue.

Without a word, Azrethemne and I began to dig. We uncovered the buried man's bare shoulders, then his arms, then his chest, blue-white as the rest of him, cold to the touch. He gasped for breath, sucking in great gulps of air.

Then Azrethemne let out a cry of amazement and disgust and turned away. I kept on digging for several minutes more, unable to stop.

The man had no genitals, or legs either. His upper body just went on and on, his endless ribcage like that of some huge serpent, his flesh the same continuous blue-white. He lay on the sand, limp, wheezing. I had uncovered at least fifteen feet of him. The rest of him seemed to pass horizontally into the sand, buried no more than a foot down.

"It's no good," he said. "I saw Black Veiada too. I'm part of the island now."

"What island?"

"Haven't you figured that out? In every direction, the black sea. You're surrounded. There is no way off, but that black ship. Please, please. It's cold. Cover me up."

Azrethemne couldn't bring herself to actually touch him, but from a distance she heaved handfuls of sand, and we covered him back up to the neck, then crouched beside him.

"*What* are you?" I said.

"As you see. As I said. Part of the island. Once I was a man and had a name. But I've lost all that. You do, you lose everything, when Black Veiada comes for you at last. Think of it as a big melting pot. She melts us down like old, broken bronze statues, bent knives, rusty lanterns. She wants the raw material. When she comes for you, when you see her, you will change very quickly."

"*No.*" I said.

"No," said Azrethemne, and for the first time she seemed truly afraid.

"You can't help it. Perhaps you will become like me. Perhaps no more than this." He heaved a hand up through the sand, then let sand trickle through his fingers. "Maybe I will be like this too, in due time."

"But *where* are we?"

"In some halfway-formed world. One of those dark regions you can fall into when there is no god or goddess to keep everything in place. Think of it as some stray bubble in the foam of creation, but a creation that's running out, like water spilled on a leaky floor. In sorrow you come here, or in madness, or maybe led by some magic so powerful and strange that once you use it you can't find your way back. I don't remember how I got here. But you know all this. You're here. That's enough. The *how* does not matter. It merely *is*."

He closed his eyes. He sighed, as if greatly wearied from the act of speaking, and from raising his hand. His hand and forearm lay on the surface of the sand. I buried them.

"Please," I said softly. "Tell us more. Who is Black Veiada? What can we do to overcome her? We have to. We have to know. It's very important—"

His eyes fluttered open once more. I could barely hear his voice. "Perhaps she will show herself once more. Then you will know…everything…too late. As for what you can do…nothing. You're here, aren't you? She has you now."

"It won't be like that," said Azrethemne firmly. "No. We'll get away. We'll just keep on going—"

The eyes closed, but I could still make out the voice.

"You're very strong to have come this far. No one has done as much in centuries. But still, no matter how far you go, you always return to the point where you started. There is no other way."

"But why?" I demanded. "Why?"

"The island, you see, only has one side."

We left him. Hand in hand, walking slowly, dreading whatever we should find, we walked and walked for an indeterminate amount of time, until the landscape began to rise like a series of little, motionless waves. We climbed a dune.

I heard the sound of waves.

We looked down on the shoreline, where thousands of people stood on the sand or out into the oily water, and beyond them, the great, black deathly barge rose and fell, as huge as the black, featureless sky.

It was in that moment that something within me changed, that I understood I had stopped running away. From then on, I would confront Black Veiada. I would rescue Kodos Vion if I could. It wasn't merely because there was no place left to run, but because I felt, keenly, the desire to help my friend, and to help Azrethemne too, who was brave, who was good, who was strong, who did not belong imprisoned forever in some twilight land of lost souls.

I didn't care what happened to myself.

We sat down, overlooking the beach, and waited.

"Come witch," I said aloud. "Black Veiada, come. I am ready

for you."

* * * *

She came once more, in a dream. I was not aware of going to sleep. I think Black Veiada merely reached out and touched me, drawing me into the dream.

She stood before me upon the dune, oblivious to Azrethemne as if she could not see her, or did not deign to. She offered me the goblet once more.

"Drink, friend of Kodos Vion, and all will be clear. You need to understand. You are the one among thousands who must understand, and in the end act of your own free will. Now are the stars fallen into place like tumblers in a lock. The time is at hand. Drink."

I drank yet again that strange bitter and sweet wine. My senses were heightened. I heard the blood rushing within my veins. I felt every particle of dust in the air as it fell against my face.

I wanted to scream at her, to call her murderess and thief, but somehow her voice soothed me. I did not run away this time.

"It is the wine of vision," she said. "Now, behold."

And I saw Black Veiada as she had been when she had her name because of the color of her long, beautiful black hair. Jewels sparkled in it, like stars in the midnight sky.

She stood before me, there, on the top of the dune, overlooking the beach, and the darkness of the sky cleared behind her, like a curtain drawn aside, revealing unfamiliar stars, in constellations new and strange.

Then we were no longer on the beach at all. I saw her in many places, at many times. She was a slender girl, a princess of a city carven all of polished black stone, where the winds of the world were captured and tamed in the high, black towers, and lay at her feet like sleepy leopards. Even then she was a witch, and I could not condemn her for it, for she had a great and burning desire to know the secrets of things, the mysteries of heaven and earth and of the countless half-worlds, the things known by the Goddess and those hidden even from the Goddess.

I saw Black Veiada as queen, reigning in glory over that city and country compared to which even Ai Hanlo, or any other place I had ever known was but a squalid collection of hovels.

Yet it was because of this glory that the Goddess came to envy Black Veiada. Because Black Veiada was the most powerful witch who ever lived, who could reach out and touch the Moon and change its phases, or halt its passage across the sky, the Goddess feared her.

Further, Black Veiada loved a man, a mighty warrior and king without peer in that age. The two were to be wed, and in their union all the world would be drawn together, so that men would worship king and queen alone and have little use for any other. For this, the Goddess hated her.

The Goddess herself had been mortal once. In Black Veiada's youth it had been little more than a century since a storm of divinity had whirled around some girl and raised her up. Such things happen by nature. When a god or goddess dies, divinity dissipates, like a dying wind, and there is a period of darkness and confusion, but in time, as inevitable as a new sunrise, the holy winds regain their strength, and gather, and rage, howling, and another god or goddess is created, and the interregnum ends.

When her epoch was still new, when the Goddess was still partially human, she had human emotions, magnified by her condition, but human nonetheless, and she was jealous and afraid and truly terrible in her anger.

I saw, in my vision, the night of Black Veiada's wedding. Two royal trains gathered on a terrace beneath a huge silver dome held aloft by spiderweb-thin arches of some impossible glass. All the city was ablaze with lights. The full Moon rose over the sea. The winds, which were the queen's servants, sang softly amid the dark towers.

White flowers rose out of the pavement, like fountains bursting with foam in slow motion, rising up, taller than trees, opening out as the moonlight touched them. Maidens in sweeping dresses made a solemn procession through the forest of blossoms, while the king's warriors stood at attention, their armor gleaming in the pale light, their swords raised on high. Children in white held candles and rang little bells. Overhead, great ships of metal and glass drifted in the sky, silent as clouds, trailing luminous streamers.

The lords of the land stood silent. Priests gathered. At the very center of the terrace, under the dome, the king and queen waited, each holding a crown to be placed on the head of the other.

There came a moment of hushed expectation. Even the winds were still.

Then the sky split apart with a blinding light, and there was a great shout; and the earth shook and the sea rose up in wild waves.

The Goddess herself rose up beyond the horizon, towering over the world, clad in the wildest aspect of the dark side of her nature, her face filled with madness, with rage and hate. None could look on her. The crowds fell down and covered their faces, or else died as they stood. The Moon was shadowed, covered over by her hair. Lightning flickered as she moved. Huge serpents writhed around her waist and arms, spitting fire.

The black towers toppled, and the fires roared, blasting the roofs off the whole city. And the people cried out for their queen to save them.

She stood on the terrace, as the silver dome disintegrated around her.

There came another flash of light, and another, and another. In my vision, now, only I could see all that happened. I saw the bridegroom king raised up in a whirlwind and strangely transformed, his eyes glowing brilliantly, burning with the fire of the Goddess. One of the courtiers, shielding his eyes with one hand, reached up with the other and caught the flailing king by the ankle, but, as soon as he touched him, burst into flame and blew away in a puff of ash.

The king's face changed for a moment into a glittering crystal mask, then back into flesh, but terrible to look upon. He was standing in the air now, atop the whirlwind, high above the city, growing taller, less distinct, like one turning into a cloud. He stood beside the Goddess and she embraced him. He looked once more upon Veiada with longing, but then his newly divine nature overwhelmed him, and he did not look again.

I saw how it ended, the sky filled with smoke, the city tottering, sliding beneath the ocean or falling into newly opened chasms in the earth which devoured it like hungry mouths. The silver dome came down like a cloud of shards. The glass arches fell like tinsel, raining over corpses and charred flowers and the few, struggling survivors, who did not survive much longer. Only Black Veiada escaped in the end, by her magic, closing space around herself like a cloak.

I saw her later as a wretched wanderer. I felt her endless days as if they had been my own. I dwelt with her in caves and forests, in every desolate place, always hiding from the sky and the sight of the Goddess. Only her pain kept her going. In the darkness, then, hidden away, she learned more secrets, gained more powers. She extended the span of her life. Her hatred would not let her die. All this while mankind knew nothing of her, and worshipped two divinities, the great and terrible Goddess foremost, and, to a lesser degree, her Consort. Statues to the pair were raised in every land, showing the two embracing, serpents entwined about them both.

It was the custom of Veiada the Exile, when she stole upon these statues on cloudy nights, to smash them to pieces.

I saw the years and centuries pass. The wine of vision revealed to me how the Consort came back to Black Veiada.

On a certain night the witch sat, deep in a cavern where the stone fangs of the mountain dripped. Moonlight shone dimly through a tunnel, touching a little pool. The witch sat away from that light, in total darkness.

Then the light went out. She looked up, at first thinking only that a cloud had covered the Moon.

Pebbles rattled in the tunnel. Someone called her name.

"I am here," she said.

The voice called again, and again she said, "I am here."

Moonlight reappeared. Now startled, frightened, she ran to the tunnel mouth. There was no one there. She scrambled on all fours up the steep way, scattering stones, until she came to a ledge high above a valley. There she sat, looking at the Moon.

A cloud covered it, and more clouds filled the sky, swirling around the mountain. Lightning flickered.

On the ledge, in the darkness, as thunder rumbled low and far away, the two lovers met and embraced.

It was the first of many such meetings. Always, she waited there and always he arrived thus, in a cloud, invisible in the darkness. It seemed to her after a while that his touch became more gentle, his voice more what she had once heard. He was returning to his humanity, slowly becoming as he had been so long before.

There is more than I can tell. In the end, though, the Goddess found them out. In my vision I felt the anger of a goddess, which is more terrible than may be described. She descended out of the night, seized the king by the throat, and raised him into the sky. He did not grow huge this time. He was a small, wriggling thing, like an insect plucked from the ground by a great bird.

I saw it all, even as Veiada fell to the ground and covered her eyes. *I* saw it, in my vision.

The Goddess tore him to pieces, flung his limbs to the ends of the Earth and beyond, into the dark, half-worlds and the spaces between. When she had done this, she stood over Veiada with the king's heart in her hand. She made a fist over it, and the fist burned like the sun, bringing a sudden and unexpected dawn to the world.

Then she let the ashes of the heart trickle through her fingers, scattering them on the wind like Death dispensing a pestilence.

At the very end I saw Veiada, wrinkled, broken, clad in mourning, adrift on a black barge between the worlds, recovering the pieces of her lover one by one when by chance she found them.

"Now I think you understand," she said, taking back the empty goblet.

And the vision left me.

* * * *

I awoke into howling wind and stinging sand. Azrethemne was shaking me and shouting, though I couldn't make out anything she said. Sand caked my face like a mask, plastered there by my tears. I tried to tell her what I had seen, but it came out all garbled, drowned out by the wind.

When I could see again, I made out the familiar hillside, the beach, and the sea. Through a wavering curtain of sand I could make out a few stars in the sky, and the black barge bearing down on the island, so huge that it blocked out those scant stars even as I watched.

Everything was changing before me. The sea roared. Waves broke, and, for once, foamed. The air rapidly cleared, and I saw clearly, every detail of the barge visible, every rotting board, torn sail, flapping tatter of rigging. The thing rushed upon us inexorably, more vast than Ai Hanlo Mountain, obliterating the beach and the thousands of lost, damned folk standing there.

I cringed and screamed and tried to crawl away behind the dune we sat on, but Azrethemne held on to me.

The barge *broke* over us, like a wave, no, like an avalanche of ashy debris, enormous fragments like crumbled paper floating in the air, disintegrating further, choking us with dust. There was a strong smell of decay, of graves newly opened.

Gradually the dust rose into the sky, hiding the stars entirely, until we seemed to be sitting beneath a huge, gray bowl, but in time this too faded away, and the stars appeared again.

We found ourselves sitting, not on sand, but on cold, dry pavement, surrounded by walls of black stone. Houses rose many storeys on either side, their windows gaping dark. The wind over the rooftops made a sound that was almost a voice, almost singing. Shutters flapped.

Then I heard a footstep.

At the end of our little alleyway, Black Veiada stood waiting. She was still old, her hair a stringy gray, but she was dressed like a queen.

"Now come," she said, " and help me at last."

"Yes," I said. "I will."

She held out her hand. I got up and walked over to her and took it. She began to lead me away.

"*No!*" Azrethemne screamed. "Don't! Think of yourself. You were going to be heroic, remember? Come back. Don't give up like this. *Think of Kodos Vion!*"

Indeed, I thought of Kodos Vion, and for one last time I thought of my brave Azrethemne. There was no time to explain that I had forgotten nothing, that for the first time ever in my existence I *was* being heroic, or at least trying to. I merely turned back to her and said, "You are not a part of this. Escape if you can. One extra soul more or less won't be noticed."

"*Come back!*"

Her voice faded away quickly. Then she was gone altogether.

* * * *

The rest is a jumble, a swirl of sight and sound:

Veiada led me into a broad avenue. Above us, the city rose into the night sky, tier upon tier, gleaming in the starlight. The wind sang in the towers. The streets and houses filled with voices as we passed, as if thousands of inhabitants long dead now returned to life as their queen once more walked among them. There was a flicker of motion in a doorway. From a window, a name was called. Footsteps sounded on a balcony.

For a while, we might have been flying as we rose from level to level, as we followed the great stairway that engirdled the city like a serpent.

I saw faces, then, thousands of half-visible, misty figures drifting alongside us, bearing torches and lanterns so faint and so dimly flickering that I could barely tell they were there.

The winds sang. The people sang. Their voices were as one.

Faces appeared in the stones too: a woman seemingly carven into the corner of a building, coming awake suddenly, eyes snapping open, but blank, the wind howling out of her gaping mouth. Pillars became writhing masses of black marble, with hundreds of faces and limbs drifting within them, turning, heads and shoulders sometimes protruding, as if struggling to break free. From these, too, wind and howling voices came.

In a courtyard, where the pavement was somehow transparent as glass, I saw, moving beneath the ground, the blue-faced snake-man I had helped dig up and rebury on the beach. He was mouthing something. I couldn't make it out.

Onward Veiada led me. As we neared the highest level of the city, suddenly every window was ablaze with light, as if a million stars had gathered there.

We moved like flecks of foam in the tide of the great multitude, all of one purpose, to one destination. I could see the people clearly now. Their torches blazed. They shouted and sang with great joy, but I did not feel their joy. It was as if I were viewing some ghostly re-enactment of a former time.

"Where are they going?" I asked.

"To the wedding of their queen," Veiada said to me.

* * * *

I didn't know what to expect in the end, but in the end I felt only a certain inevitability.

We reached the uppermost part of the city. Here, the silver dome still lay in ruins, as it had for so many centuries. Brittle skeletons of glass pillars gleamed in the torchlight, as the place filled with people, as they crowded against walls, swarmed onto ledges, leaned out windows.

But the place was also strewn with corpses, burned and shriveled husks, and with heaps of bone. As I walked among the charred stalks of the gigantic flowers, I realized, to my growing dread—for all the people sang with oblivious joy—that there were fresh corpses here too; and I was brought up suddenly as I came upon one I recognized. It was the boy from the Inn of Sorrows. His face was very pale. His throat had been slit, and gaped like a second, dark mouth.

The winds sang. The people sang. Black Veiada led me.

In the middle of the terrace, in the act center of the circular ruin of the dome, a large hole had been gouged into the pavement. A hole like a grave, filled with ash, and carefully embedded in that ash was a coffin of polished wood, in which a giant lay, a huge man clad all in gold like a king, with a crown on his head and his hands crossed upon his breast. His face was perfect white, like marble.

As I watched, Black Veiada reached down and parted his hands, placing them one after the other at his sides. She opened his robe, exposing a cavity filled with soft light but nothing else.

The giant had no heart. His lover had not been able to recover *all* of the pieces of him.

Then Black Veiada, Queen Veiada, stood over the coffin of her beloved, flanked on every side by her ghostly priests and ministers, clad in a gorgeous robe of scarlet inset with black gems, and wearing a crown of bone-white spikes. She held a shallow dish in both of her hands, in which, glowing, beating even yet and very much alive, was the heart of my friend Kodos Vion.

The wind sang. The voice of the people rose in crescendo. Phantom children like wisps of smoke drifted by, holding candles. White-draped maidens like puffs of mist off a lake at dawn made solemn procession through the ruined flowers, gathering around us.

Veiada spoke a word of power, and the giant stirred and opened his eyes. But there was no intelligence in them yet.

A goblet was pressed into my hands and a priest said, "Drink this, so you may understand at last."

I drank, and tasted the wine of vision one last time. Countless voices, sensations rushed at me. I could hear so many voices, share so many minds, look out through so many eyes all at once. I heard, I felt every one of those countless songs. I felt, too, the souls of all those people awakening into something that was almost life, and I knew, too, for an instant, the infinite despair of all those "lost ones" who had lost their hold on life and fallen out of the world into this other place, the ones who had been "melted down" as the snake-man had phrased it. But even this was overwhelmed by the anticipation, the joy of Queen Veiada, as the sand on the shore is overwhelmed by a raging tide.

I felt the stars moving into place, one by one, like tumblers in a lock.

And, very briefly, very faintly, I was aware of Azrethemne's presence nearby. I felt her terror and her despair at the sight of me standing passively before that coffin, as the Queen held Kodos Vion's heart and I made no move to take it. It was Azrethemne's own determination, intense to the point of madness, that I *must not* surrender to Black Veiada, however she had been wronged in the past. I seemed to hear her actual voice saying, *Remember Kodos Vion. Do not abandon him.*

All these things came together, and I understood.

I reached out and caught Veiada by the wrist. She held on to the disk with a frantic grip. I could sense her astonishment, even fear. The singing stopped. The ghostly children stood still. The wind was hushed.

"Stop," I said. "Great Queen, *take my heart instead.*"

My voice was like thunder in the sudden silence. The city trembled.

Black Veiada stepped back, holding on to the disk more tightly, encircling it with one arm.

"Please," I said. "Spare the life of Kodos Vion. Take my heart instead. I am not worthy. I am nothing. So there will be no loss. I *understand* what you are doing and why. I have tasted the wine of vision and seen all. I even understand why you took Kodos Vion's heart rather than mine in the first place, because he is greater than I am, more vital. But if I gave up my own willingly, without fear, wouldn't that make up the difference? He was afraid. I will not be."

She smiled coldly. I could not bear her gaze. I lowered my head and looked into the giant's wide, blind eyes. His mouth had fallen open, gaping.

Black Veiada said, "What good is your heart, when the blood that flows through it is cold as spring water? You are right. Kodos Vion was more vital than you could ever be. I needed a great heart. Yours cannot be substituted."

"Then why am I here? Why, at the very last, am I here at all?"

"To make a contribution. That much should be clear to you."

She spoke another word of power, and the air seemed charged, about to burst into flame. I knew that the moment had come, the single perfect instant in which all her plans could be brought to fruition. The stars were right. There was no Goddess alive to interfere.

There was only me.

Her eyes met mine, and all the strength went out of my limbs. I fell to my hands and knees, into the ashes, clinging weakly to the side of the coffin. The stars, the looming towers, the lights, the faces of the spectators all began to spin, to whirl faster and faster around me. Once more the wind found its voice, howling and triumphant, filled with raucous, signing voices.

And everything was clear: I was there to die. That was my role. I had come of my own will, after a fashion. I had offered myself up in sacrifice. Somehow I was the final, necessary ingredient to Black Veiada's design.

A priest handed me a dagger.

The crowd gave a great shout.

The Queen took the heart in her hands and lowered it into the coffin as I knelt with the dagger point pressed just below my breast bone, aimed upward.

And suddenly, like a man standing on the edge of a cliff about to jump, I realized that I didn't want to die after all. It was as plain as that. I wanted to get up and say, "No, if I can't save Kodos Vion, I don't want any part of this."

But my will was taken from me. There came an intensely

vivid vision of the Queen taking this giant by the hand and walking with him into the sky, reaching out as a new goddess with her consort to touch the Sun and Moon and move the stars in their courses. It was as if I were a part of them both, sharing their consciousness, doing these things myself as I stood astride the world, so far removed from my former existence that to think of my time as a hack poet in Ai Hanlo was to suffer a kind of death, but only a little death, an irritant from which I could freely and easily turn away.

The eye has not seen, nor the ear heard, nor can the mind conceive of what awaits.

For just an instant I wondered what had become of Azrethemne, but I felt no passion, just a faint sorrow.

* * * *

The jumble, the swirl of lights, the ending:

It was Azrethemne who saved me. She rushed through the crowd. I saw her face looming over me, her mouth forming words of some sort, but I couldn't hear anything over the roaring wind. Something struck my wrist and the dagger went flying. I knelt there, stunned.

And Black Veiada screamed. All the city cried out in terror and wrath. Lightning exploded out of the dark sky. The ground shook. Masonry fell. Tiles slid from rooftops.

I shielded my dazzled eyes, and when I could see again, the terrace was empty of any crowd, but Azrethemne stood there, a bone in her hand, raised high like a club. Down it came, smashing, smashing—

She struck the corpse-king as he lay there and his head shattered like a porcelain globe. Again Veiada screamed. It had all happened between one second and the next—

Azrethemne struck. The thing in the coffin raised its arms in a feeble effort to protect itself. A forearm exploded into shards. The thing wriggled up, tumbling over the side of the coffin, headless, somehow screaming through the open ruin of its neck, wallowing in ashes, groping about with one arm while the stump of the other waved like a useless flipper.

Black Veiada hurled herself at Azrethemne, howling, transformed, almost an animal now, a hag again, her mouth distended, snapping long fangs like those of a dog. The two of them thrashed among the bones and ashes and corpses. The two of them screamed together.

I don't know why I did what I did just then. I didn't have time to think about anything. I merely acted. I seized the headless king. His remaining arm came off in my grasp, and I beat him with it, pounding his body with it, then with my fists, until he was reduced to a shapeless, crumbling worm of not-quite-flesh, writhing in the ash pit. I found a bone, snapped it against the pavement, and used the sharpened end to cut into the chest of the monstrosity.

The cavity was empty. The heart was not there.

But I found it a moment later, glowing in the ashes at my feet like a dying ember. It wasn't beating. For an endless, awful, eternal instant I held it in my hands, helpless as I realized that I had no idea what I was supposed to do with it. I was no surgeon or magician, who could put it back inside Kodos Vion.

Then it burst like a bubble, and my hands were empty.

"It is too late now," said Black Veiada wearily.

I turned around. She had heaved Azrethemne aside. The girl lay amid the bones, panting. The Queen stood over her, weeping. For the first time she seemed utterly human, and I shared her sorrow.

"Help me," I said. "If there's a way. Take my heart and give it to Kodos Vion. It's too late for you, but—"

She changed even as I watched, like a paper figure curling in a fire, becoming a bent crone. Her eyes met mine, but her gaze communicated nothing. To this day I don't know if she hated me or pitied me or understood me or merely no longer cared.

She folded the air about herself like a cloak and was gone.

* * * *

Azrethemne helped me to my feet. We stood on an empty, ruined terrace. The torso of the dead king was little more than a ribcage wrapped in tattered gold. The flesh fell away to join the ash around it.

"You are a true hero," she said. "Don't call yourself *nothing* ever again."

I could only weep. My mind was filled with confused, contradictory thoughts. I had won, but I had failed more profoundly than words can say. I had failed Kodos Vion. I had failed myself.

Below us, level upon level of the ruined city was devoured as the sea rose. The island was sinking.

Above, the stars began to go out.

Then cold, oily water washed over our feet.

* * * *

More tangled memories: I was falling, far, far down like a stone in an endless well, into darkness. There was a shock of cold. I gasped and my mouth filled with foul water. My lungs were bursting. I struggled against a current. My ears burned.

I broke the surface, shouting for Azrethemne. Even if I was to die now, there were still things I wanted to explain to her, excuses I wanted to make. I wanted to thank her too, more intensely than I had ever wanted anything. It seemed impossible that I should lose her just now.

Then I saw her, running toward me across the surface of the sea, her pale legs flashing. I called out to her once more, but she did not pause, instead running right past me, toward a bright light. She shouted as she neared it. I think her cries were of joy. When she reached it, the light winked out and she was gone.

I hoped she would remember me, at least.

I could only wait for death, rising and falling with the waves, gazing up at the last, failing stars. My body began to go numb.

Then I saw lights coming toward me over the water. It wasn't a ship, but a building. That was impossible. I had to be going mad, at last.

Light streamed from windows.

Perhaps mad, then, but not quite ready to die, I decided, I swam with all my failing strength toward the open door. Warm hands caught hold of me and hauled me inside.

I found myself in Korevanos, the Inn of Sorrows. The innkeeper had rescued me.

He sat me in a chair and shook me and slapped my cheeks. He served me warm wine, not the wine of vision this time, but just a beverage. The inn was empty, but for the two of us. In time he hauled me to my feet and led me to a stairway. Above, in the darkness, timbers creaked.

"Most extraordinary," he said, "for someone to *come back*. You must be special somehow. But you can't stay here. Go. There are many exits from Korevanos. Some of them will take you back into the world. Climb these stairs. Keep on going until you come to the light. No not pause. Beware. There are many perils."

He gave me a push and I stumbled up the stairs, weak and dizzy, but determined to go on. It was like climbing the swaying rigging of a ship. I made my way along dark corridors. Indeed, there were many perils, many temptations. Voices from the darkness threatened or beseeched. Faces floated in doorways, calling out to me. Rain, snow, and hot cinders blasted me. Once there seemed to be no floor beneath me, and I was walking on the night sky, kicking up a foam of stars.

At last I saw a light ahead of me, and I ran toward it. A crocodile with the shoulders and face of a woman lay in my path.

"Don't go," the creature said. "It is death. Stay here with me."

I jumped over it as its face distended, flowed, and the snapping jaws just missed me.

Then, stumbling, blinded by sunlight, I collided with someone who shoved me backwards. A low stone wall caught me behind the knees, and I landed in warm water with a splash. For a second I struggled. My hands hit bottom. I was sitting on solid stone. I blinked, and looked, and saw that I was in a fountain, in the middle of a square. Above me, over the rooftops, the golden dome of the Guardian's palace gleamed in the afternoon sun. I was home, in Ai Hanlo.

I laughed aloud as I stood up, as people backed away, thinking me a lunatic. Then I calmly washed my face and drank, and stepped out of the fountain, dripping, regarding the mass of spectators who had gathered.

I suddenly realized that I was not far from the house of Kodos Vion. I ran. People scrambled to get out of my way.

* * * *

The house of Kodos Vion was *not* decked out in mourning. No funeral platform was set up in front. Instead, the doors and windows were draped with flowers. There was music from within, and laughter.

I shoved a startled servant aside. The great hall of the house was filled with revelers. I grabbed a woman by the arm.

"How can you *do* this? Kodos Vion is *dying*!"

She looked at me strangely, pulled herself free, and laughed. "Oh, *that!* It was nothing. His heart came back. He got well so fast it was a miracle. Nobody knows why. Miracles are like that."

Now that the Goddess is dead and nothing makes sense, I thought to add, but didn't.

I heard Kodos Vion was calling out my name. I stood there, dripping and ridiculous as he pushed his way through the crowd.

"Where in the seven thundering hells have you *been*, boy?" He grabbed me by the shoulder and nearly shook me off my feet. "*Look* at you! Been on a sea voyage? It looks like you forgot to take a boat! *Goddess!* You're a good lad and all, but my guess is you got so drunk you tried to take a bath with your clothes on."

He laughed so hard that he bent over, steadying himself on my shoulder. Others joined in. The whole house echoed with this hilarity.

"No," I said quietly. "It wasn't like that."

"Then *what*? You'll have to write a *poem* about it!"

More thunderous laughter.

I turned my back on him without a word and walked away. The laughter became stunned silence.

"Wait! Where are you going?"

I turned around and looked into the gaping faces.

"I don't know."

Then I walked out of the house, along many streets I had known all my life, and out of the city through the Gate of Evening. I kept on going for many days, until finally, delirious with thirst and hunger, I came to the cave of an anchorite, deep in the wilderness.

When I was able, I told the holy man of my adventure, and something of my life before.

"I don't understand anything," I said.

"No," he said. "You reached understanding quite early. You have yet to live by that understanding, though. That is where you must begin."

Later, I told my story to a priest, who questioned me at length about the worlds beyond the world; and again, I told it to a poet, a real poet, who listened carefully but didn't ask any questions. I heard him perform the tale once. He had changed a lot, greatly improving the character of the protagonist. Then I came to realize that *I* had to tell the story over and over, not to perform it or to move an audience and receive any reward, or even to convince anyone, but so that I might see it more clearly in my own mind, grasp it, and make it real.

What became of Azrethemne? I believe she is safe. I am sure that she found her way back into the world at last. As for Kodos Vion, as the years went by I still felt a kind of love for him, but he was someone out of a past life, a phantom of memory and nothing more. Except when telling my tale, I never spoke his name again.

IMMORTAL BELLS

Hadday Rona had incurred the enmity of the Brotherhood of Yellow Sashes. Therefore he fled through the streets of Ai Hanlo. He had lived in the holy city for all the twenty years of his life, and he knew the narrow ways, the avenues that were so steep that steps were cut into them as they climbed Ai Hanlo Mountain. He knew the corners, the public squares, the shrines, the rows of shops; but now the familiar was made strange. There was danger everywhere, and he ran in the night, his lungs raw from the damp winter air. Leaning housetops nearly touched overhead, shutting out even starlight. He groped his way, terrified as his boots made sucking noises in mud, sure each sound would reveal his whereabouts to his enemies.

He heard a shutter slam. He jumped into a doorway and stood rigid. There was laughter somewhere, and muted voices. Then silence. He envisioned knives being drawn, and felt the hard gaze of unseen eyes. But when he looked this way and that, he saw nothing, and made his way along a wall. Suddenly there was a burst of light, like the sun roaring in his face. A man came out of an inn bearing a sizzling torch. Hadday covered his eyes and ducked behind a barrel. A cat snarled at him, slashed his boot with a claw, and scampered off.

Hadday ran. He lost all sense of direction. The city became a maze, every street corner, the opening to every alley the same, featureless, filled with darkness and danger and with waiting assassins belonging to the Brotherhood of Yellow Sashes. He had known nightmares like this, in which he fled endlessly, never seeming to get anywhere, as if he ran in place, his legs getting heavier and heavier, while death closed around him. He wished that it would end, even if death were the resolution. He could not go on like this.

He leaned against a post, gasping.

Lights blinded him from every direction. Cymbals clanged. Horns blew. People poured out of the houses, around corners, holding torches and lanterns. A dancer in a black and white costume whirled among them, trailing rags and streamers, shouting the holy names of the Goddess, juggling black and white hammers. Behind the dancer came the core of the procession. A statue of the Goddess was held aloft, a thing of black and white glass, mirrored inside, Hadday knew. It would break into gleaming splinters at the right time and the right place, smashed by the hammers in commemoration of the death and dissolution of the Goddess.

He had been to this festival many times. Now he only wanted to get away.

Behind the statue came a line of priests, singing, holding aloft boxes containing smoking skulls.

He could do little but allow himself to be swept along with the crowd. He was pushed and dragged by the press of bodies like a chip of wood in a raging torrent.

They came to a square, on the far side of which a man stood on a wagon, surveying the crowd. He wore a yellow sash. His eyes met Hadday's, and he scowled, reached under his jacket, and jumped down from the wagon, pressing his way through the jostling throng.

Hadday screamed, but his cry was just one more in the tumult. Desperately, like a drowning man trying to swim through water that somehow becomes thicker and thicker, he struggled to the edge of the crowd.

Then once more he was running through empty streets so dark he could see nothing at all in front of him, splashing and slipping through puddles and over muddy cobblestones. Sometimes he thought he heard footsteps behind him, and deep, deliberate breathing.

He came to a street lined with the shops of metalsmiths and jewelers and bell-makers. In the darkness, in his exhaustion and dread, it seemed to ripple and distend, growing infinite in length as he staggered along.

At last, when he could go no further, he turned, and fell down a few stairs against a door. For a moment it seemed to ripple like a curtain and give way. Then it was solid again.

The door swung open, a bell jangling. It was all Hadday could do not to cry out in fright. He crawled inside and closed the door behind him, then sat against it, breathing hard. There were definitely footsteps outside. Someone ran past. Then nothing more.

The inside of the shop was utterly dark, but filled with sounds, the tinkling of tiny bells like wind chimes, and the faint shivering of larger ones. There was an almost subliminal music in the air, as if a thousand sleeping bells stirred and whispered in a language he could never know. He stood up, groped about, and touched cold, smooth, vibrating metal, and as he did the whole rhythm changed subtly, as a spider's web swaying in the wind might alter its motion ever so slightly when it catches a mosquito.

The young man listened, and the sounds seemed to recede infinitely far, as if there were no end to the place. He heard the beating of his own heart, his breathing, and the scraping of his boot soles as he moved slowly, carefully through the lightless shop.

His foot found a stairway. He climbed, and still the restless bells were all around him. The stairs creaked.

He came to an upper room. Shutters were open, and faint starlight shone through translucent glass. He could barely make out two motionless figures seated at a table. He approached cautiously, reached out, and touched one of them. Stone. It was a statue. His fingers explored the face, found a rough beard, and vastly detailed wrinkles around the eyes.

He stepped back into a mass of bells, which fell to the floor with a clangor. Panic-stricken, he looked around for a place to hide, darted this way and that, colliding with more bells.

Again he was dazzled by light. All around the room candles flared up. Dangling lamps spouted gentle flames. His shadow danced over the walls, over banks and rows of bells of every size and design.

The bearded figure at the table turned to look at him, then turned to the other, an old woman with a shawl, and said, "He can see us. He has the sight of the Anvasas."

Hadday only stared in astonishment. He had touched a statue. He was sure, if he could be sure of anything. It was impossible for them to be living people now, unless he were going subtly mad, as a result of some poison given to him by the Brotherhood of Yellow Sashes.

The woman smiled in a motherly way.

"Boy, you are tired and hungry. Join us at our supper."

He sat, and the woman ladled some stew into a bowl and set it before him. The man poured him some wine. Without questioning, he ate and drank. All around him the bells stirred, as if sleepless spirits moved among them.

The man leaned over the table. His face was unfathomable. Hadday was afraid of him. He wasn't of the woman.

"You do not see as others do, or you would not have found your way here. You have the Eye of the Anvasas."

And Hadday knew that he was helpless and could hide nothing from these two. He took out the leather bag he wore on a thong around his neck, opened it, and took out a globe of perfectly clear crystal the size of a plum.

The man snatched it from him before he could react, and held it up to a candle, turning it in his hand.

"Yes, it is the Eye of the Anvasas." He gave it back to Hadday. "It does not come to anyone without a reason. How did you get it?"

"I—I—" He wanted to lie but he knew he could only tell the truth. "I am a thief. I stole it. From the Brotherhood of Yellow Sashes. They displayed it on an altar in front of their lodge. As soon as I saw it, I knew I had to have it, no matter what. Something came over me. I don't know what drove me. I jumped over the railing and grabbed it, in front of everybody, and fought my way through the crowd. I don't know how. It's as if some demon inside me…I can't explain.…"

The two stared at him without speaking. Stuttering, he went on.

"I can't—can't—I don't even know what it is, or if it's worth anything. Normally I steal purses, or jewelry from stalls in the marketplace, or.… But this, I—"

"Perhaps it was tired of where it was, and wished to be moved," the man said. "There is a tangled thread of destiny within it. It goes where it wills, and causes itself to be found… or stolen."

"But how?"

"Who knows? It is of the Anvasas, by which many things are made possible that could not, otherwise be."

"The what?"

"You have not heard of the Anvasas, ignorant one?"

"No, I—" Hadday felt more bewildered and helpless than ever.

"Only now, that you have the sight, can you perceive the Anvasas. What is it? Some call it a city, some a country, some a gateway leading out of the world. It is the product of the vast science of men who lived before the time of the Goddess, men who could touch the stars. Now, masterless, the Anvasas goes on, manifesting itself in many ways. There are those who say it is a living thing, like a vast colony of seaweed, always dying at one end and being born at the other, immortal, drifting through seas beyond time and space, outside of the world and the sky and the days and the years, only able to touch the Earth now that the Goddess is gone and there is nothing to keep it away. Holiness lies fallow in our age. *Now* the Anvasas is visible to those with the sight."

Hadday put the crystal sphere away. He sat rigid, clasping the edge of the table with both hands.

"I don't understand any of this. What are you talking about?

What is going on?"

"We can explain by telling you a story," the woman said. Again she smiled, and there was something in her smile which calmed the young thief.

"I will begin," said the man.

* * * *

"In a certain city there dwelt a certain man."

"His name was Manri," the woman interrupted. "He lived in the time of the death of the Goddess, as we do, but long ago, here, in Ai Hanlo. He made bells."

"Yes," the man continued. "He was the master bell-maker of all the city. It was an ancient art, even then. Its secrets had been passed from his father's father's father to him, and no one questioned this, or asked him what it was, nor did they pester his apprentices. Not even the Guardian of the Bones of the Goddess sought out the secret, for all that the fame of the bell-maker spread far. He sold his bells to the Guardian and his court, to all the great families of the city, and to kings and lords and priests in every part of the world.

"What is so special about a bell? Nothing, if it's the kind you hang around a cow's neck. But these bells were *perfect*. They were almost holy things. It was within this bell-maker's power to put a little piece of his soul into each bell. And he was not diminished by this. His soul spread throughout the world. He put a drop of his blood in the metal, too. Then, because his soul and the blood were shared, he was readily able to give each some strange and rare and wonderful shape, and to sculpt the very sounds that would issue from each bell, and give each an inscription which rang in the mind of the beholder even as the bell itself rang with the motion of its tongue.

"I cannot tell how it was done. That was the secret. But the thoughts of the maker of bells were as calm and still as a frigid pool in an underground grotto. By the secrets of his art, by years of discipline and magic, he strove to make himself as perfect as his bells.

"Otherwise none of his bells would have been good enough for the most solemn occasions, for ringing in commemoration of the death of the Goddess, and for summoning her successor to rise, in time, out of the Earth. When the Guardian performs certain rituals, as secret as those of the bell-maker but wholly sacred, he is accompanied by acolytes ringing delicate, perfectly formed bells. Nothing less will do. To ring in holiness, a bell must be perfect. To ring perfectly in joy and sorrow, so too it must be perfect.

"Thus the bell-maker had to achieve perfection, in a sense."

* * * *

The teller paused, and Hadday stared around the room, at the many bells, wondering if this were just something the old man had made up to glorify his profession. Still, he listened politely. The couple had treated him with kindness. And the Brotherhood of Yellow Sashes was waiting outside.

"Manri was married," the woman said.

"Yes," the man said. "A year after he inherited the position of master bell-maker, he took to wife Tirham, a magician's daughter from Zabortash. She was as exquisite as any of his bells. Her eyes, they say, shone like diamonds, and she was dark and slender, and her hair flowed to her waist, black as night, and gleaming, as if filled with stars. She was gentle, and wise too, and sometimes when she spoke it was as if the hearer had been led into the world for the first time, and his life had truly begun.

"No one ever felt such love as Manri for his bride. You should have heard the bells ringing on their wedding day! All over the city, all over the world, bells broke out in spontaneous peals of joy, often to the astonishment of their owners.

"Tirham's father came to the wedding, a full Zabortashi magus, clad in black with a tall hat. He folded the air around himself in his home in the far south, and when he unfolded it, he was in Ai Hanlo, without having crossed the distance in between. But he was not a grim and forbidding figure, as many magi are. He was merry. He performed feats of magic for the bride and bridegroom and their guests. He folded the air about himself again at the end, and was gone."

"Seven years passed," said the woman.

"They lived together in happiness, in perfection for seven years. They had seven children, three sons and four daughters. The city was at peace. Even the Guardian felt a calm settle over the city. The bones of the Goddess never stirred. There was peace everywhere one of Manri's bells could be heard. At that time, it was impossible to get a mournful sound out of any of them.

"I think the Powers envied Manri and Tirham after a while. I think that's why what happened, happened."

The teller paused again, trembling, as if he had come to a part which was painful to recount. The woman prodded him.

"Then Manri had a dream," she said.

The man resumed.

* * * *

"A thing like a huge black bird, only covered with hair, and with a human face, came for him in the night, snatching him out of his bed. He cried out for Tirham, but in an instant his soul, his awareness, was out the window, even while his body lay still beside his wife. He dangled by the hair from the thing's claws as it soared over the city. He felt the pain in his head, the cold of the upper air.

"He was carried to a ruined tower in one of the dead places, where once stood a city older than the Goddess. There were spirits of the waters there, waiting for him, floating like golden skeletons of fish through the walls and floors of the tower, drifting in the air. And there were things of the earth, a monster like a man from the waist up, but beneath it a riot of useless limbs; and something that walked upright, with the head of a crocodile and the wings of a raven, but the beautiful, glowing body of a man. Animate shadows flickered in the periphery of vision, always in motion.

"Manri knew he was in the present of the Dark Powers, surviving splinters of the dark aspect of the Goddess. But he was brave. He did not cower before them.

"The crocodile man spoke first, saying, 'Tirham shall be ours. We shall take her slowly at first, then all of the sudden, as it pleases us.'

"Manri's resolve broke when he heard this. He cried out in terror and despair. He begged them to take him instead, but they would not do so. He was still sobbing when he was returned to his bed, and he awoke.

"Tirham comforted him, saying, 'It is only a dream you had. We are still together.'

"But even as she touched him he could tell she was feverish. She sickened quickly in the following days. There was nothing anyone could do. Manri watched, helpless, wretched, as she declined. Then one night, very late, he was awakened by a sound, and he saw her standing in the doorway of the room in which he slept.

"'You should not be out of bed,' he said. 'You must save your strength. The night air is bad for you.'

"Then he noticed that her face shone like a lantern, and he was filled with dread.

"'I have strength enough for my journey,' she said. 'Do not be afraid. It is neither warm nor cold for me. The Dark Powers shall not have me. Be comforted. I shall walk past them, never leaving the road.'

"'What do you mean?' he cried. 'What nonsense is this?'

"He ran to the doorway, but she was gone. Even as he stood there, his eldest daughter came to him, tears streaming down her face, to tell him that Tirham had died.

"Manri's grief was as great as his love. Even long after Tirham was buried, the black banners hung outside the shop, and Manri wept. Bells rang day and night of their own accord, both in the shop and all over the city. If before it had been impossible to get a mournful sound out of them, now it was impossible to get anything else, even from the smallest and most delicate of them. Everyone shared Manri's sorrow and pitied him, but in time they called on him to give up his endless weeping. Even the Guardian came to him with many priests, but he would not be comforted. The bells rang, and sorrow spread like a miasma over Ai Hanlo. Far below the ground, the Bones of the Goddess stirred.

"This could not go on. Manri's sons resolved to travel to Zabortash, to find their grandfather, the magus, and seek his help. But they did not know the way, or where he dwelt, and they knew the journey could take years. Nevertheless, they set out.

"And still Manri mourned.

"At last the Eye of the Anvasas manifested itself, causing itself to be brought to the bell-maker. He sat one night in his shop, working on the delicate gold ornamentation around the rim of a bell, while around him bells shivered in sorrow and the air was thick with sound. But suddenly the sound changed very slightly, and Manri knew there was a stranger at the door.

"No one ever discovered the man's name. He passed the Eye to Manri and was gone. The bell-maker stood in the doorway, holding the crystal sphere, wondering what it was. But even as he did, his vision was altered, and he discerned the Anvasas. Golden smoke came pouring along the street like water, ankle-deep on the pavement, washing against the houses, pouring down the short flight of stairs, over Manri's threshold, into the shop.

"He walked up to street level, then began to run before the smoke, half afraid, half aware he was being directed, all the while clutching the Eye. When he came to the Sunrise Gate, there were no watchmen around. He forced the gate open. Then he looked out on a golden sea. All the world had been covered over but for Ai Hanlo Mountain, which stood like an island.

"And gliding toward him over the mist was a great galleon, the most magnificent he had ever seen, as ornate as the finest of his bells. Indeed, like a bell, it trembled with muted song as it neared him. This was the Anvasas, as it appeared to him.

"There was someone walking toward him across the golden sea, from the ship. He stood, straining to make out some feature, but with the luminous mist rising, for a long time he could only discern a long white gown, and a staff such as travelers carry.

"It was only when the figure was very close that he recognized the gown, the staff, and the travelling boots he had given to Tirham to aid her in her journey out of the world.

"He let out a yell of astonishment and ran to her. The mist held him up. They met a little ways from the gate and embraced. She was no ghost.

"'How is it you are returned to me?' he asked. She put her finger to his lips. 'Do not ask. Only welcome me back.'

"'You are welcome, *welcome!*' he said, his voice cracking. And he led her into the city, running before her in his excitement, then waiting for her to catch up. All around, his bells rang with sudden exaltation. People looked out of their windows. He did not know if they saw the mist or the ship which was the Anvasas. He did not care.

"Slowly the mist receded. When he got to his shop, there was only a little pool of it at the bottom of the stairs.

"He led Tirham inside, and fumbled nervously with candles, trying to get one lit, so he could see her more clearly.

"It was when he did that he shrieked and tore his hair, yanked her staff from her, and ripped her gown away.

"No living woman stood before him. It was not Tirham, but a stone statue, a perfect likeness, exquisitely wrought. The bells clamored. His daughters came to him, puzzled and frightened. They could not silence or comfort him. It seemed he would go mad, and the whole city would also, for the ringing of the bells.

"The neighbors came, some with wax in their ears, saying, 'It is a beautiful memorial. Keep it and be still.' But he was not still. When he fell into an exhausted sleep at last, still the bells rang and jangled. Some of the huge ones split and fell into pieces, thundering.

"The people asked, 'How can this cruel thing be?' The Guardian of the Bones of the Goddess came with his priests and soldiers in slow procession. For once, no bells preceded him. He knew by his holy vision that the statue was of the Anvasas. 'You must accept it,' he told Manri.

"'No, Lord,' said the bell-maker. 'Not even you can command such a thing.'

"'We shall see,' said the Guardian, who then set a cordon of soldiers around the shop.

"Day and night the soldiers stood there, with wax in their ears to dampen the sound. The nearby houses and shops were deserted. Manri's children were allowed to go in and out and see to his needs, but he was not permitted to leave. Daily he sat amidst the pealing bells, blood running from his ears at the sound, staring at the statue of his wife. It came to life slowly. After a week, its limbs relaxed. After another, it began to lumber about the shop, crashing into bells, overturning tables and work-benches, stumbling against his forge where he melted metals. The stone face was expressionless. It spoke, its voice rasping, grinding. 'Husband...do you...not know me? Where is my husband?' It would come groping toward him. He had to scramble out of the way to avoid being trampled.

"But slowly it became more human, its voice more like Tirham's. One day he found it kneeling before a trunk, going through her clothing. The face turned toward him as he entered the room. There was an expression on it now: surprise turning into delighted recognition.

"'I am naked,' she said. 'I have to put something on.'

"Manri surrendered. Weeping, he fell into her arms, and found that her flesh was soft and warm. She spoke to him in familiar, intimate whispers, as only Tirham could. They made love. The bells stopped ringing.

"Throughout the rest of his life, he lived only for each day, never questioning, just accepting each sensation, each instant as it came. Since Tirham was genuine to all his senses, there was no question in his mind that she was indeed his wife."

* * * *

Again the teller of the tale paused, and looked directly at Hadday Rona, the thief.

"Now you know the power of the thing you have stolen. You know what it can do. Can you imagine for what purpose it has come into your possession?"

Hadday was afraid now. He rose to leave.

"Wait," said the woman. "There is more. Stay and listen."

He sat down.

She told the rest of the story.

* * * *

"Manri the bell-maker grew old, but Tirham did not age. This did not make him question. Nothing did. She was as he had always remembered her, as beautiful as she had been when they were first wed, and he was content. He counted himself lucky. In time, he told people that she was his daughter, then his granddaughter. He didn't hear very well in his old age.

"When he died, it was she who would not be comforted. She had become so much like the original Tirham that she truly loved him with the same intensity that he had loved her. Once more the bells rang uncontrollably. They exploded into fragments. It was dangerous to be near one.

"But this time the agony did not go on as long. This Tirham was of the Anvasas, and she could perceive it directly, without need of the Eye.

"She sat disconsolate in her room above the shop, staring out over the Endless River and the plains beyond.

"The wind blew a leafy vine through the window. It brushed against her face. She held it, puzzled. Then she looked out the window again and saw, not the river and the plain, but the floor of a forest, deep and boundless. The base of a tree blocked half the view.

"She understood because she was of the Anvasas, and

crawled through the window, emerging into the forest from a hole in a vine-covered mound. The forest was solid and real. She did not fall into the street, below the window.

"She walked for a time in utter silence beneath the trees. Somewhere the sun was setting, and the green faded. Shadows lengthened, and pooled, and filled the forest.

"Then she saw a light ahead and came to a campfire, and found her husband sitting beside it.

"'I was expecting you,' she said.

"Together they returned to the city and dwelt in the house of Manri and Tirham, making bells of consummate perfection, which never broke or rang of their own accord. The two of them aged as they chose to. They had a way of bending the light that fell on them, deceiving the beholder. They could assume any appearance they wanted. They were immortal. They watched their children grow old, and their grandchildren, and they caused themselves to be forgotten and assumed new identities."

* * * *

The woman fell silent, and there was only the faint sound of the bells in the darkening room as the candles burned low. In this light, Hadday realized, the two faces before him looked very much like stone.

"I think I..." His heart was racing.

The man and woman both nodded.

To the man he said, "You are Manri." To the woman, "You are Tirham."

"There are many like us," the woman said, reaching over to hold her husband's hand gently. "We discovered that soon enough. We are seedlings of the Anvasas, scattered throughout the world. No one can recognize us, except for those who have the special sight."

Hadday fingered the bag around his neck.

"Another thing," the man said. "The children of the Anvasas do not bleed as mortals do. Our blood runs clear. If you have the sight, you can see it."

Trembling, Hadday let go of the Eye. He took out a knife and slashed his left palm. He stared at it for a moment, then, making a fist, got up and ran from the bell-maker's shop.

* * * *

The city wasn't there when he got outside. Only the shop stood, absurdly, in the middle of an utterly barren plain. He looked back once, but did not go back inside. He was resigned to his fate. He understood that once more the Anvasas had revealed itself.

He crossed the plain beneath a steel grey sky. Hours passed, or perhaps days. There was no change in the light. He lost all sense of time, and became delirious with thirst and hunger. The air was stifling. It was hard to breathe.

Again he looked back, but the shop had long since disappeared in the distance.

At last he saw a thin column of smoke above the horizon. He headed toward it. A dark speck resolved itself into a tumbledown hut. The smoke was rising through a hole in the roof. He stood for a time before the door, savoring the cool shadow of the overhanging roof, then went in.

An old man crouched before a bubbling cauldron, his back to Hadday.

"What…?" was all he could say. His throat was dry. He was filled with dread.

"You wonder what is this thing, the Anvasas. I shall tell you. You wonder what the Eye is. I shall tell you. The Eye is part of a machine that's at the center of the universe, spewing forth the Anvasas like smoke from a fire."

"I—" Hadday stepped forward.

Agile as a monkey, the other scurried around to the other side of the cauldron.

Hadday reeled in astonishment.

The old man had no face. His head was smooth and featureless as an egg. He reached into the boiling water with a pair of tongs and drew out a face, a mask of flesh.

The face was Hadday's own. It spoke with his voice.

"In one of the languages of the ancients, the term 'Anvasas' means 'messenger,' for the Anvasas is the messenger which travels to the worlds and between the worlds from the center of All. But that was half a million years ago. In a more recent tongue, it merely means 'truth.' Behold, Hadday Rona, the Eye of the Anvasas has opened your own eyes, and you perceive the Anvasas directly. The truth is before you. The cloak is removed from your soul. The shutters are flung open in your innermost tabernacle, and everything you ever were, everything you are, everything you shall be is made plain by the light. Now hear the truth, all of it, concerning Hadday Rona—"

The young man tore the bag containing the Eye from around his neck and threw it. Screaming, covering his face with his hands, he ran from the hut.

The other shouted after him, "The Eye of the Anvasas has withdrawn from the world. It has returned home. You are its instrument. That is part of the truth."

There was more, but Hadday did not hear.

* * * *

He was falling. Water splashed, then filled his boots. He flailed his arms.

But he only stood thigh-deep in the Endless River. He waded toward the shore. He saw Ai Hanlo through some reeds. He climbed onto the bank and turned away from the city, and kept going until at last he came to the land of Nagé.

He never stole again. He apprenticed himself to a scribe, and in time read many books and pondered many mysteries. Eventually he married a woman of that country and loved her deeply, and lived with her all the days of his life, confiding in her all things except what he had seen in the palm of his hand as he sat in the shop of Manri the bell-maker.

BETWEEN NIGHT AND MORNING

Between night and morning, in the last dark hour, Velas Ven sat in a tavern, in a back street of Ai Hanlo, thinking deep thoughts as his wine swirled slowly in his cup. He was a storyteller of great renown. Wherever he went, people would cry out, "Velas! Velas! Speak to us of wonders!" Sometimes he would hire a boy to go before him, alternately blowing a trumpet and shouting, "Gather and listen! Velas Ven is coming!"

But now he sat in this tavern, in a booth by the window, alone but for the taverner who had fallen asleep at the counter, alone with his thoughts. He wanted to be a philosopher. Storytelling was just bright colors. It was not enough. He wanted to know how there could be any meaning or purpose to life in the time of the death of the Goddess, when even the foremost of men, the Guardian of the Bones of the Goddess, could only listen as the last echo of her dying faded away. Soon the very last holiness would be gone from the world. He wanted to know how history could continue, how mankind could ever hope for more than endless stumbling in the dark, groping for a future when there would be no future. Velas Ven wanted to be the one to discover the light.

Tonight was a night of festival. He scarcely noticed, there in the tavern, in the darkness. He was oblivious to the revelers outside, to the music and laughter and shouting which could still be heard even at this hour. He knew that even now a huge double statue of the Goddess in her Bright and Dark Aspects was being carried slowly through the city to the sound of flutes and rattling tambourines, to the flash and acrid smell of burning powder.

The statue was nearby. It had to pass along every street before dawn. That was the custom. The sounds from outside grew louder. But he was like a disembodied spirit, barely able to perceive the world of men, trying to withdraw further.

He drank, and his thoughts closed around him like shadows.

A short time passed and his gaze drifted to the dim figures he could see through the translucent glass of the window. There was a burst of light, then applause, and people running. Voices rose in an almost raucous hymn.

The main body of the crowd moved on. There were only a few stragglers left when Velas saw, quite distinctly through the glass, an old man in a ragged cloak. He seemed to swim in a black and gray haze, and the glass distorted the light of the lantern he carried into wavering lines, but he himself was quite clearly visible, as if, just for him, the glass had become impossibly clear.

The man raised his lantern, illuminating his own face. He gazed directly at the seated Velas Ven. Their eyes met, and the storyteller was dazzled, as a rat is by the gaze of a snake, but in a different way, too, for he was not afraid. He slid from his booth in trembling expectation. He saw in that gaze, in those eyes, a revelation, and he knew it for what it was.

He ran out of the tavern. The cold air was a shock. The sky was dark, filled with brilliant stars. Far away, bonfires burned. The celebrants had moved on. He was almost alone in the lane.

The old man hesitated for a moment at the edge of the receding crowd, then passed from sight. Velas ran after him. Soon he was surrounded by people, pushing his way through. White-clad girls and black-glad old women pressed against him, the girls holding black candles, the old women white ones. They sang. They asked him for coins. He put a copper in the first palm his hand met, then struggled to break free.

Then he was face to face with the man with the lantern and

again, even though he was no longer peering through glass, only this one figure was clearly visible. The rest were gray blurs. The sounds of the festival receded to a faint murmur. Velas moved through the crowd as if through smoke. He stood within arm's reach of the lantern bearer.

The lantern flickered in the wind.

"Reverend Father," he said, making the gesture of respectful address with his right hand. "Have you come to tell me something?"

But the other did not speak. He walked swiftly away, his footsteps echoing, the flame of the lantern sputtering. The people around him, the revelers, were like swirling mist.

Velas followed. They walked for what seemed like hours, but time was suspended, and the night did not end. They passed through many districts of the city, crossing the great square of the fountain, walking along the base of the wall of the Inner City, beyond which no common man may go. They wound their way among the tall, silent stone figures in the Garden of Statues. The lights of the festival were faint flickerings, like lightning on the horizon, and the celebrants were only half-glimpsed shapes, moving shadows, suggestions of sound. He was alone, but for the stranger who led him.

Once, the old man turned and looked back at him. When he saw that face again, and those serene, terrible eyes, only that gaze and the memory of it were real to him. He followed, through a city of illusions.

At last they turned down another narrow lane and came to another tavern. The old man we down a short flight of stairs. For an instant, the lantern disappeared around a corner. Velas ran after him, slipping on the muddy, wooden steps, catching hold of the railing. Wood creaked. At the bottom he splashed through an inch of water, then came to a door.

There was nowhere else the stranger could have gone. Velas banged on the door. From within came sounds of revelry and laughter, tankards banging, a stringed instrument being played.

He shouted again and the door swung inward, and he couldn't

hear his own shouting. The sounds were larger than life, like thunder. He staggered into the room. Smiling faces pressed near his. Hands caught hold of his arms, steered him to a bench.

"Wait!" he said. "I can't stay here! I have to go! I don't understand—"

The laughter only got louder. A cup was placed in his hands. He looked around for the old man with the lantern, but could not find him. He tried to rise, but was pushed back down into his seat. Two or three laughing, red-faced fellows took hold of his forearms and raised his cup to his mouth. He drank deep. The wine was stronger than any he had ever known.

Soon he was caught up in the frantic celebration, forgetting everything except the single moment in which he lived. He stood on a table and proclaimed his tales, the most wondrous he knew, embellishing them as he spoke. There were raucous shouts, ridiculous suggestions. He incorporated them into the tale, and it grew like a living thing, writhing like a serpent even as it was created.

Later, amid as much noise as ever, he somehow came to be on the floor under a bench with a naked woman in his arms. They made love there, laughing.

Still later, another woman, fully clothed, caught him by the ankles and dragged him out from under the bench. He was laughing, too, as she helped him straighten his garments, and as she hustled him out of the tavern, up the stairs, and into the street.

The hour had not changed. The festival continued. The unmoving stars shone brilliantly in the dark sky.

The woman grabbed him by the shoulders, turning him around.

"I am not angry with you," she said. "I knew what kind of man I married. I wanted you. I knew you would still be ready for me."

In the back of his mind, Velas Ven was aghast, for he did not know this woman, and he was sure he was not married. But he was carried along by sensations more intense than anything real. His mind was working strangely. He had become detached from what was happening for just an instant, and then he sank completely into each experience and knew no future or past, or any abstraction. He lived in an eternal now.

The woman who seemed to be his wife led him to a fine house. Servants met them at the door and took his cloak. Others conducted them upstairs into the bedchamber, then retreated hastily. He made love again, to this woman whose name he couldn't remember, but whom he was sure he had known for many years. He remembered many things as they lay side-by-side afterwards, very few of them from the life of Velas Ven the storyteller. He was settling swiftly, gently, into someone else's life.

The woman stroked his hair.

"My Odanek," she said. "Could I ever have wanted anyone else? I have lived all my life to be the wife of Odanek. He is greater than all other men."

He wondered who Odanek was, but soon forgot about it, caught up in the mere sensation of being there in that bed with that woman.

Much later, after she had gone to sleep, he got up to relieve himself. He couldn't find the chamber pot, and it occurred to him that he didn't know his way around this house. So he went to the window and opened the shutters.

No time had passed. It was still that same, last hour of the night. The stars shone. The festival went on.

In the street below, the old man stood with the lantern, gazing up at him.

Behind him, the woman muttered, "I love you, Odanek."

He turned to look, and saw that she had someone else in her arms.

Suddenly he was afraid and filled with shame. He was an intruder, terrified of discovery. The woman and her lover did not seem to notice him, so he carefully gathered up his clothing and crept out of the room. He dressed in the hall outside, looking every way. No servants appeared. He made his way down the stairs and out of the house.

He shivered in the night air, suddenly aware that he had forgotten his cloak. But he didn't dare go back for it. He hurried around to where he had seen the old man.

Someone was relieving himself out the window.

"Odanek, come back to bed," came a voice from within.

Velas heard a footstep. He turned just in time to see the lantern disappearing around a corner. He ran to follow. Again he met that awful gaze, and nothing else seemed real. He drifted through the insubstantial city.

* * * *

The stars gleamed overhead. He ran in darkness after the stranger, pushing his way through a crowd that was alternately solid and indistinct. He saw the lantern drifting into a walled garden and followed. Once inside, there was no trace of his quarry.

"Papa! Papa! Come play with us!"

He looked down in astonishment. Two little girls, six or seven at most, tugged at his trouser legs. He did not know them. They could have been any of the city's countless children. They carried paper lanterns, as children often did on festival nights.

"Papa! Come!"

He made his way along a winding path between hedges, to a circular lawn with a fountain in the middle of it. Palely glowing night flowers, planted in concentric rings around the fountain, swayed gently in the night breeze. Water splashed.

"Papa!"

Three more children ran to greet him, two more girls and a boy. He did not ask their names. He merely followed them.

One of the girls got out a flute and began to play. The others took him by the hands and danced in a circle, turning him slowly at first, then faster, swinging their paper lanterns. Light washed over the hedges, over the fountain. The night flowers glowed more brightly when the light touched them. The splashing water flickered through the air like a rain of luminescent pearls.

On the waxed paper sides of the lanterns were black silhouettes of birds and beasts. Somehow, by a trick of light and shadow, they came alive, separating themselves from the lanterns. It seemed that great black birds whirled in the sky overhead, while black leopards crept through the hedges, their eyes glowing like coals.

Then he was aware that the children had let go of him. He staggered dizzily.

They were dancing around someone else.

"Papa! Papa!"

"Come children," said the other man. "Your mother wants you home now. Kavni, Ushias, Raedmon, come on." He herded them away. "You too, Surren." The girl with the flute stopped playing and hurried after them.

No one seemed to notice Velas Ven. He was invisible to them. It was only when he stood alone in the garden once more that he realized that the other man's voice had sounded very much like his own.

He had not seen the other man's face.

Then he was not alone. The old man appeared across from him, on the other side of the fountain, holding the lantern.

"What spirit are you?" Velas demanded. "Why have you come to me?"

The other merely turned away. Velas followed.

* * * *

Later still, but after no time had passed, in the same hour, he stood guard on the vine-covered, decaying battlements of the Inner City, gazing into the night, out across the vast array of the Outer City below, where the light of the festival moved among the houses like some glowing, amorphous animal. Beyond, starlight reflected in the broad expanse of the Endless River, and beyond that fields and distant mountains were hidden in the darkness. The air was so clear that he could even make out some of the distant peaks, darker than the sky, blotting out a few stars along a jagged horizon.

It seemed that he had been there for a long time. He stood with another soldier, warming his hands over a pot of coals. Nearby, a huge, curving horn hung from a wooden frame. Someone would blow on that horn to announce the dawn, as soon as the first glow of sunrise was seen from the walls. He had done it often.

He chatted idly with his companion. The night remained dark. The stars had not moved. The other soldier's conversation brought up memories of campaigns in distant lands, of forced marches, long hours in camp, and longer hours on this wall, waiting for an enemy that never came. The city had not been threatened since his father's father's time.

Velas Ven did not remember any of this, but it came to him. It was part of another man's life.

A pair of soldiers came to relieve the other two, who walked away, their spears slung lazily over their shoulders. Velas Ven was left unnoticed by the coals.

* * * *

In the same hour of the night, he came to an academy of scholars and took his seat in their great reading room. Torches and braziers cast long shadows on the walls. The bookshelves were shrouded in darkness. Here and there shuffling figures in ankle-length robes moved along the shelves, holding candles, peering, groping for the volumes they sought.

He sat at a desk and strained his tired eyes once more by the light of a little lamp. The pages before him were written in a script and a language strange to Velas Ven, and covered with abstract figures and diagrams, but he understood them. He had the memory of long years of research. His whole life had passed in this academy. Now he was very old. He struggled desperately to find what he sought, the answer to some great mystery, before death claimed him.

There was a pain in his chest. He labored for breath.

He came to the last page of the book, looked up, and extinguished his lamp. The master of the academy came over to him, gently put his hand on his shoulder, and said, "Have you found the answer?"

"Yes, I think I have."

"Then come into the lecture hall, and tell it to us."

The old scholar rose from his bench. All torches, braziers, and lanterns were put out or carried from the room, leaving Velas Ven sitting at a desk in the dark.

He groped after them, but could not find the lecture hall. Finally he came to a door, fumbled with a latch, and pushed it open.

Outside in a courtyard, the old man was waiting with the lantern.

* * * *

Still the stranger's gaze held him, but he was angry, and able to exert himself.

"Have you come to haunt me? To lead me forever? To drive me mad? Explain yourself!"

Then the other spoke for the first time. His voice reminded Velas Ven of his grandfather's, until he realized that it was what his own voice would sound like when he grew old.

"I come in fulfillment of your wishes. You will come with me one more time, and everything will be clear. You have my promise."

The old man drifted over the ground like a puff of smoke. Velas followed him along a deserted street. The stars sparkled overhead, unmoving. The festival was far away now. He heard no footsteps but his own. The lantern floated in the air before him like a moth.

They came to the open gate of a cemetery. There, stone images of the dual Goddess stood on either side, their arms joined in an arch overhead, holding a stone sun.

Within, a crowd of mourners gathered around an open grave. Many held lanterns and torches. He lost sight of the old man in the crowd. He pushed his way through, gently, asking again and again, "What funeral is this? Who has died?" But no one answered. No one acknowledged his presence.

He came to the forefront of the crowd. A priest droned something, holding aloft a reliquary containing a splinter of a Bone of the Goddess.

The old man with the lantern stood in the grave, next to the open coffin. No one seemed aware of him, except Velas.

"If you want to understand," the old man said, "come here. Look into the face."

But Velas did not look. He closed his eyes tight and stood at the edge of the grave, hugging himself, trembling. The night air was suddenly very cold.

"No," he said. "I won't look. I don't want to see."

Hours seemed to go by. He lost all sense of time. When he finally opened his eyes, he was alone in the cemetery with the old man. It was still night. There was no open grave.

"Very well then," the old man said, holding the lantern up by his own face as he approached Velas.

Velas saw the other's features very clearly. He screamed. The light was blinding. He fell to his knees, holding his hands over his eyes. The flame of the lantern roared all around him, consuming the world.

He fell.

* * * *

Velas Ven awoke stiff and sore, face down in cold dust. He rolled over and sat up, blinking. There was light. He was afraid, but after a while he saw that it was only the dawn come at last, gently touching the monuments in the cemetery. High above, on the wall of the Inner City, a soldier blew on the curving horn.

* * * *

He told stories, speaking of wonders, of fantastic things, the dreams of his people. He told of common things too, of everyday lives, of lovers, children, fathers, soldiers, tradesmen, and many others. He even made the scholar's lot seem an adventure. He made his audience feel the trembling excitement of discovering a treasure at last, after many years of labor among books.

And he told of sorrow and loss.

He was even more popular than before. His stories were written down and read in the great courts. Once he was brought before the Guardian himself. After he had finished his reading, the Guardian of the Bones said to him, "You have described these dreams and these many lives more vividly than anyone else, as if you were a kind of universal spirit, able to look into every man's heart, to share and live out every man's life. But there is no apparent moral. What does it all mean?"

Velas Ven shrugged and laughed. "Holy Lord, how should I know? I'm not a philosopher."

He was asked that question many times. He always gave the same answer. Sometimes he gave it sadly.

Quite late in his life, he married a woman named Nomonig and they had one daughter, Ael. She was a brilliant girl. She asked many questions.

Once he took her aside and said, "Daughter, the Goddess died long ago. She is buried beneath our feet, at the heart of Ai Hanlo Mountain. Her power is almost gone. But sometimes a little bit of it, like vapor, seeps up through the cracks in the pavement. Our minds shape it, and we in turn are shaped by what we have unknowingly created. These events are called miracles."

Ael was grown and had children of her own when Velas finally died, very old and very tired. At the funeral, before the open grave, while the priest droned on and held a reliquary aloft, one of Ael's children tugged on her sleeve and whispered, "I thought I saw Grandpa pushing through the crowd. He covered his face and fell down on his knees. I think he was saying something."

She replied, "Hush, child. It is only the wind stirring up the dust."

THE SHAPER OF ANIMALS

"When my husband's horse came home without him," the Lady Nestra often said, "I knew there was no hope. One of his boots was still in the stirrup. I knew then that I had lost my Lord Caradhas, the most matchless of husbands. The City of the Goddess was saved at the battle of the Heshite Plain. Etash Wesa was overthrown, and the world was spared the one who had proclaimed himself the new god, but I died in that battle too. My soul bled. A great wound had been torn in my heart. My life was over, though my body still went through the motions of life."

All the upper class visitors to Ai Hanlo, where the Bones of the Goddess lie in holy splendor, knew of the Lady Nestra, and avoided her, for she was in mourning, and had been for a long time. She appeared at the great festivals, in the spring and autumn. Of old, when the Goddess was alive, those festivals were times of spectacular manifestations, when Her power would be witnessed by all, and the signs and the seasons would be changed, and miracles occurred freely. But, after the death of the Goddess, the festivals were merely gatherings, to renew the ancient rites, it is true, but mostly people came just to celebrate themselves and the passage of time, and to trade. No one prayed for miracles anymore, except the wretched mendicants who gathered in the public squares, and the Lady Nestra.

She was still young and beautiful, yet when she appeared in public draped all in black, she was like a sudden chill that moved through the city, and a hush seemed to follow her when she walked daily around the battlements of the wall of the inner city, beyond which no commoner may pass. She would pause each time over one of the shrines set in the wall, where the mendicants gathered, and call down to them, and join in their pleadings, that some lingering fragment of the Godhead might touch her, and grant her a miracle.

The members of the court could not avoid her, for she was a great lady. She commanded people into her presence, hardly realizing what she was doing, and as social necessity dictated. Inevitably, she would tell of her sorrows, and often she would weep long and hard, and others would weep with her.

It was whispered that she had draped the whole city in mourning for a funeral that went on forever, but no one could deny her.

So it was that others came to pray, and many petitioned the Guardian of the Bones of the Goddess, the holiest of men, that somehow, someday, the Lady Nestra would find peace.

* * * *

There was a knocking at the door of her chamber one night. Lady Nestra looked up from her writing, but did not rise from where she sat. The door swung open, and the Good Guardian himself, Tharanodeth IV, entered alone, his long robe sweeping the floor.

At once Lady Nestra dropped from her chair onto her knees.

"You may rise and sit," he said.

She sat. "Holy Lord, I am greatly honored."

He waved his hand. "It cannot continue," he said gently. He took a stoppered vial and a little ivory box out of a pocket and placed them on her writing-table. "It cannot continue. The very Powers are without rest."

Still she only looked at him with longing, not daring to hope, and again the Guardian spoke.

"Have you some image of your husband?"

And, very tenderly, Lady Nestra unwrapped a silver dish she

had received on her wedding night, into which her husband's features had been worked in fine relief.

"Ah, excellent," the Guardian said. "You must seek into the darkness with these things. In this vial is the wine of vision. Pour it into the dish. Then open the box and add the powder that is inside. It is made from the dust of the tomb of the Goddess. You need know no more than that it is very powerful. Stir it into the wine, then look, and see, and believe what you see. Beyond that, merely hope. Hope that enough of the echo of the passing of the Goddess remains, and that the Powers have not wholly dissipated."

As the Guardian made to leave, Lady Nestra opened a coffer filled with rare jewels, but Tharanodeth did not even pause on his way out the door.

It was on that night that the Shaper of Animals arrived in the holy city, for all Lady Nestra did not know of him. Indeed, no one witnessed his advent, but when dawn came, his wagon was merely there among the many others in the Courtyard of the Upraised Hand, where tradesmen and merchants gathered for the festival. He didn't seem to have any draft animals. Perhaps he had merely appeared out of the air, but in the first light of day he opened his shutters and his door, and hung out a sign with birds and beasts painted on it in bright colors.

Perhaps he had come solely for the Lady Nestra, a miracle shaped by the Guardian from the fleeting traces of holiness that lingered over the Bones. But by mid-morning a fat, mustachioed jester had entered the wagon, then come out again with a white monkey that laughed at his jokes. And a poet entered, and left with something like a peacock that sang in an exquisite, half-human voice; and a girl-child bore away a large-eared ball of red fur which listened to her every secret.

Perhaps the Shaper came for these people too, and many more. Or, perhaps, even the Guardian did not know of his presence, or what the wine of vision would reveal to the Lady Nestra. No one can ever know, for all things are uncertain in the time of the death of the Goddess.

* * * *

The Lady Nestra wept softly the following night, as she placed the silver bowl on her marble writing-table. Slowly she poured the dark wine into the bowl, obscuring her husband's image, all the whole reciting a rhyme, every stanza of which ended with the name of the man she had loved and lost. She added the powder from the ivory box, while her maid went about the room, extinguishing candles one by one.

She stirred the wine with a silver rod. The pale grey powder swirled in the center. Then, as the last candle was snuffed out, the wine began to glow a deep red, the swirling mass dark against it.

She called her maid over. The woman's face was a pale oval in the faint light, her eyes wide with astonishment and even dread.

"Rilla, what do you see?"

"Only the magic light, Lady."

"Then leave me," Nestra said. "This thing is not for you. Go and wait outside the door."

The maid curtseyed and went. Torches flickered in the corridor outside, and the light from the bowl diminished as the door opened, then brightened again when it was closed.

Lady Nestra leaned low, watching intently as the mass of dust became a solid disc. Now the bright fluid swirled around it, like clouds around the eye of a storm.

She spoke words in a secret tongue, and points of light appeared in the dark circle. She spoke again, and they were stars, and she was looking through the silver bowl into the night sky.

Something was moving there, in the darkness. Wings passed before the stars, and something darker than the sky took shape, a great bird flapping slowly across the star field.

"I am here," Lady Nestra whispered. "If you are the one I seek, come to me."

The thing came. For an instant she shared its vision, and

saw Ai Hanlo whirling, rushing up at her, and she recognized the wall of the Inner City and the great, golden dome of the Guardian's palace. Then the view narrowed, and the bird was hovering outside a shuttered window, above a small garden.

She looked up and listened to the wings flapping and scratching against the shuttered window of her room. But she did not rise from where she sat by the table.

A voice came from without, first a confused babbling, like some animal's attempt to imitate human speech. Then the voice softened, and said very distinctly, "Beloved." And finally it said, "Dearest Nestra, it is I, Caradhas."

She peered into the bowl once more. The bird was still there, but it drew nearer, and she could see that it had the face of a young man with pale skin and dark hair. It was the face of Caradhas.

Therefore she got up, taking the bowl in her hands with desperate care. Still the wings scraped and fluttered outside the window.

"Now guide me," she said, speaking into the bowl.

Behind her, metal creaked. She turned around suddenly, the gasped with terror, afraid she had spilled the contents of the bowl. But the image merely rippled.

She looked for the source of the sound and saw a tapestry billowing in the darkness from a draft, pressing against her husband's armor where it stood in a corner. The sword scraped against the thigh piece.

For an instant she had hoped—

But that was not the way of this magic. In the bowl, the bird was rising out of the garden outside her window, drifting on the air over the roofs and battlements and tangled lanes of the holy city.

"Rilla, come here at once."

The maid re-entered, reverent with awe when she saw her mistress standing there with the glowing bowl.

"Lady?"

"Did you hear it? At the window?"

"No, Lady. Nothing."

"But I heard it," said Nestra. "We must go. I am sure this time."

The maid reached for the black cloak Nestra always wore, but her mistress shook her head and indicated another which hung on the peg beside the black one, but was never worn. It was blue and red, embroidered in threads of many colors against the background of a gold circle, showing the double aspect of the Goddess, bright and dark, one figure astride a dolphin, with the sun in her hand, and the other holding a tree and wearing a crown of stars. It was the cloak her husband had worn to the battle of the Heshite Plain.

Rilla led her mistress out of her room, gently guiding her by the arm down a flight of stairs, across a common hall where a few late diners and their servants looked on in silence as Nestra passed with the bowl of Seeing, and out into the night. All the while the Lady never took her eyes off the image, but merely described what she saw to her maid, and allowed herself to be led. When they came to the gate leading out of the inner city, into the lower or outer city, the guards there did not question her, for they saw the bowl and recognized that this thing was of the Goddess.

Nestra followed the bird, and was led by Rilla, through many districts where few ladies would venture alone at night, but they were not molested. So, in time, she came to the wagon of the Shaper of Animals. She paused then, and the image of the bird suddenly vanished. The bowl shone with pure white light, brighter than a lantern. All around, campfires burned low and wagons and tents were dark. Loud snoring came from a window overlooking the yard. Farther away, a dog barked.

The Shaper's wagon was dark and silent, but she approached it confidently, her footsteps scraping gently on the paving stones. It was only as she placed her foot on the first of three steps below the door that lights came on in the windows, slowly, like the opening eyes of a great beast lazily rousing itself from sleep.

Rilla gave a little cry and shrank back.

"If you wish to wait outside, you may," Nestra said. The door of the wagon swung slowly outward of its own accord. She entered, holding the bowl gingerly. She was not aware of her maid following her.

The inside of the wagon seemed far larger than the outside, half-illuminated by the light from her bowl. Shadows flickered. She had the impression of a deep forest and of thick vines and leaves that gleamed with a touch of gold, but her eyes somehow couldn't define anything. The whole place was like a rippling reflection by moonlight, and again, it seemed alive, as if every part were an outgrowth of every other part; and the very darkness sighed and shifted.

She turned to her left, then to her right, trying to see by the light of her bowl. Then a lamp rose in the center of the room, seeming to float in the air. It was a heavy, silver thing, like the head of a horse, open-mouthed, with fire in its teeth. By this light she saw, in the back of the wagon, shelves of bottles with things floating in them, but she had no chance to examine them closely.

The Shaper of Animals stood up in the darkness, behind the horse-head lamp. His face was long and pale, his beard silver, and he wore a silver robe; but his huge, hunched shoulders were not like those of a man, and he did not move as a man would on two legs. Beyond that, Nestra could not define his strangeness. When he shifted his great bulk, there was a sound half like leaves rustling, half like the tinkling of coins.

"You are the Lady Nestra, wife of the Lord Caradhas," the Shaper said in a gentle voice.

"I am."

"Give me the bowl."

She gave it to him, then tried to snatch it back.

"Wait!"

He ignored her and calmly raised the bowl to his lips. She watched bewildered as he slowly drank the contents. After a long, silent pause, he handed the bowl back to her.

"You do not need this anymore," he said. "It has served its

purpose."

"I saw in it—"

"You saw in it what you wished to see, what you needed with the deepest yearnings of your heart to see. Therefore you have come to me, for it is my profession to provide people with what they truly want."

She swayed. She thought she might faint. He motioned her to a chair. She hadn't noticed any chair before, but there was one. She sat, nervously running her hands over the armrests. They felt like mere polished wood.

"*Can it be?* Truly?" She could not find the words to say any more, for all her mind screamed her husband's name. She sat there, trembling, drenched in cold sweat.

"Lady, by my art I shape animals, causing each one to be the perfect companion for each individual person. Each of my creations is unique, as each customer is."

She stiffened. "A pet? You mean the perfect lapdog? I don't need a *pet*." She put up a brave front, but she was more frightened than angry.

He spoke to her soothingly, like a parent to a pouting child. "I assure you, Lady. It will be far more than a pet. Consider this: you peered into the night with your magic, seeking the one thing which might end your sorrow, and you found me. Has your magic, which is of the Goddess, misled you?"

"It cannot," she said weakly.

"Then it is more than a pet I offer you."

She took off three rings from her fingers and tossed them toward the Shaper. She didn't hear them hit the floor.

"You require a fee. Will these do?" He did not even glance down.

"As you say, Lady."

"Very well then. Perform your art."

He looked at her. Their eyes met, and for an instant she felt utterly naked before him, as if he could see everything that was in her mind, and understood her innermost fears and desires more than she did. She had never felt so helpless, not even on that first day, when her husband's horse had come back riderless. She covered her face with her hand and leaned forward, weeping, almost tumbling out of the chair.

"Perform your art!"

"Lady, I have performed it."

Something fluttered faintly. She looked up. The Shaper was before her, holding a cage covered with black cloth.

"Take this," he said, guiding her hand as her fingers grasped the silver handle. "In three nights, sorrow no more. But, whatever else you do, never remove the cloth before the time, nor allow anyone else to remove it, even for an instant."

She hefted the cage. Whatever was inside weighed no more than a few ounces. Something hopped and, again, fluttered. She was sure it was a bird. But it made a sound that was not at all birdlike, more like a child humming.

"Do you understand my instructions, Lady?"

"Yes."

"Go then, and may you find peace."

She left, and as soon as her foot was off the bottom step outside, all the windows of the wagon faded into darkness. Rilla was waiting for her. Without a word, she handed the silver bowl to the maid and covered the cage with her husband's cloak. She and Rilla made their way through the empty streets to the gate of the inner city, where they were once more allowed to pass without question.

It was the hour before dawn.

* * * *

When she reached her chamber, Lady Nestra carefully placed the covered cage on the table, then fell down exhausted and slept through the day. She dreamed of her husband then. She saw him as he had been on the day he rode to his death, tall in his gleaming armor, mounted on a white stallion, alternately waving to her and giving orders to the troops, while pennons flapped around him and a crowd of the common people shouted his name. She had been so proud that day as she stood on a little balcony above the crowd, in view of all, the greatest lady of the land.

Now the whole scene was repeated in her dream, so vividly that she could feel the sun through her heavy, stiff garments and smell the sweat of the horses and the dust rising in the air. But the sounds faded suddenly, as the sounds of revelry from within a tavern fade when the shutters are closed. Pennons continued to flap, but their motion was as silent as the drifting of clouds. The voices of the people were no more than a faint murmur on the wind.

It was then that Caradhas turned around in his saddle and said, "Wait for me but a little longer."

She awoke with a cry. Rilla was standing over her. She bade the servant sit beside her on the bed, and the two women embraced. Nestra wept, and haltingly told of what she had dreamed.

"Wait for me but a little longer," came the voice again. Nestra screamed, broke free of Rilla's arms, and searched about the room frantically, pulling side curtains and tapestries, opening closets and trunks. She had heard the voice clearly and distinctly, and she knew she was no longer dreaming.

Then she stared at the covered cage atop the marble table, and stood still, covering her mouth with her hand.

"Lady?" said Rilla. "What is it? Are you well?"

"Didn't you *hear* it?"

"No, Lady. I heard nothing."

And Lady Nestra replied, in the same tone she had used before, "This thing is not for you."

Rilla got up and reached for the cloth covering of the cage.

"*Do not!* Upon your life, do not touch it!"

The maid drew away, as if she had been reaching for a cobra. "Shall I leave you, Lady?"

"No," Nestra said gently. "I do not mean to be harsh. I am not angry with you. Come here and sit with me for a while. My husband is coming back. It is the excitement. It sets me on edge.

He is coming soon."

"As you say, Lady."

* * * *

Throughout the rest of the day and into the evening, Lady Nestra directed Rilla and her other servants to make the chamber ready. What had been plain before was now gorgeously ornamented. Rare tapestries were hung. The finest carpets covered the floor. The white marble table had been replaced by one of porphyry, and on it was placed a decanter of the finest wine, and two cups. The cage remained, covered with black cloth.

And Lady Nestra still wore the black gown of mourning.

"I will change it when he comes," she said.

Her servants answered politely when she addressed them, but otherwise retreated into their work. She could tell they all thought her mad. She laughed aloud at the thought, then sobbed as she felt a pang of doubt. Rilla turned to her, alarmed. Nestra sat down on the bed and sighed.

"I am not completely unhinged yet. Be patient with me."

"Yes, Lady."

The whole matter did not bear close examination. All this was because of a dream, a voice, and something in a cage, which she had not seen—

She put the thought aside, forcing herself to hope. Around her, the servants steadfastly ignored her laughter, her tears, and then her silence.

As the darkness of the second night came, she sat alone in a room like the throne room of a king. All through the night she spoke with her husband. She listened carefully, her ear to the covering-cloth of the cage. At first there was only hopping and fluttering within, but then all motion stopped, and the voice came which she could mistake for no other.

"Beloved, I am very near. Before another night has passed, you shall see me with your eyes."

She sat on the edge of the bed, her hands clasped tightly

together, as if each would restrain the other. More than anything else, she wanted to tear aside the covering and look on the miracle that was taking shape within the cage. That voice alone overwhelmed any possible skepticism. She merely wanted to *see*. But the Shaper's warning came back to her, and she did not touch the covering.

The conversation continued for a while, touching on pleasant things, shared memories from their past, from childhood, even from their wedding night. Near to dawn she leaned back on the bed and fell asleep, and dreamed that Caradhas was sitting beside her, softly humming a song they both knew from long ago, combing her long hair as he did. His armor was draped over a chair behind him, as if he had just returned from the wars. Outside, very far away and muted, multitudes shouted to celebrate the victory.

Again she slept through much of the day, and when she awoke, she was humming the song. She ran her hand through her hair and was quietly pleased to find her comb where Caradhas had left it.

* * * *

As the evening of the third day approached, she summoned Rilla once more and told her, "Lay out my finest, brightest gown. It is spring. The festival is very pleasant. My husband and I will go out into it."

The maid was trembling as she laid out the gown. Nestra said to her, "You think I'm mad, don't you?"

Rilla was struggling to hold back her tears. "Lady, it's just that…please, do not be angry with me.…You have always been good to me. I know you are a good person. I want…to be able to believe everything you say. But you see things I do not see. You hear things I do not hear. And now…I don't know what to think anymore."

Nestra took her gently by the hand and said, "Just believe me this once, for a few hours yet. Go now. Very soon, you shall see and you shall hear and everything will be very easy to understand."

"Thank you, Lady," Rilla said. She hurried from the room.

The shadows deepened and wavered in the candlelight. Lady Nestra sat alone in the room, listening to the sounds of the festival beyond the shuttered window, fingering the bright gown, never taking her eyes off the covered cage.

For a long time, there was no voice, no sound from beneath the cloth, and she sat, watching and waiting, for the first time unsure of what she was expecting to come out of this little cage which was no more than two hands high. But she did not think about it very much. She merely trusted what she had already dreamed and heard, and she passed into a kind of reverie, in which there was no sound at all. The world beyond the shutters faded away. She could hear one of the candles sputtering and hissing as it burned down into the holder.

Then there came another sound, like a footstep. It was inside the room. She couldn't tell where. It seemed behind her, perhaps by the window. But she did not get up. She did not turn around. She merely waited, her mind feverish with joy and anticipation.

Clothing rustled. A shoe scraped on bare floor, then was muffled by carpet.

Nothing stirred within the cage.

"Beloved Nestra." The voice came from behind her.

She let out a startled cry, almost a scream, and lunged for the cage, ripping off the cover. Then she stood, terrified at what she had done, ready to die as she saw that the cage was empty. It was a flimsy thing, the wire bars widely spaced. The little door was missing. Nothing could have ever been imprisoned in it.

"Beloved Nestra, here I am. Turn around."

A hand touched her shoulder, and she turned around, letting the black covering fall to the floor.

Caradhas held her in his arms, unchanged since the day she had last seen him, for all that he wore no armor. She glanced over her shoulder once. The armor was still standing in the corner.

"No, here I am," he said, and he kissed her and held her very tight, as no ghost or phantom could.

* * * *

They spoke of many things. They shared the rare wine from the decanter. Once they danced to music they could only hear as they imagined it, and she said, "No, stop; this is foolish."

"Let us be fools then," he said. "You are the greatest lady in the land. Who is to stop you?"

Much later, as they lay side-by-side in the bed, she knew that she had never been as happy as she was at this moment. She wanted time to stop, here, now, and linger forever. She did not want to go on to mere living, day-to-day. She wanted to be suspended, like a dragonfly in clearest amber.

Gray dawn showed in the crack between the shutters.

Somewhere, beyond the garden outside, on the battlements of the inner city, a soldier sounded the long, deep blast which heralded the new day.

Caradhas stirred beside her.

"I have been thinking," she said.

"Do not think. Do not question. Merely accept what your senses tell you. Live in this perfect moment."

She turned to him, startled at how he seemed to know her very thoughts.

"But I must. What will we do tomorrow, and the next day, and the next? How can you have truly returned?"

"Through the art of the Shaper, you see what you see, you hear what you hear. Is this not enough?"

"No. What happens next?"

"For me," he said, "nothing. For you, whatever it is will happen to you alone."

She had been told once that when a warrior receives a terrible wound in battle, sometimes it is like a light blow at first. The pain does not come at once, and he still may perform one more deed in the brief interval left to him.

In the brief interval, she was able to say, "I do not hear you."

"You hear, you see, you feel," he said. "All these are true things. It is also true that this morning I shall leave you forever. Even the Shaper cannot sustain this miracle forever. That is why I tell you to live only in this moment, before it passes."

She screamed loud and long. She wriggled from his grasp and crawled out of the bed, dragging her black gown with her, blundering into the table. The wire cage clattered onto the floor.

"You are not my husband!"

She got to her feet and backed away from the bed, clutching the gown in front of her. He rose slowly, taking up a little lamp from the nightstand. His face and chest gleamed almost golden in the faint light.

"I am as you see me."

"*What* are you? You're something created by his horrible magic."

"I am what you most wanted. The Shaper saw that in your mind."

"No! No! No!" She ran to the suit of armor in the corner, drew out the sword, tried to wield it, dropped her gown, stooped to cover herself, dropped the sword.

He stood over her. He set down the lamp and took her hands in his own very solid, warm hands. They stood in silence. After a moment he let go, picked up her gown, and wrapped it about her gently.

"This is a thing you must understand. The Shaper saw your need. Therefore he created me."

"What *are* you?"

"This flesh is not the flesh the mother of Caradhas bore in her womb, if that is what you mean. But my words are his words, and my thoughts are his thoughts. My memories of you are his memories."

"How?"

"Some were drawn out of your memory. You are the true shaper. More than that, the rest of the mystery, comes from the age when the Goddess was yet living, and may not be understood."

"What is the Shaper?" she said, barely able to form the words. "Is he a god?"

"I think the he too is one shaped, out of need. More than that is part of the mystery."

"But you are *not* my husband. This is all a fraud, an illusion. It does not make me content. No, it tears open the wound. Now I am more wretched than ever. I should have known it was impossible. The dead do not return."

"Dearest Nestra, this flesh is not your husband's flesh, but in me his mind has been recreated. His thoughts have returned. The most terrible thing about his death for you was that he went away suddenly, unexpectedly. There was so much the two of you had to say. He had no chance to say goodbye. Now, in a way, he does. My words are his words. Will you listen to them, and hear what you hear, and accept them merely as words?"

She broke away from him, ran over to the bed, and sat down, huddling in her black robe.

"I feel like I want to die," she said. "Then I will be with Caradhas."

The lamp went out. He spoke from the darkness.

"These are the words of your husband, Caradhas: I cannot return to you. I merely ask that you remember me, but grieve no longer. You have mourned for ten years, and still you are young. Your life is before you. You are twenty-nine. I want you to live. Partake of the present and look to the future. Remember me, but go on: Do not ask how or why, but believe that it is truly Caradhas who says this to you."

"I truly believe you," she said.

She wept for a long time, softly, and was vaguely aware that the shutters opened of their own accord. Something whirred by her and out the window, small, fluttering, like a sparrow. As the day brightened, she ceased her weeping, and looked up, and saw that she was alone in the room.

A little while later Rilla came timidly in and found her sitting on the edge of the bed, holding the empty cage in her hands.

* * * *

Lady Nestra slept most of the day, and slept the night alone, but on the following morning she rose, put on her bright gown and her jewelry, called her women together, and went with them, out into the great festival of the City of the Goddess.

THREE BROTHERS

The chamber in which the three brothers dwelt was round, like a pendant worn on the necklace of a god. It was golden without and within, and had triangular windows set in the sides, through which the brothers could gaze into the darkness which is outside the flow of time, and called Eternity. Sometimes the chamber swayed, and the glowing crystals of the chandelier that hung from the ceiling rattled.

They rattled.

Zon, the eldest of the three, if age could mean anything in their state, looked up impassively.

Thandos, the middle brother, sighed but did not speak.

As light and shadow flickered over the curved walls of the chamber, Kudasduin, the youngest, said, "I am weary. I want to go into Time again."

"You are foolish," said Zon.

"You will take the years on your shoulders like a burden," said Thandos. "They will break you."

"No, they will be as light as dust. I am not afraid."

"Why?" said Thandos.

"Why do you want to go?" said Zon.

"There is a longing within me, an emptiness which must be filled."

Zon, Thandos, and Kudasduin, three master magicians of a race of master magicians, who had escaped age and death in their time chamber so long before that not even they recalled their origin, did not argue among themselves. They were, in a sense, three aspects of a single mind. When one of them had a thought, all felt it and were altered, even as a river is altered, however subtly, when a stream flows into it.

They sat down at the controls of their chamber, in chairs of living metal which flowed and rippled and hardened again to embrace them. Their hands played over levers and globes of silver and of brass, of jade and of carven bone.

The chamber seemed to dip. The crystals stopped rattling.

Zon raised a mask to his face and looked through it, into Time. He saw the millennia in a continuous strip, light and dark, and he searched for a place where the fabric of continuity was weak, where the time chamber could enter in.

He found one in the time of the death of the Goddess, when the Earth rolled blindly through the universe with no hand to guide it. All things were in disorder then, and much was possible that would not have been in any other age. The ribbon of years was worn thin, and the Chamber could pass through.

It came to rest in a field.

Thandos rose and opened the door. All of them felt a prickling, a chill as duration flowed in and touched them.

"I will look outside," he said. "There will be nothing of interest to see. When we know this, we can depart."

He left, closing the door after him. Zon and Kudasduin waited. Through the windows they saw only a flickering light, like an aurora.

* * * *

When Thandos returned, he was subtly changed. His brothers sensed it immediately, but they could not define the manner. Perhaps there was another wrinkle on his face, perhaps a touch of silver in his beard.

He sat down, gasping for breath, as if he had run a long way. His brothers leaned over him. "Well? What did you see?"

"A fire. A child running in a field. Nothing of interest."

Thandos and Zon looked at Kudasduin. There was a moment

of silence.

"I have to go," the youngest brother said.

"I do not understand why," said Thandos.

"Perhaps when I return, you shall."

"Go then," said Zon. "Return, and we shall see."

* * * *

First Kudasduin raised a trapdoor in the floor of the chamber, and he and his brothers descended into a cramped space, where they gathered around a stone font. Within, a blue fluid glowed, the light of it illuminating their faces. This was the very stuff of Eternity itself, which powered the chamber and kept it inviolate.

With a pair of tongs, Kudasduin lowered a glass bottle into the font, then took it out and stoppered it. The fluid did not ripple, nor was it diminished.

"If I venture deep into Time," he said, "I will need this to get back."

"Go only to the edge, as I did," said Thandos. "Look but briefly, then return."

"I will know when to return," Kudasduin said. He left the chamber.

* * * *

The auroral light was the interface, where the chamber intruded into the world. Kudasduin walked through it as forces wrenched him, as the flow of moment into moment settled on him, indeed, like a burden. His limbs were heavy. He struggled to breathe.

But he was not afraid. These were new sensations, the first he had known in many aeons. He was, above all, a scholar, one who set out to study all things, even what it felt like to pass from Eternity into Time.

He was entranced at the feel of wind on his face, at the soft soil beneath his feet. He was slowly beginning to remember what it had been like to live in the world; before he and his brothers had set out in the chamber.

He had forgotten so much, he knew. Dazed, confused, he wandered until the pain slowly faded, and he was no longer an intruder into the time flow, but part of it. He looked up at the night sky and saw the stars, the constellations different from any he had ever known. The stars, the darkness, the chill air, the cry of a night bird all combined to bring him into a kind of ecstasy.

He came to a rolling plain, where naked ground showed between patches of snow. He stood on a rise of land and looked into the distance.

There was a fire, as his brother had reported, lurid and flickering, filling the horizon, outlining jagged shapes.

Dark, huddled figures streamed away from the flames, into the night.

And, as his brother had reported, a girl child clad in a tattered white gown ran across a field, waving her arms, her long, pale hair streaming behind.

Kudasduin hurried toward her, wondering what this could mean.

The child saw him and ran in his direction, shouting something he could not make out.

A horseman in black, scaled armor followed her, his lance lowered.

She almost reached Kudasduin. He saw the hopeless terror on her face. Remembrances stirred.

Fear was another thing he had experienced long before, when he had lived in the world.

"Help me! Help me!"

He noted all this with interest. He stood and stared, failing to understand.

The lance caught the girl between the shoulders and flung her off her feet, but it fouled in the tangle of her clothing, and the horseman collided with Kudasduin as he dragged the corpse along awkwardly, trying to shake the weapon loose. The magician was hurled aside. Then the lance came free. The horse reared, and the rider swung the lance like a club, clipping Kudasduin on the side of the head.

He caught a glance of a face between slits in a dark helmet, contorted with hatred. Then he hit the earth hard and lay still, stunned. He heard the horseman thunder off, and managed to roll painfully to one side. Beyond the corpse of the child, several cavalrymen met, slowing to a trot, circling, while one of them stood up in his stirrups, waved a gleaming sword over his head, and shouted, "Kill them all! Let no one escape!"

They galloped off across the snow, toward a dark stream of refugees.

Kudasduin lay still for a while, his head throbbing. Blood was wet on his face. He regarded the burning city in the distance. Then, quite nearby, there was a shriek, followed by incoherent babblings and deep sobs. He got to his feet unsteadily, and beheld a woman kneeling over the dead child, tearing at her hair, swaying back and forth.

"My baby…they've killed my baby…" Another child, a boy much smaller than the girl, tugged at his mother's arm as Kudasduin approached.

She looked up, then rose to run, but only sat down again, resigned, hopeless, holding her son in her arms.

Kudasduin stood before her and said nothing, slowly beginning to comprehend, as more and more feelings and memories returned to him. There was a sense of urgency. He wanted to be away from there and thought of returning to the time chamber right then, of running toward the auroral light which only he could see.

He took the bottle of fluid out, held it up, and considered it. The glow was a brilliant blue, like a beacon.

Then he put it away. He hesitated. He did not want to leave the woman and the boy. He wasn't sure why.

"You—you," the woman gasped. "You're not one of them. You're not! Say you won't kill us!"

She lunged forward, grabbed him by the knees, and knelt

there, hugging him, weeping.

"They're all around. They're killing every one. We can't get away."

"I will help you," Kudasduin said slowly.

She looked up into his face, her expression one of wild exaltation.

"Yes! Yes! You are a god, or a Power, or spirit or something! Help us! Take us away from here!"

"You'll have to let go of my legs first."

She let go as if she had been embracing a hot iron.

He reached down and took her gently by the hand, helping her to her feet. The boy stared at him with wide eyes, then yanked on his mother's coat and pointed.

"Mommy, look."

A dozen horsemen had broken off from a column and were thundering toward them, black against the snow, invisible as they crossed bare mud.

Something snapped inside Kudasduin, bringing him fully awake, fully aware, as if he had suddenly come to life and realized how dear life was. He understood that he was a part of what was going on, not a detached observer.

He hauled the boy up over his shoulder and ran, dragging the woman by the hand. There was a grove of trees ahead, in a little valley. He made for them, forgetting all else, actually afraid, his breath labored, his legs pumping, his boots splashing through mud and slush. The horsemen bore down on them.

Then they were among the trees, scrambling through underbrush. Behind them, the horsemen plunged into the forest. There were shouts from every direction. A horse shrieked and reared up, and a cursing rider crashed through snapping branches. The three fugitives huddled beneath an uprooted tree. A cavalryman leapt over them. Another disappeared behind the huge clod of soil that had come up with the tree's roots.

After a while, the sounds of pursuit were farther off. When they had faded altogether, the pocket of forest seemed a little world unto itself, dark, quiet, bitterly cold. Kudasduin could not hear the sounds of slaughter. A rise of land hid the light from the burning city.

The three of them came to a hollow, where a stream flowed between rocks. They fell down, exhausted, and drank. The water was so cold it burned. They huddled together throughout the night. The ground hardened. The stream froze. A wind sent ice and twigs clattering down from the treetops.

The boy slept in his mother's arms, the woman with her head in Kudasduin's lap. He draped his cloak over her, and hid his hands up his sleeves. He sat awake for hours, pondering, remembering what it meant to be human. At times he was afraid, at times disgusted, in the end filled with hope.

* * * *

The morning sky was grey between the trees when the woman stirred. Kudasduin awoke.

"Thank you for helping us. Who are you? How did you come here? Are you a magician?"

She sat up beside him, cradling her still sleeping son in her lap. Her hair was tangled and matted, her face smeared with soot, and her clothing reduced to muddy tatters, but still he could tell that she was beautiful. It came to him what it meant for a woman to be beautiful.

She looked at him expectantly.

He smiled. "I can hardly answer so many questions at once. I am called Kudasduin. I am a scholar. Yes, I am learned in those arts which are called magical. I came here…from very far away, farther away than you can possibly imagine."

"Can you take us there?"

Kudasduin felt the bottle in his pocket. He said nothing. Above them, wind rattled the branches. The smell of wet, burnt wood was in the air.

After a while, he asked her, "What of yourself?"

"There is not much to say. My name is Sansha, My boy is Evorad. My girl is dead. So is my husband. He died when they broke into the city. They came suddenly in the night. What else can I tell you? I was a weaver, but now I am nothing. Everyone, everything in my life is gone, except my boy."

"These soldiers, who are they?"

She looked at him in utter bewilderment. "Please," he said. "I am from very far away. I do not know."

"But—but, how can anyone not have heard of Etash Wesa?"

"I have not heard of him."

"I'm almost afraid to speak his name."

"Tell me what you can."

Haltingly she told him of Etash Wesa, a monster who had once been a man, and was now somehow removed from the physical world. Etash Wesa began to fill the dreams of a certain king, tormenting him night after night, manifesting himself by day in horrible ways, until the king was driven mad, and was wholly the instrument of Etash Wesa, who sent the king's armies forth to ravage all the lands, to march on Ai Hanlo, the holiest of cities, and seize the very bones of the Goddess which lie there. Etash Wesa wanted to become a god of darkness and terror and death.

Kudasduin remembered something more from his past. He remembered how one could be corrupted by the power of his arts. He knew the dangers, the temptations, and he wondered if he and his brothers had not been changed, very subtly, until they were less human than Etash Wesa.

"Can this…magician…be stopped?"

"Maybe the Guardian of the Bones can stop him. I don't know. In the meantime people suffer and die."

"You do not have to die," Kudasduin said with firm certainty. He noted her puzzled expression.

The boy woke up. "Mother?"

"Hush. It's all right."

The boy was still. He did not complain about the cold, or hunger. Kudasduin cared for this woman and this boy. He understood this clearly now.

"If we can get across the fields," Sansha said, "and into the greater forest, before the day gets too bright, then we'll be safe. We can't stay here. They'll find us before long."

She got to her feet. He started to rise, then paused.

She screamed.

Underbrush crashed all around. There were triumphant shouts. A dozen warriors rode down on them. He held Sansha and the boy to himself, turned this way and that, and saw that there was no escape.

"Die! Die!" the horsemen shouted.

Quite calmly, deliberately, Kudasduin the magician took out the glass bottle he had filled from the font in the time chamber, opened it, and poured a measured quantity of fluid onto the ground.

There was a flash of blinding blue light.

They were falling. There was no impact, only a cessation of motion.

* * * *

Kudasduin was the first to regain consciousness. He sat up and found himself in the same hollow by the stream. Sansha and Evorad lay beside him.

The horsemen were gone. The whole place had changed in a thousand different ways he couldn't define. The air was fresh and warm.

Sansha awoke and shook her son awake, then looked around, wide-eyed in wonder. She grabbed a nearby branch and studied it intently, as if every leaf were a marvel.

All the trees had leaves on them. They shut out the sky. Birds sang in the branches.

Sansha's amazement only increased. Kudasduin picked up a cavalryman's spear. The rusted head fell from the rotten shaft.

"How—?" the woman whispered. "What did you do?"

"I cannot tell you how. I moved us forward in time a little ways, until our enemies were no longer around us."

"How far forward?"

"Does it matter? In Eternity, all times are the same."

When they ventured out of the woods and looked over the plain, there were no marauding armies. The grasslands were clear of corpses. In the distance, where the city had been, were only low, grassy mounds. They examined the ruins. The tumbled stones were green with years. Birds nested in the broken shells of houses. There was a monument, a statue broken off at the ankles so that only the feet remained. The inscription on the base was nearly worn smooth.

"We are alone," Sansha said. "I think I understand you. You are an exile. So are we all, now."

For a long time he said nothing, and then he asked her, "What shall we do?"

"Don't you know?" she said bitterly, but more in sorrow than in anger. "You're the magician. You know everything."

"No. Please understand. I am a stranger here. I don't know everything. I have come to learn many things. Guide me, will you?"

So they set forth, and wandered through many lands. Nowhere did they encounter anyone Sansha knew. Nowhere did they hear the name of Etash Wesa spoken, and when once, at an inn, Kudasduin asked about him, the hearers made signs and hurried away, leaving them alone in the room. They left that town quickly. The world was apparently free of the armies of the possessed king, but Etash Wesa was remembered.

"It is all one in Eternity," Kudasduin said, and Sansha did not seem to understand what he meant. As he felt the experience of the days, the texture of time, of eating and sleeping and walking, of mingling with strange people; as the sights and sounds of the ancient Earth settled on him and changed him even as a river is changed by the streams flowing into it, he became less sure of what he meant himself.

"I have had a dream," he announced one morning as they sat at breakfast around a campfire by the side of a road. "I dreamed I had two brothers, and they were waiting for me, still as statues in a round, golden room. I dreamed they were frozen outside of

Time, enduring forever, alive but not alive. They moved very slowly inside their room so that in the centuries of my dream I saw one of them blink an eye and the other raise his hand, and that was all. But I felt for certain that they wanted me to go to them."

"Will you go?" Sansha asked.

"No. It's just a dream. It's fading now."

They came into Zabortash, the land of the magi, where the full moon ripples in the air of the tropic night, and tall birds with glowing eyes wade in the sluggish rivers and call out with the voices of men. There Kudasduin had much converse with scholars, even with the grand magi, and once or twice with the wading birds, which were rumored to live for centuries and to have overheard much from the ghosts that whispered in the swamps. He was as much a mystery to the magi as they to him. About his conversations with the birds, he said nothing. All this while Sansha earned money for them by weaving common cloth, and also those special fibers known to the Zabortashis, which are made out of dreams.

Kudasduin learned much, and he made copious notes, but still he was without understanding, and he knew that his mission into Time was not yet over.

They ventured north through swamps and forests, along the banks of a great river, until they came to a place called the Edge of the World, where the trees of the jungle grew so thick that they formed a solid barrier, miles high, which shut out the sky.

They began to climb, with Evorad slung on Sansha's back. For months they sojourned in the branches, travelling both vertically and horizontally, never touching earth until they came to the Hanging Land, a tract two miles long and one thick, suspended in the tangle of the treetops. They found a metal citadel there, and were guests of winged philosophers.

And the chief philosopher, a man nearly eight feet tall with spindly legs and arms like rods, whose silken black wings touched either wall of his cell, looked into Kudasduin's soul with a glass, and into his dreams and memories. In the end he said, "You are not as others, and again you are as others. Go where you will and come to the end which the Goddess dreamed for you before she died. Know that she was of Eternity, before she fell into Time and perished, and she could look into the past and future even as you turn your head, to right or left."

Then the philosophers took Kudasduin, Sansha, and Evorad in their arms and bore them up, flying for half a day through the winding ways of the treetops at the World's Edge. In the dim evening they broke through into the clear sky. Below, in the night, the forest looked like a vast black sea, rippling in the wind. They flew horizontally for the full of the night, until they came to solid ground beyond the edge of the trees, and set the three down. They drifted away into the sunrise like a flock of birds.

Sansha was numb with wonders by now, and said nothing, and the boy was still. Kudasduin lay down and dreamed again of his brothers, and in the centuries of his dream each second that his brothers lived through was a year to him. He had no idea how long he had been gone, nor any concern over it.

When he awoke, the dream swiftly faded, and it troubled him no more. But he was indeed troubled by what the philosophers had told him, and by the mystery of the world around him.

* * * *

At last they came to Ai Hanlo, the holiest of cities, where lie the Bones of the Goddess. There the wind from the grave of the Goddess, which is called Fate, clouded Kudasduin's mind even more, until for long periods he completely forgot about Eternity and his two brothers waiting for him in the time chamber. He took Sansha to be his wife and Evorad to be his son. In time they had another son, Evoraduil. Again Sansha worked as a weaver, and Kudasduin consorted with philosophers. All the world was new to him, all the world filled with wonder, and he observed every part of it, and wrote his findings in a great encyclopedia. Before long he was famous as a scholar throughout all the Holy

Empire, but when men praised his wisdom, he said, "No, I am the most ignorant among you. I know and understand so little."

Humility was added to the list of his virtues. Soon students gathered around him, paying rich fees to be instructed. His days were filled.

All the while he kept the stoppered bottle he had brought with him out of Eternity. Before long, he was no longer sure what it contained or what it was for. He wrapped it carefully in a cloth, placed it in a little coffer, and put the coffer in the bottom of a trunk by the foot of his bed.

So the years slipped by, and he lived like other men, even as the winged ones had seemed to prophesy. Then one day he chanced to be in the great square of the city, seated on the edge of the fountain there, lecturing his students, when right in front of him an ancient, feeble man, who seemed to have taken half the morning making his way across the square with the aid of a stick, fell down on the pavement and lay still.

One of the students went over and came back, reporting that the man was dead.

"What caused his death?" Kudasduin asked.

"Merely age," the student said. "The fellow had been around so long it was inevitable."

Kudasduin looked at his own reflection in the water of the fountain. He saw that his hair and beard were white. Suddenly he was afraid. He rose, dismissed his students, and hurried home. But he did not go in. He stood in front of the house, pacing back and forth, wringing his hands, muttering nervously, while memories flooded back. He remembered the time chamber.

He put his ear to the door and heard his wife within, talking to his sons. He couldn't bear to confront them, so he ran away and hid until late that night, when he returned with stealth and, taking the smallest lamp he owned, crept into the bedroom. Careful not to wake Sansha, he unpacked the trunk and got out the stoppered vial. He went from the house as quietly as he had come, then ran through the streets until he came to a small gate, which he knew to be unguarded.

He walked with long strides across the plain, away from Ai Hanlo, toward the distant hills, searching for the auroral light where the time chamber intruded into the world. He wasn't sure where it was. Then he thought of the bottle. Perhaps if he opened it, he would be back in Eternity.

He took it out, and was working the stopper loose when he heard someone running breathlessly toward him.

It was Evorad, now grown to be a man. He put the bottle away.

"My father, where are you going? Why have you left us so secretly? I woke up and followed you. Even now Mother does not know that you are gone."

And Kudasduin cursed his own folly, and felt remorse, and said merely, "It is nothing, I would have come back in the morning. I came out here to study the stars."

The two of them spent the rest of the night gazing at the wheel of heaven. When Kudasduin finally saw a light on the horizon, it was not a sign of the time chamber, but of dawn.

* * * *

"What is death?" he asked his students one day. He had over a hundred of them. They no longer met in the square, but in an academy.

"It is a journey," someone offered.

"I am already on a journey," he replied. "I have come a long, long way. How is death any different?"

"Your present journey is but a prologue, a preparation. You have travelled through all this life, only preparing to depart. The long road is still before you."

"I do not understand."

And this was a great marvel, that the wisest man in the land did not understand.

Later, Kudasduin's granddaughter, Evorad's child, came running to him and said, "Grandmother is dying. Come quickly."

He could not come quickly because his joints were stiff, but, with the aid of a cane, he made his way to Sansha's bedside.

Her face was sunken and lined, her hair a flawless white. She opened her eyes slowly. She spoke in a whisper. He leaned forward to hear.

"I thought you would be late," she said. "I didn't want to leave without seeing you first."

"You're not leaving. There is much to be uncovered. You must help me explore the world yet."

He looked up at the doctor his sons had summoned. The man shook his head sadly and turned away.

"You are always uncovering things, my scholar," Sansha said. "Can you do without one more mystery?"

"You are the mystery. I have not uncovered what it means to live with you, to love you. I have only begun my investigation."

"You will have to fill your encyclopedia with incomplete results, with guesswork."

He wept long and hard. His sons and the doctor left him alone with Sansha.

She coughed once and stopped breathing.

In panic he looked around, wondering what to do. He felt utterly helpless. All his researches, all his knowledge was for nothing if this could happen.

He noticed the trunk at the foot of the bed. He heaved the lid up, tossed aside clothing, books, bags of coins, jewelry, clutter, until he came to the little coffer. He took the bottle from within, pulled out the stopper with his teeth, and hurried to Sansha.

His hands trembling, his face a grim mask, he forced open her mouth, and poured some of the blue fluid down her throat. He had one desperate hope, that her death was still like new-poured wax, not yet hardened. He hesitated but a moment, and even then grew afraid that it was too late, before he stuck his finger into the bottle and touched some of the liquid to his tongue. There was no sensation. It tasted like air.

Time pooled around them, like water dammed up. He saw his wife's spirit, sitting up out of her body, not yet ready to take the first step on its long journey. He coaxed it gently back into her, then, as reversed time began to flow forward again, and the instant of her death arrived once more, he breathed into her mouth.

"Husband," Sansha said a while later, opening her eyes.

Later still he went to the window, held up the bottle in the sunlight, and saw that there was only a single drop of the fluid left.

* * * *

They lived together for many more years, their descendants so numerous they seemed to fill half the city. In time, Kudasduin retired from the academy. He became the subject of fabulous tales, of legend and even myth. He continued to write his encyclopedia. Later volumes were attributed to his successors, or other men of the same name.

"I am just beginning my explorations. Always, I am just beginning. Everything is a prologue," he would say to Sansha.

"What have you discovered so far?"

"That being alive is a mystery. That being human is a mystery. That love is a mystery without an answer."

"That is enough. Must you seek further?"

And he told her again, as he had many times, all he could remember of the time chamber, of his brothers who waited for him frozen in Eternity, of his desire to return to them.

He showed her the bottle. She turned it over in her hand and gave it back.

"You have such wonderful dreams," she said.

He shrugged. "I suppose I do. But I don't know which is the dream. Do I sit in the chamber, dreaming of Time, or am I here, dreaming of Eternity?"

She kissed him gently. "You are here."

* * * *

One night he fell asleep at his desk while writing a page of his encyclopedia. Sansha came to him and touched him on the shoulder.

"Yes, yes, I know. It is very late. But I have so much to do. I have no understanding. My mission is not complete."

"It is too late," she said. "I am leaving now. I came to say goodbye."

"Leaving? You can't. Where are you going?" He looked up and saw that she was dressed in travelling clothes all of black, that her face was lighted from within like a paper lantern. He knew what these things meant and began to weep, begging her to remain behind.

"I have already gone," she said. "You cannot follow."

She receded from view. He heard no footsteps. He hurried after her. She vanished around a corner in the hall. He paused by the bedroom, and he saw her body, clad in a nightgown, leaning half out of the bed in a grotesque position, already stiffening.

Quickly he went to the trunk and got out the bottle. He regarded his wife's corpse for just a second, then ran after her spirit.

When he saw her again, she was far away, along a road. He called out her name. She did not turn. She did not answer.

He felt the fabric of Time rushing against him, holding him back, but he struggled on, like a swimmer against the current. Soon the road was filled with travelers, many dressed as Sansha was, their faces glowing, men and women of every race and nation, all of them walking on their last journey out of the world.

"Sansha! Sansha! Come back! I don't understand yet! There's so much we haven't done!"

He pushed his way through the crowd. He leapt up and saw her across a river of heads and shoulders. He waved and shouted, but she did not turn, and on and on they went, joined at every bend in the road by countless thousands.

At the very last, there was a flickering light ahead, an auroral light. He got out the bottle. He made it to Sansha's side.

"Come with me," he gasped. "Come back. It isn't too late."

She faced him, and, very briefly, she knew him.

"It is too late," she said. Then she walked into the light and was gone.

He was afraid, confused. He did not follow. He stumbled through the crowd and left the road.

He seemed to be standing in a field. He was unutterably weary.

He opened the bottle, and poured the last drop onto his tongue.

* * * *

"You have returned," said Zon.

He was too weak to close the door of the chamber. Thandos closed it.

"I have seen…wonders."

"You are wondrously transformed," said Thandos, regarding Kudasduin's wrinkled face, his silver hair, his bent back and withered limbs.

"I have found a wonder of wonders, a mystery of mysteries, the reason men bear the pain of age and death. All this and more."

"I must have overlooked something," said Thandos. "I must go again, as you did, and see what you saw."

"Yes," said Zon. "It is to be investigated. Go, Thandos, and come back and report. I shall question our brother while you are gone."

Thandos put his hand on the door, then paused. He asked Kudasduin, "What is out there?"

"I…cannot say. All things and nothing. In the end I did not understand it."

"Then I will have to go out and see."

"No!" Kudasduin screamed, lunging at the control panel. His aged heart burst. He was dead in an instant, but his body fell against the lever he had been reaching for.

The time chamber was flung far from the world, into the darkness of the abyss.

COMING OF AGE IN THE CITY OF THE GODDESS

We live in a time of strange and terrible miracles.
—Telechronos

I.

"The Herald of the Goddess came to me last night," Aerin said. "He stood outside my window. I know that's who it was. He'll come back for me tonight."

He was fourteen years old and trying to be very brave. He sat up very straight on the wooden bench in the boot room of the house. Outside, wagons rattled by. Women shouted in hoarse voices. A piper played flat, squealing notes. It was market day in Ai Hanlo.

His sister Mora was a year younger than he. She sat beside him on the cramped bench and spoke in a hushed tone.

"Yes. I saw him too. I thought I heard him call my name as I slept, but of course he didn't, because he lost his voice on the day the Goddess died. But I sat up, and saw him through the crack in the shutters."

"I did too!" said Vaenev, who was ten. He crouched across from them, underneath a shelf.

"You didn't!" hissed Mora.

"I did! I did!" He jumped up, hitting his head on the shelf, which was only a loose board. Boots and shoes tumbled down.

"Be quiet!" said Aerin. "But I did...."

"He's lying," Mora whispered. "He just wants to tag along."

Vaenev made a face and stuck out his tongue.

"I don't know if he did or not," said Aerin. "Nobody can know, except him."

"I did," said Vaenev so softly they couldn't really hear him.

The three of them sat in silence for a while. Vaenev fidgeted with the fallen shoes.

"We'll have to tell Mother and Father," Aerin said finally. He looked into their faces. Mora was clearly frightened. Vaenev was sullen. He didn't show much when he was afraid, Aerin knew. His brother didn't like to seem the youngest. But now, in just one more night, none of them, not even Vaenev, would be children any more.

* * * *

Their mother wept when she heard the news. She set aside her needlework and leaned back in her chair and wept softly for a long time. Aerin's face went red. He didn't know what to do. He felt helpless at the very time he wanted to be strong. He merely watched the tears running down his mother's face.

Mora took her mother by the hand and said gently, "It'll be all right."

"I know. I know. It will be."

Aerin could tell she didn't believe that. Vaenev stared at his feet, flexing his toes. When a servant girl wandered in, their mother calmly told her what had happened.

The girl put her hand to her face, her mouth forming a wide "O."

"All three *at once?*"

"None of your business! Go fetch my husband *right now!*"

The girl ran from the house. and returned a few minutes later with the children's father. He wore an apron, and was covered with flour up to the elbows.

"Aerin, tell him," Mother said.

"We…last night…the Herald came."

Father looked quietly at Aerin, then at Mora, then at Vaenev. "All three of us," Aerin said.

For a time, Father comforted Mother.

"You and I were both Summoned. We both had our Revelations. We're none the worse for it."

"I know," she said, "but still I am afraid. They'll be changed. Will they even know us? What if we lose them completely? Things like that happen. the Goddess is dead. Who's to prevent it?"

"Hush. Nothing will happen to them. They're just growing up. You've been listening to idle gossip."

"There was the little girl of—"

"Hush."

"All three…at once.…"

"It's better that way. It'll all be over at once. Then there will be nothing to worry about."

Father wiped his hands on his apron and addressed the children, almost as if they had just arrived in the room.

"Well. I'll get cleaned up, then we'll go see a priest."

* * * *

The three children were dressed in their very best as their parents led them up narrow streets that were so steep they had steps cut in them. Aerin wore a velvet tunic with a belt of woven gold, Mora a white gown with a sash and shoes embroidered in silver thread. Vaenev's tunic was white and starched. he looked uncomfortable in it.

None of them said anything. Aerin studied the faces of the people they passed. Sometimes he saw a kind of understanding. Many were indifferent, a few awed or afraid. Once an old lady made a sign of good luck, furtively so only he could see it.

It occurred to him that such things must happen every day. He knew that the population of the city was declining, that there were great, abandoned districts, but still there were enough people left that children must be having their Revelations constantly.

He had heard of it. He had seen children led away before. A friend of his had been through it all, but would say nothing about it. Aerin wasn't sure how he had been changed, save that he had become secretive. But all those things were abstractions. It was so different, now that the thing was happening to him.

High up Ai Hanlo Mountain the lower city met the upper in a broad square with a fountain in the middle of it, beneath a wall. Mendicants gathered there, waiting for the times when the priests would appear atop the wall and bless those below. But they never passed beyond that wall. No man of the commons ever did. The inner city was reserved for the Guardian of the Bones of the Goddess and his court.

Still, there was a door in the wall which anyone could open. Father opened it. The five of them crowded through, into a little room that was completely dark when the door was closed again.

Father dropped some coins into a bowl and rang a bell. After a few minutes footsteps came from somewhere in the darkness. A shutter slid back, and they could hear the priest breathing.

"Yes?"

"My children," Father said. "They've seen the Herald of the Goddess, all of them."

"All? How many children do you have?"

To Aerin, the priest's voice sounded old and tired, perhaps a little bored.

"Three, Reverend One."

Mother spoke. Aerin could tell she was trembling. "Is that… bad? That…all three at once, I mean."

"No," the priest said, and now his voice had become friendly and reassuring. "There is nothing wrong with all three at once. When the Goddess was alive, all children who were twelve years old saw the Herald at the same time. It happened every year in the spring. It must have been easier to manage that way. But that was centuries ago, and now that the Goddess is dead, her power is fading. Her Herald still comes, but he comes whenever he will. But still he is the Herald, bringing revelations, and it is all the same. So let us go and prepare."

The priest came out. All of them filed into a little, private courtyard. There he gave each of the children crowns of stiff cloth, half black and half white, with black ribbons hanging from the white side and white from the black, symbolizing, Aerin knew from many recitations, the dual nature of the Goddess.

And then he knew why he was afraid. With the death of the Goddess, her will had been extinguished, but fragments of her power remained, undirected, settling at random. What came to him in the night could be from her evil aspect as readily as from her good. That was the way of things. The world was uncertain.

On the way back to the house, people covered their faces as the crowned children passed. Now everyone who beheld them knew for certain what had happened, and it was bad luck to look on someone on the night of their Revelation.

When they got there, Mother and Father hung black and white ribbons out the windows and placed a wreath on the door.

"We'll be at Grandmother's," Father said. "We'll come for you in the morning. Then we'll celebrate." When the priest wasn't looking, he made a good luck sign for all the children to see. Then he and Mother were gone.

The old priest prepared the ritual meal, and Aerin, Mora, and Vaenev ate: unleavened bread, greens, and water, the diet of an anchorite. When they were done, he said to them, "You three know what a Revelation is, don't you?"

"Yes, Reverend One," they said in unison.

"Good. Then you know that on this night the Herald of the Goddess will bring each of you a message, a separate and different one for each, a fragment of the godhead, even as the Herald is himself such a fragment."

"But Reverend One," said Aerin, "are we not all fragments of the godhead?"

The priest smiled. "You are a bright boy."

"I have studied."

The priest began a long explanation of how all living things emanate, ultimately, from the divine, and how at the end of each cycle of the Earth's long history, when the god or goddess dies, mankind continues for a while like the ripples in a pool after the stone has settled to the bottom, but always diminishing, the world becoming ever more barren, until sometimes there are only a single man and woman remaining, and a single seed, before a new god or goddess is reborn. At the end of time, which cannot be far off, the process will simply stop.

Then the priest noticed that Mora was listening patiently, but with a pained look on her face, and Vaenev was staring at the ceiling.

"In any case," he concluded, "the Herald is an active *thought* of the Goddess, given form by her will, and sent to each of you so that you will learn, in some way, what direction the rest of your lives will take. You will all experience different things. Each experience is private and holy. Therefore you must not speak to one another after you have retired for the night, nor must you ever tell anyone what you have seen. To tell it is to lose it, and to lose it is to wander directionless forever. Do you understand all this?"

"Yes, Reverend One."

"Then I'm sure you understand, but I must ask you anyway: do you understand how terrible a thing it is to lie about a Revelation? If any of you have not truly seen the Herald, you are surely lost. I am required to ask this, and to hear your answers. Have you truly seen the Herald of the Goddess?"

"I have seen him, Reverend One," said Aerin.

"And I," said Mora.

Aerin looked expectantly at Vaenev. Mora was trembling.

"I have, too," said Vaenev.

"Very well, then. I want you to consider how lucky you are. Did you know that not everyone gets a Revelation any more? It happens less frequently every year, as the power of the Goddess fades. And some people don't get them until they're very old, when it's too late. That's why the world is such a confusing place."

Aerin wondered if the priest had ever gotten one, but he dared not ask.

Then the priest blessed them, pressing to the forehead of each a reliquary containing a splinter of a Bone of the Goddess, and he was gone. He left the door open behind him. None of the children rose to close it.

Again, Aerin, Mora, and Vaenev sat in silence for a long time. Mora began to cry. Vaenev took her by the hand.

"Don't be afraid," he said plaintively.

"It's not that. It's…just that tomorrow we'll all be different. We'll never be like we are now, here, together. I don't know how, but we'll change."

Aerin was shocked to find himself wondering what would happen if he simply ran out the open door and kept going.

Then Vaenev had an idea. He got out a game they had played many times before, an affair with dice and colored balls and a carven board. For the last time, as children together, they played it, and when the time came, they left the game out on the table and went upstairs, each into their separate bedrooms, which were lined up along a corridor. Each had a window opening onto a balcony. They opened the shutters, each of them, and leaned out, pausing at the sight of one another. No one spoke. They went back into their darkened rooms and waited.

II.

I am the oldest, Aerin told himself. *I must not be afraid.*

He lay in the darkness, knowing that he was afraid. He prayed silently to the Goddess, even though she was dead, that her fading power might be enough to bring him safely through this night.

He didn't know if he slept. He was too tense to sleep, but after a time he seemed to come back to himself out of a blurry dislocation. Perhaps hours had passed, perhaps only a few minutes.

There was a footstep on the balcony outside. Instantly he was completely awake, his heart thumping. He saw nothing, heard no further sound, but he knew in a manner beyond reason that his time had come.

He rose from his bed.

A board creaked on the balcony.

"I am here," he said weakly. A little dizzy, he walked over to the window. It was intensely dark outside, the night darker and quieter than any night in the city ever could be. He climbed out the window, onto the balcony, groping for the railing. Grasping it, he stood shivering in the frigid air. Beyond was only a void. There was no starry sky. No light burned in any window of the city. There was absolute silence, but for the beating of his own heart and the sound of his own breathing.

He realized with mounting excitement that this darkness, this silence were part of his Revelation.

"I am here," he said again.

A light exploded into being inches from his face. He reeled back, arm up to shield his eyes, passing through the space where the railing should have been. He hunched his body against the expected fall, but only found himself staggering, bent over, on hard pavement.

The light diminished into a kind of torch. The hand that held it was skeletal, naked bone. He saw the face of a skull enveloped in pale white light, burning faintly like a candle, like a half-living thing with flesh of endless fire.

The thing hissed at him. He took a step toward him, and again he recoiled. It wore what had once been a fine gown, fringed with gold, but was now ragged.

"Aerin. Come."

He did not run away. This, too, was part of his vision. He looked around once. He did not see the house. The light of the torch revealed dark windows and ledges of buildings he did not recognize.

"Follow," the torchbearer said, and he followed, along a street to an intersection. Dark, empty houses loomed above them. Shadows flickered. Footsteps echoed. Above, there was only absolute blackness, as if a canopy had been draped over the city or the stars had been extinguished. The way slanted

upward. The street had steps carved in it. Still there was no other light, no other sound. The darkness was like a tunnel. He followed the light of the burning man. Familiar things emerged slowly; a doorstep, a post, a rain barrel, a cart; only to vanish behind in the gloom.

When they came to the great square before the wall of the inner city, the torchbearer stopped. There was another waiting there for them, also bearing a torch in a bony hand. Again there was a skull face covered in gentle flame, flickering softly in the night, but this apparition wore the garments and jewelry of a lady of high birth.

It curtseyed before him. Rings rattled on finger bones.

"I am A-Tanae," it said.

He nodded slightly, unsure of what to do. The name meant something, and then he understood. There were many old stories that began, *In the days of the first Guardian, a thousand years ago, there lived a girl named A-Kenru...or a boy named Ka-Hadin...*but nobody had had names like that in as long a time.

Others came, from every direction, out of every part of the outer city. He saw their torches far away, mere drifting motes in the darkness. Then they were with him, and each skeletal creature introduced itself. Some had ancient names, some modern ones. Each had a face like a skull soaked in alcohol, burning softly. They wore a fantastic array of jewels and sweeping cloaks and peaked caps and satin and gleaming metal and rags. When there were more than a hundred of them, he realized that he was part of a procession, at the heart of a glowing snake that wove through dark streets and coiled before a huge gate beyond which no commoner might ever pass.

For them, the gate swung open and the inner city was revealed, bathed in the same pale light. Flames flickered from every window and doorway, hissing softly, consuming nothing. The pavement itself burned.

Aerin started forward, determined to be unafraid. The flames touched him and he felt nothing, but as they touched the feet of the skeletal company the fire rose up between the empty bones, giving a semblance of glowing flesh. The faces were like lanterns, too pale and insubstantial to be alive, but the distinct faces of individuals, sculpted out of flame. He saw that he was being led by a square-jawed man with a braided beard. A-Tanae was a long-faced lady with a ring through one nostril, as was the custom in ancient times.

They passed through ivory doors outlined in fire, along beautifully decorated corridors that burned blue. The flames were everywhere, the whole inner city one vast phantasm of shaped vapor. The tiniest details, the furnishings of a room, the draperies, even the pens on a writing desk, were things of living light.

At last they emerged into a vast room beneath a golden dome. Here a vast pit of fire burned silently, and the flames were of gold.

Across them, on the other side of the room, the Herald of the Goddess sat on a throne atop a dais. Aerin knew him by his robe of glittering black and silver scales, his peaked hat, his lantern, and his horn. Their eyes met. The Herald was calling him.

For an instant, the boy paused to wonder, and to be a little bit proud: all these mysteries were for him alone, for his long contemplation. The meaning of his vision would not become clear without years of effort. Did it mean he was destined for some greatness?

The Herald set aside his horn and his lantern and rose from the throne. He descended the dais to greet Aerin, then led him back up to the top and stood beside him, making a sweeping gesture with his arm above the fire pit.

As they watched, the torchbearers filed slowly into the pit, each of them merging with the flames, vanishing into shimmering gold and absolute silence.

When they were all gone and Aerin and the Herald stood alone, the Herald spoke, impossibly, for he had no voice, but Aerin heard him nonetheless. The words formed in his mind.

"Look now, and see the meaning and fulfillment of your

vision."

Something rose out of the flames, as vast as a mountain being born, an enormous skull, blackened, with shriveled flesh clinging to it. A neck and shoulders were revealed, as if a monstrous corpse were sitting up.

"Aerin," it said. "Come to me, Aerin. You are mine, Aerin."

Now the boy's courage left him and he screamed and turned away, but the Herald caught him firmly by both shoulders and turned him back again, like a parent directing a reluctant child.

"You must go to her. You are looking on the Goddess as she is now, in death. Your fate and your future are with her."

And Aerin, determined not to be afraid, to set an example for his sister and brother because he was the oldest, determined to follow his vision through to the end; and touched with pride and almost dead with terror, he walked slowly down the steps of the dais and into the fire pit.

The flames clothed him and the flames held him up. He walked through them like a spirit across the surface of a lake.

The mouth of the Goddess gaped wide.

* * * *

It was strange, he realized much later, that he was burning all over but there was no pain.

Fire filled him. He opened his mouth and orange flame billowed out, dazzling his eyes. He stretched out his arms, and columns of fire rose from his upturned palms.

He rose with smoke toward the golden ceiling and drifted through a skylight.

Below, the city appeared as it would on any night, a tapestry of soft lights, lanterns in windows, torches on battlements. Beyond, the river called Endless gleamed silver beneath the full Moon.

There were stars in the sky.

He drifted, still enveloped in fire, until the river was beneath him, and he looked down into the Moon's reflection.

Above, the Moon was full. Below, it was a waning crescent, a tiara worn by a beautiful woman whose flowing black hair sparkled with stars. Her face was, in some way his mind could not grasp, awesome and terrifying beyond anything he had ever known.

Their eyes met. Her memories flooded into him. The past was revealed. In an instant, he knew all the history of the world.

III.

Mora crouched beneath her window, her ear to the wall, listening. The house was silent. She did not know how many hours had passed, but it seemed that most of the night was gone. There was no sound from either of her brothers.

She went from being excited to being afraid to being slightly bored. What if nothing happened? What if she had no vision at all?

There was a footstep on the balcony. She stood up and peered out the window. No one was there. She climbed through and went to the railing, looking out over the familiar streets of the neighborhood, and up the mountainside to the Guardian's golden dome as it gleamed in the moonlight. She turned back toward the house when she heard the footstep again, to her right. She whirled, and by some transition too subtle to follow was no longer in darkness, but in light, no longer on a balcony, but standing in the middle of a grassy field.

She put her hands over her eyes to protect them from the glare, then let them drop when her eyes adjusted.

The sky overhead was blue, the sun bright. Far away, over miles of waving grasses, a mountain rose, covered with the ruins of a city long abandoned. Beyond the city, a broad, muddy river curved through the land.

"Come. Join us," a pleasant voice said.

A youth and a maiden stood beside her, both naked and bronzed with the sun. She saw that she was naked, too, but very pale. The sun and the warm air felt good on her skin. She walked along a dusty path. That felt good, too.

The couple led her over a low hill, to a place where statues stood in a circle, hundreds of feet high, all of them so ancient that their features had all but been erased by the wind and the rain and the sun. Only the vaguest outlines of faces remained. Some had no faces, and were just columns of crumbling stone.

Inside the circle, hundreds of naked people, all of them young and flawlessly beautiful, lounged on a soft green lawn, eating fruit, drinking from golden goblets, laughing and joking, or making love. A young man played on a kind of flute. Several women danced around him.

"Here, drink."

The maiden who had led her gave Mora a goblet filled with red wine. She drank, expectant. The sensation of the wine inside her was intensely pleasant, warm, almost an ecstasy. She felt dizzy. The goblet dropped from her fingers. She sat down on the grass.

When she felt steadier, she looked up. The scene was the same as before, only most of the people were no longer human. They were tall and delicate, and had the heads of birds. Some had soft, downy feathers, growing out of marble-white skin. Only about one in four was as she had originally seen them.

"Come, join us in our celebration," the maiden said. She helped Mora to her feet. The ground swayed. The statues seemed taller, looming, leaning down upon her. The faces seemed to move, the stone mouths to form silent words. The sky was spinning. the sun a searing, swirling ring overhead.

She was dancing with the others In a great circle among the ruined statues, around a bonfire, all of them drawing ever closer to the fire until her skin ran with sweat and she was faint from the heat and smoke and exertion.

The flames parted like a curtain, and a thing stepped out, something like a man with the black, fierce head of an eagle. She was thrust into its arms. She struggled helpless in the iron grip, choking on the scorched smell of hot flesh. The rough feathers of the creature's chest scraped her face. Talons cut into her back.

Around them, the revelers danced. They began to sing:

Take the flame inside you.

IV.

Vaenev heard a footstep in the darkness.

He ran to his door, fumbled with the latch, and groped his way out into the corridor. He came first to his sister's room. He pounded softly on the door.

"Mora, please. Let me in. I'm afraid."

His voice echoed in the dark, empty house.

He went to Aerin's door, whimpering. He crouched down and scratched at the wood.

"Help me, Aerin. Help me."

Floorboards creaked at the end of the corridor. He looked up.

"Is that you?"

V.

The parents returned in the morning to find only Mora, naked on her bed, bleeding from long gashes in her back. She was feverish, and lay near death for many days, while her father and mother nursed her. Sometimes she screamed in the night. Later, when she seemed to come back to herself, she brooded for long hours and would say nothing of what had happened to her.

A priest was called, but she would not tell him anything either, although it was lawful for her to do so. After examining her, the priest said to her parents, "These are holy things which have come to pass, and by their holiness they are made even more terrible. When the divine touches each of us, we know it by our terror. Do not seek an explanation. There is none. With the Goddess dead, holiness is directionless in our age. We may only hope that these random miracles are like fortune sticks, randomly cast, from which meaning may be drawn. We may hope for a revelation, that we may know the day when our epoch is to end, and a new god or goddess will be born. You, especially, may hope that this will have been the final sign, that there will be no more destruction of innocents. Take comfort in that. Do not despair."

But the priest saw that the parents would not be comforted. There was little he could do. He hung a charm over the girl's bed and went away.

Within a few weeks, it was evident that Mora was with child. By the end of the first month, the child began to speak within her womb. The priest returned, with many attendants this time, and they bore her away in a litter.

Aerin, the parents later learned, had been discovered in the very throne room of the Guardian, marvelously transfigured, filled with a kind of fire that did not burn. He spoke much, and shouted and sang and wept. He had many voices, some those of people dead for thousands of years. His parents could not get in to see him. The sentry at the gate of the inner city shook his head sadly and said only that there was a ward in the palace where such people were kept, so that clerks might write down their every utterance, and the priests might study the transcripts and interpret any prophecies that might be found.

Vaenev eventually turned up stuffed in a rain barrel with his throat cut.

* * * *

The parents could not be comforted, even after a year had passed. Often they wept together, or just sat in the darkness at night, listening to the emptiness of their house. It was to them that the Revelation came, not to the priests.

Once, when they sat thus, a voice spoke out of the air, "Mother, Father, do not grieve for me."

The mother let out a cry. The father said, "Who is there?"

Suddenly the room was lit, as if with a thousand flickering candles, and Aerin appeared to them, floating in the air, transfigured with light. His mother fell from her chair to the floor and covered her face, sobbing. She thought him a ghost.

"Grieve for Vaenev, who saw nothing and understood nothing, and perhaps for Mora, through whom strangeness will enter the world, but not or me. Mother, Father, I shall return to you. The memory of the Goddess is in me now, and I see what she saw. She could look into the past, and into the future a ways, as far as her power was to extend, but not beyond. She could not see the new age. Mother, Father, I see no future at all, as if my face were up against a dark curtain. The new age is upon us. When the divine rises anew, the spirit of the old Goddess shall pass from me, and I will return to you. Mother, get up. Dry your face."

His mother stood up, and reached out to touch him, but he vanished.

On that night the clerk assigned to him reported that Aerin said nothing, and slept peacefully for the first time.

* * * *

These were the last miracles. The time of the death of the Goddess ended shortly thereafter.

ABOUT THE AUTHOR

DARRELL SCHWEITZER admits that he is considerably older today than he was when he wrote the stories in this book, or the novel *The Shattered Goddess* (1982) to which this volume forms a loose prequel. His others novels are *The White Isle* (serialized 1980, book 1990) and *The Mask of the Sorcerer* (1995). *Living with the Dead* (2008) is a story cycle published as a short book. *We Are All Legends* (1981) is also a story cycle. He is the author of nearly 300 published short stories, which have appeared in many anthologies and magazines. He has been nominated four times for the World Fantasy Award, once for best novella, twice for best collection, and he won it (with George Scithers) as editor of the legendary *Weird Tales*, a position he held for nineteen years. He has also edited anthologies, including *Cthulhu's Reign*, *The Secret History of Vampires*, *Full Moon City* (with Martin H. Greenberg), and *That Is Not Dead.* He is a critic and scholar of note, and has published books about H. P. Lovecraft and Lord Dunsany. He lives in Philadelphia with his wife, the writer Marilyn "Mattie" Brahen, and the requisite number of literary cats.

Printed in Germany
by Amazon Distribution
GmbH, Leipzig